second chance
chance
girl

Also by Susan Mallery

Secrets of the Tulip Sisters
Daughters of the Bride

Happily Inc

You Say It First

Mischief Bay

A Million Little Things
The Friends We Keep
The Girls of Mischief Bay

Fool's Gold

Best of My Love
Marry Me at Christmas
Thrill Me
Kiss Me
Hold Me
Until We Touch
Before We Kiss
When We Met
Christmas on 4th Street
Three Little Words
Two of a Kind
Just One Kiss
A Fool's Gold Christmas
All Summer Long
Summer Nights
Summer Days
Only His
Only Yours
Only Mine
Finding Perfect
Almost Perfect
Chasing Perfect

For a complete list of titles available from Susan Mallery,
please visit SusanMallery.com.

SUSAN MALLERY

second chance girl

HQN™

HQN™

ISBN-13: 978-0-373-80418-4

Recycling programs
for this product may
not exist in your area.

Second Chance Girl

This edition published by arrangement with Harlequin Books S.A.

For questions and comments about the quality of this book, please contact us
at CustomerService@Harlequin.com.

® and TM are trademarks of Harlequin Enterprises Limited or its corporate affiliates.
Trademarks indicated with ® are registered in the United States Patent and Trademark
Office, the Canadian Intellectual Property Office and in other countries.

HQNBooks.com

Printed in U.S.A.

Being the "mom" of two gorgeous cats and a new tiny puppy, I know the joy that pets can bring to our lives. Animal welfare is a cause I have long supported. For me that means giving to Seattle Humane. At their 2016 Tuxes and Tails fund-raiser, I offered "Your pet in a romance novel" as an auction item.

In this book you will meet a funny, sweet and slightly naughty beagle named Sophie. She was a superstar in a previous book, *Thrill Me*, and her human parents once again gave generously so she could be immortalized in all her glorious Sophie-ness in this book. I adored writing about Sophie and was delighted to give her many adventures. From romping with a giraffe to being a doggy bridesmaid, Sophie will steal your heart.

One of the things that makes writing special is interacting in different ways with people. Some I talk to for research. Some are readers who want to talk characters and story lines, and some are fabulous pet parents. Sophie's family adores her and she brings hours of pleasure to them.

My thanks to Sophie's family, to Sophie herself and to the wonderful people at Seattle Humane (www.seattlehumane.org). Because every pet deserves a loving family.

CHAPTER ONE

Getting kicked in the stomach by a gazelle was never pleasant, but at one thirty in the morning, it was especially hard to take. Carol Lund glared at Bronwen and the gazelle glared right back.

"You don't get to have attitude, young lady," Carol told her. "I'm not the one who insisted on going out by the rocks. I'm not the one who got scraped up, yet here I am, in the middle of the night, checking on your leg to make sure you don't have an infection."

Bronwen was notably unimpressed by Carol's presence and dedication. She stomped her front hooves and turned away.

"You say that now," Carol grumbled. "But just wait until feeding time. Suddenly I'm your best friend. You're incredibly fickle."

Carol packed up her supplies. Bronwen's leg seemed to be healing nicely. With luck she wouldn't require a second night's visit tomorrow and Carol could catch up on the sleep she was missing.

She left the gazelle barn and started for her Jeep. The night was clear and cool and there were a million stars in the sky.

While Carol would have preferred that Bronwen hadn't been injured and that they'd both been able to sleep through the night, she had to admit that staring at the perfect sky was a very cool compensation. If she didn't look at the horizon, or try to pick out individual constellations, she could be any-where in the world—literally. Because the night sky was a constant.

Oh, sure, there were differences between the hemispheres and at certain times of the year, but still...stars!

She climbed into her Jeep and drove toward her small bun-galow, then pulled onto the shoulder before she got there and cut the engine and lights. She got out of the Jeep, sank down onto the ground and gave herself over to the nighttime view.

It was October in the desert which meant warm days and pleasant nights. Rain was an unlikely possibility—that was more a spring-summer thing. The closest town was Happily Inc and it wasn't all that huge, so it wasn't hard to get away from the streetlights and into true darkness. Here, on the road, she was flanked by the mountains and the golf course, with the rolling hills of the Happily Inc Animal Preserve just behind her. And the stars.

She draped her jacket on the ground so she could lie down and get the best view of the wonder overhead. She had no idea how long she'd been lying there when a pair of head-lights cut through the darkness and briefly illuminated her.

Carol sat up as a swoopy midnight blue Mercedes sedan pulled in behind her Jeep.

Of all the gin joints in all the world, she thought. She watched a tall, dark-haired man step out of his car and walk toward her. It had to be after two in the morning, yet Mathias Mitchell looked more alert than sleepy. No doubt the linger-ing effects of the hunt, takedown and getting laid.

He stopped a few feet from her. It was too dark for her to read his expression, but if she had to guess, she would say he was amused. Mathias seemed to find the world a delightful place. She supposed given who he was, with his combination of good looks, easy charm and career success, there was no reason he should think otherwise. To mix metaphors and clichés, the world was his oyster and Mathias dined well.

She, on the other hand, was simply a woman with looks and a personality as ordinary as her name.

"Lose a contact lens?" he asked drily.

"Bronwen hurt herself, so I had to go check on her. On my way back, I stopped to look at the stars."

He sank down next to her and raised his gaze to the sky. "Why not wait until you got home?"

"This is the best view in the area."

"Because you've tried them all?" He sighed. "You're an odd woman, Carol Lund. Who's Bronwen? One of the zebras?"

"Gazelle."

"Fancy name for a cow."

Carol felt her lips twitch and was grateful he couldn't see her trying not to smile. The conversation was familiar. Unlike most of the citizens of Happily Inc, Mathias had no romantic notions about the animals grazing just outside of town. "Gazelles aren't cows."

"They're close. Oh, I'll give you that they're more elegant, probably faster, too, but still, under their pretty outsides, they're cows. Just like your precious Millie."

Carol glared at him. "Don't you say that. Millie's wonderful."

"I'm not saying anything about her character, just pointing out that despite her being adorable and very tall, she is, in fact, a ruminant." He leaned close enough for her to smell the perfume clinging to his body. "Which makes her just like a cow," he added in a stage whisper.

She waved her hand in front of her face. "There's a smell."

Mathias nodded. "Yeah, she did get a little heavy with the scent."

"Did the big boobs compensate?"

"I'm not actually a breast man. My requirements are more about general appeal."

"If she's slutty, you're in?" She cleared her throat. "So to speak?"

"You wound me. There's a process."

"Not a very good one. You really need to shower before you go to bed tonight or your sheets are going to reek."

"Excellent advice. Thank you."

"My neighbor, the man whore."

She made the statement without a whole lot of energy—mostly because there was no point. Almost nothing ruffled him. Despite what he did for a living, he was the opposite of a brooding artist. Except for his questionable taste in sexual partners, there was little not to like about Mathias and she had to admit that in her heart of hearts, she was a fan.

"Have you considered that nearly all the derogatory terms about a person being promiscuous are directed at women?" He glanced at her. "Slut, whore. We have to modify them to make them apply to a man."

"What about a player or a sugar daddy?"

"No guy minds being called a player and I'm not sure any human has used the term 'sugar daddy' since 1979."

She chuckled. "That's not true. People say it all the time."

He looked at her, but didn't speak.

"Okay, maybe not *all* the time, but lots."

"Carol, Carol, Carol, you are such an innocent."

"That must be refreshing after a night with one of your women."

"It is, although I have to say, I don't understand your dislike of bridesmaids."

"I don't dislike them. I simply don't understand what you see in them. Or what they see in you."

The last was a lie. Mathias was funny enough to be charming and sexy enough to be irresistible. She would admit that even *she* had had the odd fantasy or two about him. Not that she would ever bother to act—she knew her place in the world. She was the plain peahen, while Mathias was the classic peacock. There was no reason for him to notice her and even if he somehow did, he only did one-night stands and that had never been her thing. She was much more a fall in love first kind of girl.

"What I see in them is that they'll be gone in the morning," he said as he stood. "As for what they see in me, isn't that obvious?"

He held out his hand. She reached for it and he pulled her to her feet. As soon as she found her balance, he released her, then reached down and grabbed her jacket. He put it around her shoulders.

"Come on, my little animal warden friend. We need to get you into bed. Morning comes early and cows expect to be fed."

"I should slug you really hard in the stomach," she grumbled as they walked to her Jeep.

"Such violence. You're not embracing the cow mantra of being one with nature."

"If you say cow one more time, I swear I'm going to—"

He held open the driver's door and she slid onto the seat. They were nearly at eye level.

"You're going to what?" he asked.

The dome light illuminated his features. His eyes were dark and his smile nearly blinded her with its brightness. He had broad shoulders and the honed body of a man who used muscles every day in his work.

As happened every now and then around him, she remembered that she was a healthy woman in her twenties who hadn't been with someone in way too long. Mathias had to know what he was doing—he certainly had enough practice.

Not that he would be interested in her. Not only didn't she fit his "You must be leaving town" criteria, she wasn't, you know, special. Or at least not special enough to tempt the likes of him.

"I'm going to start training the zebras to poop in your yard. Have you smelled zebra poo? It's going to make that perfume seem like nothing."

He flashed her a smile. "Time to say good-night, Carol."

"Good night, Carol."

He closed the door and walked to his sedan. She started down the road, the Mercedes following closely. A couple of miles later, she pulled into her driveway. Mathias flashed his lights, then kept going. For a second, his car disappeared as he rounded a small hill, then she saw him as he came out the other side. The lights turned as he drove onto his property, flashed twice again before disappearing into his garage.

She continued to stand in the darkness until more lights appeared, this time in his massive house on the edge of the animal preserve. There was humor in the fact that her twelve-hundred-square-foot bungalow could fit comfortably in his five-car garage with room to spare, yet he was her closest neighbor. There she was—living on the edge of the world of the "haves" and more than happy to stay on her side.

Carol unlocked her front door and went inside. She toed off her boots, then went directly to her bedroom and barely pulled off her jeans before sinking onto the mattress and sighing.

Morning would come way too early, thanks to Bronwen. Unlike some people who lived in big mansions with views, she had to get up with the sun. Her herd didn't like to wait for breakfast.

Carol quickly fell asleep only to find herself tangled in a strange dream of flying cows and Mathias begging her to kiss him. She woke to the insistent sound of her alarm and the knowledge that of the two scenarios, flying cows were by far the more likely to happen.

Mathias walked barefoot across his patio. It was still early and a light mist clung to the ground—no doubt the result of early-morning watering, but he preferred a more romantic explanation. It was the artist in him.

He took his favorite chair, set his coffee and sketch pad on the table beside him, then prepared to wait.

He wasn't sure how long ago the ritual had started. Shortly after Millie had arrived, maybe. He didn't know why she got to him more than the others. She was just a giraffe. Shouldn't he find beauty in the swift-footed gazelles or majesty in the water buffalo?

While he'd been aware of the animals when he'd pur-chased the house, he hadn't really noticed them for the first few months. He supposed they'd crept into his consciousness after he'd met Carol.

Most towns hid their dumps behind gates or far away from any suburban sprawl. Happily Inc had planned differently, putting it just southwest of the population center, carefully downwind.

In addition to running a recycling and reclamation pro-gram that was one of the best in the nation, the two men who owned and ran the dump had also purchased hundreds of acres around the landfill. Grasses and trees had been brought in. Once they'd taken root, the animals had appeared. The ga-zelles had been first, then the zebras. There were a few wad-ing birds, the water buffalo and lastly, Millie.

Mathias knew the basics—the two men who had created a unique African savanna on the edge of the California desert were Carol's father and uncle. When she'd completed her degree, she'd come to work at the preserve. A year ago, the old man in charge of the animals had retired, leaving Carol to take over. A few months after that, Millie had arrived.

Mathias didn't know why the giraffe and the woman were so closely linked in his mind, but they were. Now, as he watched the morning fog slowly dissipate, he saw Millie stroll into view.

She was a reticulated or Somali giraffe, nearly fifteen feet tall, with traditional markings. Her face was almost heart shaped, with widely spaced eyes and an inquisitive gaze.

Mathias sipped his coffee before reaching for his sketch pad. He already had hundreds of drawings of Millie and Carol, but he hadn't yet found *the one*. He would know it when he saw it, so every morning he waited.

Carol appeared when they cleared the trees. She barely came to partway up Millie's shoulder. In the morning light, her short red hair seemed almost blond. She was strong and wholly herself—a contrast to his usual type of woman, so he shouldn't have found her appealing...only he did. There was something about her lack of artifice, something about the way she was so comfortable in her own skin that made him pay attention.

Carol and the giraffe strolled together like this most mornings, after the other animals had been fed. At first he'd thought this was Carol's way of making Millie more comfortable with her surroundings. But the walks had continued long after Millie had settled in to her new home. When the small donation jars had started popping up all over town, he'd realized Carol was attempting to fulfill Millie's need for companionship.

A few minutes on the internet had taught Mathias that while male giraffes were mostly solitary, female giraffes lived in a loose group. Mothers often took on babysitting duties so they could each go forage for food. Carol's morning walks were her attempt to help Millie feel as if she had a herd.

He watched them for nearly half an hour then went inside. Before heading to the studio, he went to his sunroom where he worked from home. Not with glass—that setup would require more equipment, not to mention a very understanding insurance agent—but with pencil and pad or even paint and canvas.

He flipped through the drawings stacked on a shelf. Millie alone, Millie and Carol walking, Millie with the zebras. It was there, he thought, doing his best to ignore the ever-present frustration. He'd been close a couple of times, nearly capturing the image he wanted. It would come—he had to believe that. And when it did, he would create it out of glass. Assuming he still had what had once been his reason to live and breathe.

Ulrich Sherwood, Duke of Somerbrooke, stared out of the eighth-floor conference room window of the Century City high-rise. To the west was Santa Monica and the vast Pacific Ocean, to the east were haze-covered mountains...or maybe that was smog smudging the outline. He'd only been in Los Angeles twice before and hadn't enjoyed himself either time. This visit was to meet with lawyers—something else he didn't enjoy but which was in this case a necessary evil. A very well-financed TV producer wanted to set a modern-day *Downton Abbey* in England and Ulrich's home of Battenberg Park had been chosen as the location. Not only did the use of the rambling estate mean a hefty fee, Battenberg Park would also receive a "spruce" as the lawyer had called it. For their purposes, that meant fresh paint and a significant upgrade in landscaping. Combined, the fee and the "spruce" had made a trip to Los Angeles more than worth the time and effort.

Linda, the forty-something attorney, returned to the conference room and smiled at him. "Your Lordship."

"Ulrich, please," he murmured, knowing there was no point in correcting her to use the more accurate "Your Grace." Not only did he prefer to keep that sort of formality to a minimum, he was in the States. Here, true royalty came in the form of movie stars. What did anyone care about lineage, titles or peerage?

"Here's your copy of the contract," Linda said. "Along with a receipt for the first payment. As you requested, we wired the money directly to your bank."

"Excellent."

Linda had the firm, slim body of a woman who took fitness seriously. She looked at least a decade younger than what he would guess to be her age and he was sure, when it came to playing the game, she was far more experienced than he. He'd married young, divorced only two years ago and since then had avoided entanglements. He supposed he should have been flattered and perhaps intrigued when she said, "Now that our business is complete, I'd love to take you out to dinner. I know a great little place not far from my condo."

Ulrich knew he could easily take advantage of what was being offered. He was single, out of the country and no one would ever know. He doubted Linda wanted or expected anything other than the one night. What could be more perfect?

Only he couldn't summon the interest. It wasn't that she was nearly a decade older, it was…well, everything.

"Thank you for the invitation," he said, offering a polite smile and a tone of genuine regret. "I'm afraid I have pressing business in the eastern part of your state and I must get on the road right away."

"Where are you heading?"

Ulrich did his best not to curl his lip in disdain. "To a town called Happily Inc."

She laughed. "I've been there. A friend had a destination wedding at a place called Weddings in a Box a couple of years ago. It's cute. An interesting choice for a man like you. Are you getting married?" She sounded more intrigued than put off by the idea of his pending nuptials.

"What? No. I have, ah, family business in the area."

An American shyster stealing from his grandmother, to be exact.

Linda regarded him thoughtfully. "I'm sorry we won't be able to spend the evening together."

"As am I," he lied. "Truly." He waved the folder. "Thank you for this."

"You're welcome."

Ulrich nodded and left. Twenty minutes later he was heading east on I-10. His rental car's nav system promised him an arrival at his destination in less than four hours.

On the seat next to him was his briefcase. Inside, along with the contract from Linda's production firm, was a name and an address.

For the past half dozen or so years his eighty-year-old grandmother had been sending packages to one Violet Lund. At first Ulrich hadn't noticed or cared, until the head housekeeper had mentioned that items from the estate had gone missing. A pair of candlesticks here, a small painting there. Individually the items were of little consequence, but in the aggregate, they were significant.

He'd found out about the packages, but when he'd questioned his grandmother, the dowager duchess had informed him it was none of his business.

Ulrich had very little family left—Winifred, his grandmother, was his closest living relative. She'd helped raise him after his mother had died, they'd comforted each other when his father had passed a few years before, and he loved her deeply. There was no way he was going to confront her directly, but that didn't mean he couldn't go around her and find out about the disgusting human being who would prey on a helpless old lady.

For a second Ulrich mentally paused to appreciate the six or seven thousand miles between him and his grandmother. Because if she ever knew he'd thought of her as helpless or old, she would grab him by the ear and give him a stern talking-to. She wouldn't care that he was thirty and the Duke of Somerbrooke.

Fortunately he didn't plan to tell her. Instead he would confront the con artist and sever the contact. Then he would fly back to England and retreat to his beautiful if slightly needy home and brace himself for the Hollywood invasion.

Nothing about his mission was pleasant, but that didn't matter. For over a millennia, his ancestors had been riding or sailing or, in his case, driving into battle. Not for glory or personal gain, but because it was expected. He had been raised to do the right thing—damn the inconvenience or short-term consequences. Or in this case, the thieving ways of the mysterious Violet Lund.

CHAPTER TWO

Mathias held the form in position. Ronan focused intently as he heated the glass to a molten state. Timing was everything. The material had to be hot enough to shape, but not heated too much or it would become a blob and he would lose all the work he'd already done.

A sketch of the completed piece was pinned up on the wall of the brothers' giant studio. The finished installation would be nearly thirty feet across and ten feet high. On the left was a perfect green dragon—on the right was an elegant white swan. In between the two were morphing shapes as one became the other.

Ronan had just started the piece. He had a year to complete it and then he would oversee the installation of it in an upscale hotel in Japan. While these days he mostly worked in the privacy of his studio at home, aided by assistants and interns, he often started a project at the studio they and their brother Nick shared. Mathias liked to think Ronan wanted the comradery and the shared energy, but maybe he was fooling himself. He and his brother had once been close. A few years ago, all that had changed.

Ronan pulled the glass out of the oven. Mathias stepped into place and held the form as Ronan spun the rod. Nick applied pressure with a sharp edge. The glass yielded.

The heat was intense, as was their concentration. Success or failure was measured in seconds as the material hardened in the breathable air. Ronan studied what they'd done, then returned the piece to the oven, only to pull it out again and watch it cool and harden.

The commission would be done in hundreds of sections all carefully joined together, like a giant glass puzzle. It would consume him for weeks at a time. Mathias had seen it happen before. The start was slow, then the project picked up momentum. Usually Mathias had been a part of that. This time, he was less sure.

In his head, Mathias understood why. Everything was different now. They were no longer two of the five Mitchell brothers. He dropped the form back into the bin and walked to his work area, then shook his head. Okay, that wasn't true. They were still the Mitchell brothers, but he and Ronan, well, that was gone forever.

He studied his own morning's work. Two serving bowls in a dozen shades of amber, moss green and yellow. Unlike Ronan's creation, Mathias's was practical rather than esoteric. He made light pendants and giant vessels that were used as bathroom sinks. He created vases and platters and dishes. The latter were done in various colors to reflect the seasons. White, blue and silver for winter, pale green, pink and peach for spring, red, orange and purple for summer and amber, moss green, chestnut and yellow for fall.

There had been a time when he, too, had created art, but he'd figured out this was his path. He liked what he did— he brought beauty to people's everyday lives. If every now and then he yearned for something more, well, what was the point? Yes, he had some of their father's talent, but Ronan and Nick were the artists. He was just a guy who worked with glass.

He studied the bowls, pleased with the outcome. Every year he tried to do something to challenge himself. For this year, he'd decided to add a shape to the serving pieces. The fall bowls had the outline of a leaf. Summer had been a strawberry and spring, a daisy. For winter, he would take on a snowflake—something he still had no idea how he was going to create. Every attempt had been a disaster, but that was half the fun.

His phone chirped. He glanced at the screen and saw he had a text from his mother.

"Incoming," he said aloud, then glanced at his brothers to see if either of them had heard from her.

Nick reached for his phone while Ronan ignored him.

"Nothing," Nick said. "Guess it's your lucky day."

"Sure it is," Mathias grumbled as he read the short message.

I'm coming to see you.

An interesting statement that would have made him uncomfortable if his mother hadn't been over four hundred miles away.

When?

What he expected was for her to say sometime next week or at the end of the month, when his brother Del was getting married.

In about ten minutes. I'm in town.

Mathias swore. His first thought was "Why me?" followed by "Hell, no" followed by "Run!" Instead of following his instincts, he reminded himself that he loved his mother, even if he found her difficult, and that not dealing with her wasn't an option.

Great, he texted back, telling himself it wasn't an actual lie. More of a hedge.

"What?" Nick demanded.

"She's on her way."

His brother relaxed. "That gives us about eight hours. Why is she coming here?"

"I have no idea." He swung his attention to Ronan. "She's ten minutes away."

Mathias watched the play of emotion on Ronan's face. They were easy to read. Shock, annoyance, the need to disappear. Not all that different from his own reaction.

Five years ago he would have said the similarity was because they were twins. Fraternal, but still. They shared a bond that time and space couldn't break. Only they'd discovered they weren't twins at all—they never had been. It had all been a lie and nothing had been the same since they'd had that particular truth thrust upon them.

Ronan set the still cooling glass on the heatproof bench, grabbed his keys and bolted.

"We're not going to see him for three days," Nick grumbled. "He's got to face her sooner or later."

"You're telling the wrong guy."

Mathias walked to the entrance to the studio and waited. Ronan was already backing out of the parking space. He turned right on the street and headed for the hills. Or in his case, the mountains. Nick was right—they wouldn't see him for days.

The October afternoon was warm and clear. Rain rarely came to the desert and this wasn't the season. From now through the holidays there wouldn't even be a cloud in the sky. Come spring, the weather got a little iffy, but not often and not for long.

Happily Inc sat in the middle of the California desert, with Arizona to the east and Mexico to the south. An underground aquifer provided more than enough water for residents and visitors alike. There were mountains for those who preferred that topography, as well as an odd convergence of energy that made Happily Inc a special and magical place for those who believed in that kind of thing. More significant to daily life was the fact that the town was a destination wedding location with most of the local businesses focused on all things nuptial and tourist. The only large-scale exceptions were the sleep center north of town and Carol's animal preserve to the southwest.

An unfamiliar car pulled into the parking lot and took Ronan's spot. It was a nondescript sedan, a rental. His mother was behind the wheel and his father was nowhere to be seen. Unless Ceallach was hiding in the back seat, maybe this visit wasn't going to be so bad after all.

"Hey, Mom," he said as Elaine Mitchell got out of the car and hugged him.

"What an adorable little town. And so easy to navigate. I wasn't sure I could find my way from the airport, but it all went just fine." She turned back to the car. "Come on, sweetie."

Mathias had a second of panic, thinking his joke about his father hiding had tempted the fates just a little too much, only instead of the family patriarch stepping out onto the pavement, a brown-and-white beagle jumped down and immediately raced over to him, her ears flapping and her long tail wagging happily.

"Hey, Sophie," he said as he crouched down to greet the dog.

She ran in circles around him before jumping up to put

her paws on his shoulders and thoroughly kiss his face. He laughed, then stood to get out of the wet zone.

Nick stepped out of the studio. He looked at Mathias, who shook his head. His brother relaxed as he approached their mother.

"Mom," he said warmly. "You're a surprise." He bent over to greet Sophie.

"I know. I should have called, but I didn't."

Mathias had the uncomfortable thought that she'd deliberately not given them much warning because she'd known they would scatter if given the chance. Which sure didn't say much about them as sons.

The problem wasn't her, he thought grimly. It was their father. The man they wouldn't have to ask about because Elaine would happily tell them everything and more.

The three of them walked into the studio, Sophie bringing up the rear. At the last second, Mathias thought about all the tools, glass and ovens in the room and grabbed Sophie's trailing leash. Elaine glanced around, as if looking for someone, then her happy smile faded a little.

Mathias silently called Ronan five kinds of bastard for hurting the woman who had always loved him. But his brother wouldn't see it that way and no one had been able to get through to him, despite how they'd all tried.

"This is nice," she said with false enthusiasm. "Big and open. You all work here?"

Nick and Mathias exchanged a glance, as if hoping the other would speak first.

"Ronan has his own studio at his place," Mathias finally said. "He works there a lot."

"I see. And the gallery is close?"

"Across the parking lot. You should meet Atsuko before you go. She's the one selling our work."

"I will next time. I'm on my way back to the airport to catch a flight."

Before Mathias could ask why she'd bothered to come by, she continued, "Your father and I are heading out on tour. He's going to be lecturing and giving demonstrations. It's all very exciting to see him get the attention he deserves."

Mathias did his best not to roll his eyes. The last thing Ceallach Mitchell was lacking was attention. In his universe, he was the sun and everyone else revolved around his greatness and light.

"We'll be gone about a month and then come back here in time for Del and Maya's wedding."

"That's great, Mom," Nick said. "So, ah, why did you stop by?"

Elaine turned to Mathias as if it was obvious. "Someone has to look after Sophie while we're gone."

Mathias dropped the leash he was holding. The dog immediately took off exploring. "No. No way. I can't."

"Yes, you can. She's adorable and you love her."

Love was strong. He liked the dog…from a distance. It wasn't that she was a bad dog—not exactly. It was more that she had an adventurous spirit and only listened when it suited her purposes. If there was trouble within a five-mile radius, Sophie found it, rolled in it, then brought it home as a prize.

His mother's gaze sharpened. "Nick can't take her. He and Pallas are newly in love and Sophie would only get in the way."

Nick's expression turned smug. "That's true."

"You have that big house," his mother went on. "With a yard. Sophie will be fine with you and it's only for a month. Besides, taking care of her would be good for—"

The sound of glass shattering cut through the afternoon. They all turned to stare as Sophie yelped and raced away from the rack filled with finished plates, bowls and glasses. Mathias hadn't seen what had happened but he would guess Sophie's ever-wagging tail had been the culprit.

Elaine hurried toward her dog. Mathias swore and followed. They had to keep Sophie away from the glass so she didn't hurt herself. But as they approached, the happy beagle decided this was some kind of glorious game and darted away.

"I've got her," Nick called as he lunged.

Sophie sidestepped, whacked one of the two bowls Mathias had completed that morning with her tail and then took off for the other side of the room. Mathias managed to get close enough to stomp on her leash, which brought her to a quick stop. He grabbed her in his arms and hauled her up to safety. Sophie relaxed and gave him a doggie kiss on the chin.

Elaine smiled. "See. You're going to do great with her."

Not exactly the words he would have used. Still, he was smart enough to know when he'd been bested. He could yell and complain and generally make a fool of himself but at the end of the day, Elaine was his mother, he loved her and there was no way he could tell her no. Which meant today, it sucked to be him.

Monday nights were tournament nights at The Boardroom Pub. With weddings running the local economy, Happily Inc worked on weekends. Monday was the town's traditional party night, such as it was, and many of the residents made it a point to get out for a little fun before the next batch of wedding folk blew into town.

The Boardroom, a pub devoted to every board game known to man, celebrated Mondays with different challenges. There had been a Monopoly Junior competition over the summer. Hungry, Hungry Hippo night, along with board-based trivia games, checkers, chess. If there was a board used at any point in the game, it could be found in The Boardroom.

Carol liked Monday nights. In the past, she'd enjoyed the

chance to hang out with her friends and have fun. Lately, she was just as interested in the big crowd that showed up for the tournaments. Ever since she'd come up with the idea of buying a herd for her lonely giraffe, she'd been in fund-raising mode. There were donation cans all over town and on Monday nights, a percentage of the proceeds at The Boardroom went to the "buy Millie a herd" cause.

As she wove between the tables, she called out to people she knew. Once she reached the bar, she shook the giraffe-print-covered can and was delighted to feel the weight of it. Yes, the money was flowing slowly, but at least it was flowing. Buying giraffes wasn't cheap, nor was the very tricky transportation to get them to the animal preserve. There would be the costs of additional housing, not to mention feeding. Millie's favorite marionberry leaf-eater treats were pricey.

Still, progress was being made and that was what mattered. Carol needed her favorite girl to be happy.

After confirming the full can, she looked at the chalkboard to find out the challenge of the week, then grinned.

"You look happy," her friend Pallas said as she approached. They hugged.

"I love Clue."

Pallas, a hazel-eyed brunette with an easy smile, groaned. "Let me guess. You can always figure out who did it and where. I never can. There's too much to keep track of."

"That's why you take notes."

"It's not a game if you're taking notes. Want to sit with us tonight?"

"Sure."

They made their way to a table. Seconds before they arrived, Carol remembered that Pallas would most likely be sitting with her fiancé. Nick was a great guy—Carol liked him a lot. The problem was his brother. Because Carol wasn't sure she wanted to spend the evening sitting next to the ever dreamy Mathias.

Not that he would notice her, she reminded herself. She wasn't glamorous or special—in the animal kingdom, she was the female who would be overlooked by the alpha male. While she teased Mathias about his love of bridesmaids, the truth was his type was more specific than simply anyone who was in a wedding. He gravitated toward the most beautiful, most feminine, most alluring of the single women in town to attend a wedding.

In a word or two—not her.

She and Pallas took seats across from each other, then glanced at the menu. On tournament nights there were special drinks in honor of the game du jour, along with easy-to-eat food. Carol generally stuck with herbal iced tea rather than one of the cocktails. She had to be up early to feed her animals.

Pallas was facing the door. When Carol saw her friend's face light up with happiness, she sighed. "Let me guess. Chris Pine just walked in?"

"Better." Pallas rose. "Nick's here."

The engaged couple embraced. Nick's kiss lingered a second more than was polite, then he grinned at Carol. "How's it going? Did you hear about Mathias?"

He seemed too happy for whatever it was to be bad, she told herself as she shook her head. "I've been out on the savanna all day. What happened?"

Pallas rolled her eyes. "Ignore him. He's being mean."

"I'm not," Nick protested as he sat next to her. "But I will admit, better him than me." Nick's grin returned. "Our mom stopped by with Sophie."

Carol tried to figure out what was funny. While she'd heard about Elaine Mitchell, she'd never met her and she had no idea who Sophie was. There was no sister, so a cousin maybe? A chill raced through her as she considered the possibility of an ex-girlfriend delivered to Mathias. For reasons she couldn't explain the thought of that was incredibly unsettling.

Pallas put her hand over Nick's. "She has no idea who Sophie is, sweetie, so she's not going to get the joke."

"Sophie's a beagle. She's Mom's dog. My parents are going to be traveling for a month, so Mom brought Sophie to stay with Mathias." Nick snickered. "I'm in love, so I was spared."

A dog? Wasn't that nice? Carol liked dogs. "Why is this so funny?"

"You haven't met Sophie," Nick told her. "She's sweet and friendly as could be, but don't let those big eyes fool you. Sophie's also a terror. She's an escape artist, a food hound and all-around troublemaker. Mathias doesn't have a chance. The dog was in our studio for maybe ten minutes and she broke a dozen of his pieces. That was without trying. Imagine what she can do if she makes an effort."

Carol winced. "Is she okay? Did she get any glass in her paw?"

"She's fine. She's lucky that way. Nothing bad ever happens to her. Everyone else gets sucked into the vortex, but Sophie emerges unscathed."

"He's exaggerating," Pallas said. "I've only seen pictures, but she looks adorable. Mathias will be fine."

Nick snorted. "Tell him that," he said, jerking his head toward the door.

Carol turned and saw Mathias, a small beagle at his side and a fluffy dog bed under his arm. Sophie's eyes were bright, her tail wagging. She was every inch a happy dog.

"Oh, yeah, she's the devil," Carol murmured. "We should run while we can."

"You mock me but you'll see." Nick's tone was warning.

As Mathias and Sophie approached, Carol noticed the dog wearing a red service-animal vest. Her lips began to twitch.

Mathias reached the table and dropped the dog bed on the floor. "Don't say a word," he growled. "You have no idea what I've been through in the past few hours."

Carol glanced from him to Sophie and back. "Do you need her for emotional support?" she asked sweetly. "Does she help with flashbacks or is her job more to keep the sexy bridesmaids at bay?"

"Very funny." He collapsed in his chair. "I couldn't leave her home alone. Everything is new to her. Mom told me she's a certified service dog, so I put her in her vest and brought her."

"That's so nice," Pallas told him. She turned to Nick. "See, it's going fine."

Nick chuckled. "Uh-huh. Tell her the rest."

Mathias expression tightened. "It's been five hours. There's no way I can keep her for a month. She has more equipment than an NFL team. Leashes and collars, beds, toys, the service vest. My mom gave me a notebook of instructions. There are twenty-six pages. Twenty-six!" He cleared his throat, then lowered his voice. "She has canned food, dry food, treats, flea medicine."

"Poop bags?" Carol asked, trying not to laugh. "You know dogs poop, right? Usually on a walk. You're going to need the bags so you can pick it up and carry it with you until you get home and throw it in the trash. Oh, and make sure you tie the bag really tight when you're done because of, you know, the smell."

Mathias stared at her. "Stop it."

Nick shook his head. "Bro, she's not lying about the poop. We all do it."

"Thank you for sharing." Mathias flagged a server. "I'd like a beer, please, and if you could hurry, that would be great."

They all placed their drink orders, then Pallas smiled at

Mathias. "It's going to be fine. I'm sure Sophie's a good little girl. You'll like having her around."

"You might learn something from her," Carol added. "Dogs are loyal, committed companions. Of course that might make you too uncomfortable."

"You think this is funny."

"I *know* this is funny," she told him. "Come on. She's a dog. People have had dogs as pets for tens of thousands of years. You can suck it up for a month."

Mathias didn't look convinced.

Their drinks were delivered and the game began. On tournament night, everyone played until there was a winner at each table, then those winners would play until only one was left standing.

As they rolled dice and moved from room to room, discarding suspects and weapons, eliminated players stopped by to say hello and sneak Sophie bits of bacon and burger. Sophie took each treat gently, offering a thank-you lick when she'd swallowed the bite.

Mathias was overreacting. Sophie was obviously well trained and used to being around people. He and Nick were making her into something that she wasn't, which was just like a man. A month with a lovely little dog was exactly what Mathias needed.

CHAPTER THREE

Mathias had gone out of his way to make the rules clear to Sophie. She was a visiting pet—she was responsible for listening to him and doing as he said. As such, she would sleep in the living room and not in his bedroom. Only when it was time to go to bed, he realized that the living room was kind of a big, dark place and a long way from his room. As a way to show his willingness to compromise, he put her bed in the hallway, outside his bedroom door. Then he told her goodnight and closed the door.

All went well for eight or ten seconds, then Sophie began to cry. At first the sounds were soft little yips of loneliness but they soon morphed into full-throated howls of pain and suffering, punctuated by whines of agony.

Mathias covered his head with a pillow, but that didn't help. He told himself she would get over it and fall asleep. A full fifteen minutes later, he had to admit Sophie had some lungs on her. He crossed to the door and jerked it open. The sounds ceased as she wagged her tail at him, as if saying, "Hi. I knew you were in there. Can I come in?"

"No," he said firmly. "Be quiet. Go to sleep."

The tail wag slowed.

He closed the door again and didn't make it back to the bed before the cries started up.

Ten minutes later he carried her bed into his room and dropped it in a corner. "Just for tonight," he told her as sternly as he could. "I'm sure you miss your mom. I get that. But you have to learn to be independent, okay?"

Sophie sat in her bed, her tail wagging.

"Good night."

He turned out the light.

One second turned into ten. Sophie was silent. He relaxed and closed his eyes, only to hear something scrambling onto the bench at the foot of his king-size mattress. That noise was immediately followed by Sophie scratching at the blanket before turning around and around and around, then flopping down halfway up and more on his side than her own. Before he could decide what he was supposed to do now, she sighed and began to snore.

Mathias stared at the ceiling and told himself it was only for a month. He could endure this. It wasn't as if it was going to get worse.

It got worse. He managed to sleep through the snoring, the snuffling and twitching as Sophie dreamed her doggie dreams. In the morning he let her out before feeding her. The smell of the canned food was bad enough, but then he had to mix it with dry, add exactly one quarter cup of warm (but not too hot water), then stir it up. His mother said to add a crumbled strip of crisp bacon to the mix, but Mathias decided that was going too far.

Sophie inhaled her breakfast before his Keurig had finished brewing a single cup of coffee, then she stared at him expectantly, as if wanting more.

"Look, you'll need to talk to your mom," he told her. "I

measured everything. That's your breakfast. There's nothing else."

The hope in her brown eyes died a doggie death and the tail wag slowed. Mathias did his best to ignore her and the guilt as he grabbed his coffee and made his way back to his bedroom.

Getting ready with Sophie around was different than getting ready alone. For one thing, she was always underfoot. For another, she sniffed *everything* and he would swear, as he stripped down for his shower, she was more than a little judgy.

"No one wants your opinion," he said firmly as he stepped into the shower. "I mean it."

Sophie tried to grab his towel when he got out, drank water from the toilet and when he let her out again, she pooped enough to make a moose proud, only Mathias was stuck cleaning it up. For the record, one poop bag was not enough.

Once that was done, he was able to finally sit down and enjoy the quiet of the morning. Millie stepped out of the tall trees. Sophie took one look at her and started barking.

He told her to stop. He told her louder to stop, then he locked her in his house even though he could still hear the frantic yips, growls and barks. He returned to his favorite patio chair, closed his eyes and imagined himself anywhere but here.

"I doubt there's even going to be a scar," Carol said happily Tuesday afternoon.

"Uh-huh. That's great."

Violet Lund did her best to pay attention to the conversation. Lunch with her sister was one of her favorite times of the week. Even though they lived in the same small town, they were both busy. They'd learned that if they didn't make the effort to get something on the calendar, time tended to slip away from them.

She'd gotten up early to make chicken salad for sandwiches

and had stopped by the bakery for the cookies Carol liked. But now that they were seated at the large table in Violet's faux-loft apartment above her small store, she found her attention straying.

It wasn't her fault, she told herself soothingly. She was being tempted beyond what a normal person could expect to withstand. Because there, on the counter, tantalizingly out of reach, was a package about the size of a shoe box.

The mix of various colorful postage stamps had told her it had been sent from England—from the Dowager Duchess of Somerbrooke, to be specific. She had an idea of what was inside, but couldn't know the exact contents—not until she opened it. Oh, if only the mail lady had delivered it *after* her lunch with Carol, she wouldn't be squirming like a four-year-old waiting on Santa.

"For her modeling career," Carol added drily. "You know, with that large coffee manufacturer."

Violet turned back to her sister and tried to put the pieces together. She was pretty sure they'd been talking about Bronwen and her injuries. Bronwen being a gazelle at the animal preserve her sister ran...or managed...or whatever you called the job of person in charge. Animal keeper?

And not important, she told herself. They'd been talking about Bronwen, so how on earth had they gotten to a modeling career and who was—

The pieces fell into place. Violet sighed.

"Sorry. I was listening." Um, perhaps that wasn't her best tack. "I mean I wanted to listen. I do care about your work."

"I can tell." Carol sounded more amused than upset. "If it makes you feel any better, your buttons are about as interesting to me as my gazelle and her injuries are to you."

Violet wanted to protest. Bronwen was great and all but still just a gazelle. While the buttons were...magical. They came from all over the world. A lot were junk and of little use to her, but every now and then there were actual treasures. The rare, the perfect, the unexpected.

Once a lady in India had sent her eight perfectly matched enamel and onyx buttons edged in gold. Another time she'd received carved wooden buttons that dated back to the fifteen *hundreds*. Buttons were interesting and dynamic and a surprisingly excellent source of income. Compared to that, all a gazelle could do was eat, sleep and walk around. Still, Carol loved all her animals and Violet loved her sister.

"I am sorry that Bronwen was hurt and I'm happy she's pursuing her modeling career. She always wanted that."

Carol's brown eyes twinkled with amusement. "Shall I send her over to you for tips?"

Violet did her best to keep smiling. Her sister wasn't being unkind. Carol had no way of knowing that talking about that part of her past was painful—mostly because Violet always lied about it. Yes, she'd been a model for all of five seconds back when she'd been eighteen. She'd been famous and then it had all gone away. She told herself she was better for the experience and, on her good days, she believed it.

"My biggest advice would be for Bronwen to cut down on the snacks. The camera really does add ten pounds."

Carol laughed. "She'll be crushed. Maybe I should put my foot down and tell her she's going to have to grow up a little more before I'll let her out into the world."

"Probably best for both of you."

Her sister nodded at the package. "Go ahead. You know you want to see what that English lady sent you."

"That English lady? Nana Winifred is the dowager duchess and grandmother to the current Duke of Somerbrooke."

"You call her Nana Winifred. It's hard to be impressed."

"She adores me. I'm like family and she sends me buttons." Violet thought about saying she was happy to wait until after their lunch was finished, but Carol would know she was lying.

She grabbed the package and ripped off the protective paper before slitting the tape holding the top on the box. She took a deep breath, then lifted the lid and gazed inside.

Nana Winifred did not disappoint. Nestled in a cocoon of tissue paper were over a half dozen small plastic bags. Each contained a set of buttons.

The first one Violet picked up held seven green buttons about an inch in diameter. She pulled a pair of white cotton gloves out of a drawer and put them on. Only then did she pour the buttons onto her palm.

They were carved to look like flowers. Or maybe lotus blossoms, she thought, willing herself to keep calm. She would have to do some research, but her first, best guess was these were jade. Hand-carved jade. Chinese for sure and maybe two or three hundred years old.

"Those are nice," Carol said, her tone doubtful.

"They're exquisite. Look at the detail. It was all done by hand." Her heart fluttered. "I'm so excited to see the rest of what's in there."

She returned the buttons to the protective bag, then took off her gloves. "Thank you for letting me get a peek at what she sent. I can wait on the rest."

Her sister shook her head. "You're so weird. They're just buttons."

"I know. Isn't it great?"

A half hour later Carol left to go back to work. Violet cleaned the kitchen before heading down to her shop. She turned the sign to Open and unlocked the front door. Confident she wasn't going to be seeing any customers for the next couple of hours—most of her clients made appointments first—she spread a large cloth over the counter, then opened the package again and began to sort through the buttons.

There were the jade ones she'd studied earlier, and two sets done in mother-of-pearl. She studied a set of twelve brass buttons—obviously military and a couple of centuries old. She knew at least two New York designers who would jump at the chance to buy them.

Her front door opened and a tall, dark-blond-haired man with piercing blue eyes stalked into her shop. He looked stern. No, not stern, furious. Under other circumstances, she would have been completely intimidated—only she couldn't be. Not when she recognized the steady gaze, the firm mouth and the strong jaw.

Ulrich, Duke of Somerbrooke, might be twelve years older and even better looking—if that was possible—but everything else was just as she remembered.

In less than a heartbeat, she was that gawky fourteen-year-old again, visiting England with her mother. Violet had been beyond awkward, all long limbs and frizzy hair, with acne and braces. The phrase *unfortunate* didn't begin to describe her hideous self.

Through a family friend, she and her mother had been invited to a summer party by the dowager duchess and there Violet had fallen madly and passionately in love with the young duke-to-be, as she'd thought of him then.

He'd been all of eighteen and charming. His friends had rolled their eyes when they'd seen her, but not Ulrich. He'd been gracious and lovely and when he'd asked her to dance, she'd thought she was going to die. Right there, in front of the dowager duchess and everyone. Only she hadn't died. She'd danced and he'd chatted and she'd listened, even as her heart had been swept away.

Violet couldn't remember if he'd done all the talking or if she'd managed to cough out a word or two. What she did know for sure was that at the end, he'd leaned close, kissed her cheek and whispered, "You're going to be a beauty, Violet. Give it some time. You'll get there."

The kind promise had sustained her through six more

months of ugly. Then the braces had come off and her skin had cleared up and she'd learned how to tame her hair into gorgeous curls. Three years later one of the most famous photographers in the world had discovered her and claimed her as his muse. What followed had been a disaster, but none of that was Ulrich's fault. He'd promised her she would get there and she had. And he'd danced with her and kissed her cheek. Seriously, what more could her fourteen-year-old self have asked for?

Now she stared at the man he'd become and wondered what on earth he was doing in Happily Inc. In her store.

"Ulrich! I can't believe it. Did Nana Winifred send you? I just got a package from her and she never said—"

"Madam, I must ask you not to refer to my grandmother with such familiarity. I don't know what kind of scheme you've hatched to defraud her, but be aware that I'm here to make sure it all comes to an end. I prefer to handle this privately but I'll have no compunction about involving the authorities. I have friends in the FBI, as well as with the NSA, and I will not hesitate to contact them."

His tone was so cold and harsh, she almost didn't comprehend his words. When the meaning began to sink in, she wasn't sure if she should laugh, cry or throw something at him.

Regardless, the buttons came first. Violet carefully returned them to their plastic bags, then took off her gloves and looked at the hostile man in front of her. A man who had once danced with her and brightened her entire summer.

"I liked you better when you were the Marquess of I-can't-remember-what," she grumbled. "Now I have to be sorry I liked you at all. What on earth are you talking about?"

His icy stare cut through her. "Madam, I do not appreciate you presuming an acquaintance when none exists."

"Stop with the madam crap. If you're trying to sound like

an extra from *Pride and Prejudice*, it's working. Although there is the whole stick up the butt element to it. As for—" she made air quotes "—presuming an acquaintance, we've met. Twelve years ago, at your house. I was fourteen and had frizzy red hair and braces. You danced with me and were actually really nice." She frowned. "Something you seem to have outgrown. What on earth are you doing here and why are you threatening me with the police?"

"You are stealing from my grandmother."

His icy tone was nearly as startling as the words themselves. "Stealing what?"

"Household goods, paintings, objets d'art, silver. I will have to do some research, but I would guess their collective value has placed you in felony territory. You don't seem to be the type of woman who would thrive in prison."

She opened her mouth, then closed it. She told herself not to be afraid of him or his accusation, but that didn't stop the shaking that claimed her body.

"I haven't stolen from anyone," she said, willing herself to sound as confident and stern as he did. "You're a crazy man who's made a huge mistake."

He pointed at the box sitting on the counter. "I recognize my grandmother's handwriting. You can't deny she sent you something. Something that belongs to Battenberg Park."

He sounded so certain, she nearly doubted herself. Nearly. Violet shifted the box so he could see the contents she'd placed on the protective cloth.

"You're right," she said slowly and carefully. "She sent me buttons that she found and purchased at flea markets and estate sales." She pulled a sheet of paper from the bottom of the box and unfolded it. "This would be the receipt because I pay for the buttons before she sends them to me."

She handed Ulrich the paper. "That's what I do. My business here is only a small part of my entire company. I buy and sell buttons from all over the world. I have a network of women—most of them elderly—who find unusual antique buttons. They buy them and bill me. I pay for the buttons and the postage and the ladies send them to me. Your grandmother helped me set up my business several years ago."

He scanned the receipt, then tossed it on the counter. "You're not making any sense. No one can make a living selling buttons."

"Use a dismissive tone all you want. I'll sell these for a hundred dollars each." She shook the bag of jade buttons. "The military ones will go for nearly forty dollars. That's per button, you pompous jerk. Whether or not you believe me about my business, I have a receipt. I also have an entire spreadsheet of transactions between me and your grandmother. So you go ahead and call the FBI or anyone else you want. You're wrong about me and what I do. You've insulted me and totally destroyed a perfectly great memory. I'm only sorry I enjoyed our dance as much as I did."

She pointed to the door. "As you're leaving, you ought to think about how disappointed your grandmother is going to be in your behavior. Now get out!"

Violet was pretty proud of herself for standing her ground—mostly because her legs were really shaking. She knew she was in the right, but still, to be accused like that. It was horrible.

The Duke of Somerbrooke hesitated for only a second before turning and walking out. The moment the door closed, Violet sank onto the small stool she kept behind the counter and told herself to keep breathing. That eventually her heart rate would return to normal and she wouldn't feel so sick to her stomach.

After a couple of minutes, she stored the dowager's buttons in the walk-in safe that had come with the store. Only then did she sink onto the floor and wrap her arms around herself as she gave in to the shaking and the tears that followed.

★ ★ ★

The Happily Inc Landfill and Recycling Center was a surprisingly clean and happy place. Brothers Ed and Ted Lund had bought the business from the city nearly a decade ago and had transformed it from a smelly, overused disaster into a bustling center of commerce and innovation.

While Ed had always been interested in animal welfare—particularly when it came to animals in the wild, Ted was more of a trash guy. He'd studied waste management in college and had worked for waste management companies all around the world. He believed in every form of reusing, recycling, re-everything.

When a distant relative had left the brothers a shockingly large inheritance, they'd decided to combine their two passions into a single enterprise. Happily Inc was delighted with their proposal and had thrown in the surrounding hundred acres as a bonus. Within two years, Ed had transported massive trees from Africa, along with bushes and grasses, transforming the rolling landscape from scrub to the savanna. Drought resistant in their native land, the new plants and trees required very little from Ed. A year later, the first animals arrived.

For his part, Ted had made equally unexpected changes. Recycling was expanded from average to cutting edge. He partnered with the state's universities and colleges, offering practical, hands-on work for students of waste management and ecology. No idea was too crazy to be considered. The state's largest prison in San Bernardino also joined Ted and the colleges and developed a work-study program where inmates could sort through the recycling and earn credits. Those not interested in study could work in the reclamation center where used or broken items were refurbished and sold in the recycling store on-site.

In less than five years Happily Inc had become a recycling leader in the nation. Other cities came to study what worked and why. The store alone had become a huge moneymaker and Ted was talking with several organizations who supported the homeless to see if there was a way to get them involved, as well.

Carol had bought a perfectly good desk at the store. For an extra five dollars, she was able to have it painted candy-apple red—something that made her happy every time she saw it in her small study. As she parked by the dump's main offices late Tuesday afternoon, she thought that while her family was close and loving, they were a bit...odd. No doubt one of the reasons her parents had divorced. Her mom was simply too normal. After all these years, Samantha Lund still lived in New York City and practiced law. Carol and Violet made it a point to visit her at least once a year and kept in touch via phone calls and texts. Samantha had never visited Happily Inc. If she ever saw the dump, she would be appalled.

The thought of her designer-wearing mother walking on the savanna made Carol smile. It also reminded her she should call in the next few days.

Carol walked into the low, one-story building and waved at the receptionist.

"They're in back," Nellie told her. "Giggling over something."

Carol grinned. She doubted her dad and uncle were actually giggling but they could be laughing or chuckling or lobbing crushed aluminum cans into a recycling bin.

She paused at the doorway to their shared office and saw the two men were, in fact, working. Her dad, a tall man with red hair and brown eyes, studied his computer screen intently. Ted, a near carbon-copy of Ed, was on the phone, gesturing as he spoke. Ted saw her first. He waved her in and winked. Her dad looked up and smiled.

"How's my best girl?" he asked as he rose and held out his arms. Carol rushed toward him and hugged him back.

For as long as she could remember, her dad had been there

for her. He'd loved her and supported her, just as he had Violet. To him they were both his best girl.

Ted hung up and joined them. She received another bear hug from him. Unlike his brother, Ted had never married. He always said that Carol and Violet were his girls, too. They were, in the brothers' eyes, beautiful and special.

Carol still remembered the shock of her first day of school when she'd foolishly told everyone that she was special. The other children had quickly disabused her of the notion. When she'd said they were wrong, one of the boys had punched her in the face, bloodying her nose. They'd both been sent home in tears.

For nearly three years Carol had fought against the truth her classmates had been determined she see. When her parents split up and her world got scary, she'd been forced to accept that maybe *special* was too strong a word. Maybe she was just like everyone else. On her worst days, she feared she was actually less. And that truth had defined the rest of her life.

"We're starting a classic computer division," Ted told her as they sat down. Carol took the chair between the two desks where she could see them both. "Old computers are hot right now. The techie folks love them. Some we're fixing up and some we're selling for parts. I'm hoping we can expand the business in that direction so we can stop off-loading our old electronics to third world countries."

Her dad shook his head and sighed. Carol held in a smile. Once Ted got going on exporting used electronics, he was hard to stop.

"Did you want to tell Carol why we asked her to stop by?" her father asked. "Or should I?"

Ted blinked, as if he'd forgotten the point of her visit. "What? Oh, right. You do it."

Her father leaned toward her. "Your uncle and I have a donation for Millie's fund." He opened his desk drawer and handed her a check.

Shortly after Millie had arrived, Carol had realized the sweet giraffe was lonely and needed a herd. The cost to bring three or four female giraffes to Happily Inc, including transportation, additions to the barn and care and feeding for a year would be nearly half a million dollars. Way more than she had in loose change in her sofa cushions. She had nearly seventy-five thousand dollars from her fund-raising efforts. Only four hundred and twenty-five thousand to go.

"Thank you," she said before she glanced at the amount, then nearly fell off her chair when she saw the check was for fifty thousand dollars. "Oh my God! How did you do this? Are you sure? Are you not going to eat for the rest of your lives?"

Ted grinned at her. "We'll be eating, I promise. Business has been good. We have a couple of new contracts with other cities to handle their recycling. Your dad and I aren't giving up anything, Carol. We want to help. We believe in Millie and we believe in you."

She had to blink back unexpected tears. "Thank you," she murmured before scrambling to her feet and racing over to hug them both. "I can't believe it. This is huge!"

"You're a good girl," her father told her, his voice gruff. "We're proud of you and what you've done with the animals here. Millie needs a herd. This is our way of getting you and her closer to that."

"Thank you so much. I'm working on other fund-raising plans and I'm talking to a few people about holding a bake sale over the holidays."

The brothers exchanged a glance as if thinking that was nowhere near enough. She knew that, too, but didn't have any other ideas. She'd studied zoo management and animal care in college, not fund-raising. She'd interned at zoos, not nonprofits, which left her qualified for her job but with no clue as to how to raise enough to get Millie her herd.

"I'll look online," she told them. "I'm inspired to come up with better ideas."

CHAPTER FOUR

It was close to five and the sun was sinking on the horizon by the time Carol was able to drive home. She'd already put out the feed and done a check on the animals. One of the gamekeepers would usher everyone back into their barns and make sure they were settled for the night. She preferred to take the morning shift so she could check on them all before they headed out for their day.

Running a small but vibrant animal preserve took money and time. Visitors and grants provided the funds required for day-to-day operations. Unfortunately she couldn't find a grant that covered acquiring giraffes—otherwise she would have already applied.

She rounded a curve in the road, then put on her brakes when she saw Mathias walking Sophie up ahead. The dog looked delighted, her nose to the ground as she sniffed every inch, her tail waving happily like a doggie banner. Mathias seemed more resigned than pleased. He brightened when he saw her and hurried toward the car.

For a second Carol allowed herself to believe that he was

happy to see her specifically, rather than anyone who might distract him from his still new-to-him roommate.

He and Sophie walked around to the passenger side. She unlocked the door and he slid in, then picked up Sophie and set her on his lap.

"Save me," he said, then closed his eyes and leaned back against the headrest.

Carol laughed. "I suppose you asking me to save you is better than you offering Sophie to me."

"I would if I thought you'd take her. She's exhausting. She's full of energy, curious about everything, won't listen and is constantly begging for food. Other than that, it's great."

"Poor Mathias. Twenty-four hours down, only seven hundred and twenty to go."

He groaned. "I'll never make it."

"Sure you will." She reached out and rubbed Sophie's soft ears. The adorable beagle gave her a quick kiss, then wagged her tail as if asking where they were going next.

"Would it help if I drove you home?" Carol asked.

Mathias looked at her. "Yes, please. And if you *could* take Sophie off my hands, that would be even better."

"Not happening."

"Fine." He closed the door and fastened his seat belt. "Then stay for dinner. I'm going to barbecue steaks. You'll have to watch yours, though. As I learned at lunch, a turned back is an invitation. Someone stole my chicken burrito. I don't want to imagine what I'll be picking up in the morning, after she does her business."

Dinner with Mathias? She'd been in his house before, but never over for a meal. What was he—

She laughed. "You're afraid to be alone with her!"

"Not afraid," he corrected. "Cautious. There's a difference."

"Cluck, cluck, cluck."

"Make chicken noises all you want, this is not an ordinary

dog. She has strange powers and not all of them are used for good."

Carol was still laughing when she pulled into Mathias's drive.

He had one of the larger homes bordering the animal pre-serve. It had to be at least four thousand square feet, with views from every room and upscale finishes on every surface. She didn't consider herself much of a cook, but even she got appliance envy every time she walked into his kitchen. The miles of counter space, the gorgeous cabinets, the massive, professional-size stove.

Carol put her bag on the table in the foyer and unlaced her boots. Mathias took off Sophie's leash. The dog made a bee-line for her water bowl and lapped away. Carol wasn't sure how she did it, but somehow the dog got water on the floor, the wall and the nearby cabinets as she drank.

Mathias walked into the butler's pantry and came out hold-ing a bottle of Scotch. "What would you like? Wine? Some-thing else?"

"Are you drinking yours with a straw?"

"I wish. But seeing as you're here, I'll use a glass."

"I still have to drive home. I'll say wine."

"Red or white?"

"Red."

He collected a bottle of merlot and opened it, then poured her a glass. They each settled on a sofa in his family room. Sophie looked between them before jumping up and join-ing Mathias. She lay down next to him, her paws delicately crossed.

"She's adorable," Carol said.

"She snores."

She laughed. "Such pain."

"I'm exhausted. How was your day?"

"Good." She thought about the unexpected check. "My dad

and uncle made a generous donation to Millie's fund. Only three hundred and seventy-five thousand left." She raised her eyebrows. "Feeling generous?"

"I'd say no problem but Sophie destroyed three weeks' worth of work in about ten minutes today."

She winced. "Did she really? I'm sorry."

"You and me both. I had to bribe Natalie to look after her while I'm in the studio. I'm also looking for a dog walker to take her out a couple of times a day. She has to be kept busy so she's tired when we get home. Otherwise God knows what trouble she'd get into."

"Poor you."

"Tell me about it. So three hundred and seventy-five thousand, huh?" He shifted his drink to his other hand and absently petted Sophie. "Too bad you can't put Millie to work for some of the money. You know, get her in a movie or something. Do the animals get paid?"

"I believe they're rented."

"That's harsh. You have a unique problem, I'll admit it. You're going to have to be creative to find your way out." He frowned. "How did you get into looking after big animals?" The frown faded. "Or exotic cows, as I like to think of them."

"I'd rather you didn't."

"I know."

She sighed. "You're difficult."

"I'm charming and you know it."

Sadly, she did. "Violet and I were born in Connecticut and lived there until I was eight and she was six. Then our parents split up. Mom moved us to Manhattan while Dad took off for South Africa."

"An unexpected choice."

"He'd always been interested in animal welfare and had the opportunity to work on a large preserve. Violet and I visited every summer. It was very cool."

She'd loved everything about the experience—the simple housing, the closeness with nature, the animals themselves. When it had been time to go back to New York, she'd started counting down the days until she could return.

"I can't exactly see Violet loving it," he said.

"You're right. It wasn't her thing. She would only stay for a few weeks, then head back to the States. But I never wanted to leave. I was allowed to hang out with all the adults working there. They let me ride along and help." She smiled at the memories.

"So your dad moved back here and started the preserve?"

"Uh-huh. I finished college and joined him. He manages the business side of things and works with his brother. My team and I take care of our animals."

"I don't see a lot of your team members out at one in the morning, dealing with a sick cow."

"Stop saying cow. I'd throw a pillow at you but I might hit Sophie."

The beagle perked up when she heard her name and wagged her tail.

"Cheap talk," Mathias said, then sipped his drink. "What happens after Millie gets her herd? Are you done collecting animals?"

"We're going to have to make some decisions. We only have females. Eventually they'll pass on, so we have to figure out what we want to do. Dad and I have been talking about offering a home for older circus animals, or getting a few males and starting a breeding program. We could look at helping out some of the zoos who want to separate herds for a period of time. Millie is the only species we have that's endangered, but we could look at helping out with different at-risk species. There are a lot of options."

Mathias stared at her. "You're putting what I do in perspective. I make dishes." He glanced at Sophie. "And you break them."

"You create beautiful things. I take care of a few gazelles and a giraffe."

"Still, impressive."

The unexpected compliment made her want to squirm on her seat. "Thank you."

"You're welcome. I'm going to start the barbecue." He rose. "Now, tell me, how do you like your, um, cow?"

He'd moved away from the sofa, so she tossed a pillow at him. He avoided it easily, then shook his head. "Violence is never the answer, Carol."

"You can say that because you've never had to deal with anyone as annoying as yourself."

"Millie would be very disappointed in your attitude." He looked at Sophie. "We won't tell her, will we?"

Sophie barked in agreement.

Carol sighed as she followed them both into the kitchen. Mathias was an interesting guy, she thought, watching him pull steaks out of the refrigerator. More than interesting. Funny and sexy. If only, she thought…then told herself to get real. She would have a lot more luck wishing for the three hundred and seventy-five thousand dollars she needed than wishing someone like him would notice someone like her. Plus a night with Mathias would simply be that—a night, while the money would mean friends for Millie. A far better use of her wishing time.

Violet spent nearly twenty-four hours alternating between hurt feelings and rage. Neither was especially conducive to sleep so she was up and showered before dawn. At seven, she got in her car and went by the donut place, then headed out to the preserve. With luck she would arrive just as Carol was finishing up with her charges.

She parked by the main barn. The morning was cool, the sky clear. As she watched several gazelles came bounding out and headed across the grass. A minute later she saw the ever stately Millie walking out to greet the day. Violet collected coffee and donuts, then went in search of her sister.

Carol was in her office, waiting for her computer to boot. Her eyes widened with surprise.

"Do you know what time it is?" she asked, her tone teasing. "Shouldn't you be asleep?"

"I wish." She offered one of the coffees, then set the box of donuts on the desk. Irritation and hurt and a dozen other emotions burned. "I'm so angry, I couldn't sleep."

Her sister immediately looked concerned. "What happened? Are you okay?"

"Yes. No. I guess. I just…" She stomped her foot, wishing Ulrich's head was in the vicinity of her shoe. "For the record, English dukes are stupid. Especially Ulrich." She collapsed into a chair and groaned. "I hate him. No, I disdain him. He's loathsome."

"Okay, tell me who he is so I can hate him, too."

"You know I get buttons from all over the world," Violet began. "I got started when I was in England like twelve years ago."

"Nana Winifred," Carol said. "The dowager duchess of…" Her voice trailed off as her eyes widened. "His mother?"

"Grandmother. And she's not the problem. I buy and sell buttons. That's what I do. It's how I make my living. But does he know that? No. Instead of asking anything, he waltzed into my store with his prissy accent and accused me of stealing!"

Violet briefly explained what had happened. "He threatened me, if you can believe it."

"What a jerk. Do you need to talk to a lawyer or something?"

"I don't think so. I have records of all my purchases. I didn't steal anything. As for taking advantage of his grandmother, I buy everything sight unseen. If anyone is at risk, it's me. He's a pinhead." She sipped her coffee. "Good-looking, but still. That's no excuse."

She thought about everything he'd said. "He didn't talk to me first, you know. He just accused. There was no thought that he might have been wrong. And to think that all this time, I'd liked him."

Carol's brows drew together. "Okay, you've lost me again. What?"

"That summer when Mom took me to England and you stayed with Dad, that's when I met Ulrich. He was four years older and I thought he was so sophisticated and handsome. There was a dance. He danced with me." She didn't mention the part about him telling her that she would grow up to be a beauty. That was too private to share, even with her sister who knew almost everything about her.

"I was a kid and he was nice at a time when not many guys were. I daydreamed."

"Your handsome prince." Carol's tone was sympathetic. "Or in this case, your handsome duke."

"Who turned out to be a complete jerk. I hate him."

"You disdain him," her sister corrected mildly.

"That, too. He ruined everything. It's so unfair. I was minding my own business, and then suddenly, there he was, polluting my world." Violet reached for a donut and took a bite. "I know he can't hurt me. Nana Winifred is going to be furious when she finds out about this. I hope she slaps him." The thought of the elderly woman backhanding Ulrich across his high cheekbones brightened her morning.

"You have quite the vindictive streak," Carol said mildly. "I totally respect it and you. So you're not going to do anything."

"I'm not sure what I would do. Call his grandmother? That sounds like tattling. Plus it would break her heart and

I don't want that. She adores Ulrich." Which meant the cliché of there being no accounting for taste was painfully true.

"What's the next step?"

"Aside from whining to you?" Violet sighed. "There isn't one. I'm only sorry I danced with him." And liked it. That was the real kick in the gut. That she'd liked the dance and the man and she'd imagined oh so many wonderful things about him.

"But if I ever see him again, I'm going to tell him he's a complete and total jerk."

"You go girl," Carol told her.

Mathias glanced at the clock and knew he didn't have much time. He put down the small glass piece he was working and pulled off his protective goggles. It was nearly three in the afternoon, so approaching eight in the morning outside of Shanghai. Maya, his brother Del's fiancée, had emailed him requesting a video call. They'd settled on a date and time, although Mathias honestly had no idea why she wanted to speak to him. He barely knew Maya.

She'd been his brother's girlfriend back in high school, but he hadn't bothered paying attention to much beyond his own life. By the time she'd returned to Fool's Gold a few years ago, he and Ronan had already left their little hometown in the California mountains. They'd met a couple of times since, but that was it. So what did she want with him now?

A question that would be answered soon enough, he told himself just as his screen shifted to show an incoming call.

He hit the video button and Maya appeared on his screen. She was a pretty, green-eyed blonde wearing an oversize T-shirt and holding a mug.

"Morning," she said with a smile.

"Afternoon. How's China?"

"Good. How are the States?"

"Also good."

Maya grinned. "I hear you're taking care of Sophie for a month. How's that going?"

He grimaced. "Let's not talk about that. I've had to bribe Natalie, our office manager, to keep her in her office while I work. That dog has an uncanny ability to find the most expensive piece of glass with her tail and destroy it."

"Yikes. I'm sorry."

"Me, too. I've hired a dog walker in a futile attempt to tire her out. She gets two walks a day. She sleeps well, but loudly." He thought about mentioning the massive piles of poop, but decided against it. Maya was probably still on her first cup of coffee.

"You're being domesticated," Maya teased. "By the time Elaine's back, you won't want to let Sophie go."

Mathias leaned back in his chair. "Right. That's going to happen."

She laughed. "Okay, maybe you won't be sobbing, but I suspect she'll find her way into your heart." She took a sip of her drink. "So you're probably wondering what I wanted to talk about."

"I am."

"It's the wedding. You know it's at the end of the month, right?"

"I received your charming email invite, so yes."

"Good. I was hoping you could help with that."

"I don't understand. With what?"

"The wedding. Planning it, really."

Mathias nearly came out of his chair. "You're getting married in less than four weeks and you haven't planned your wedding?"

He was aware that he sounded painfully like a woman, but even he knew that weddings took months to pull together. There were a million details about which he knew nothing.

"I have my dress," Maya said helpfully. "That's something. Originally Del and I were just going to do the justice of the peace thing but we've been talking and we want a traditional wedding. There's a business in town—Weddings Out of the Box. I've spoken with the owner. Do you know her? Is she the one engaged to Nick?"

"She is and you should be talking to her, not me."

"I'm going to but I was hoping you would go to the meetings, too. Be my representative in person."

Mathias wanted to writhe in his chair. He wanted to stand up and say there was no way in hell. "Why not ask Nick?"

"Because he and Pallas are a couple and he won't tell her if I don't like something. Mathias, please? I've seen your work and I like how you create. Your pieces make me feel really good inside. I want that for my wedding."

Was there a conspiracy? First his mother and now his future sister-in-law, both wanting something from him. Something he didn't want to give. Something he should absolutely refuse.

"Please," Maya said quietly. "I need you, Mathias. I need your help to make this happen."

He swore under his breath before glaring at her. "You're going to owe me, Maya."

She laughed and clapped her hands together. "Forever, I swear. Thank you, thank you, thank you. I have the first meeting set up already. I'll email you the information. You're the best."

"Yeah, yeah. Sell it somewhere else. I meant what I said— you owe me."

She blew him a kiss and hung up. Mathias stared at the screen before closing the program and reaching for his cell phone.

"Hello?"

Some people's voices were distorted over the phone, but not Carol's. That combination of slightly sexy, slightly sweet came through perfectly. Mathias told himself to ignore the automatic tightening in his gut.

"It's Mathias. I need your help."

"Don't you want to start by asking about my day? Or commenting on the weather?"

"Not really."

"You're such a guy. Fine. What's wrong? And if it's about Sophie, I'm going to tell you to suck it up. She's a sweet little girl and you are more than capable of taking care of her."

"Thanks for your undying emotional support," he said drily. "I'm calling because my future sister-in-law wants me to help plan her wedding. I don't know what she's thinking, but I would be a disaster and I need you to help me."

"Shouldn't you call Violet? She's the one with the style sense."

"I don't want Violet."

He spoke without thinking and then was stuck with the truth hanging out there—flapping in the breeze. He wanted Carol, he had for a long time. Things being what they were, he wasn't going to do anything about the wanting, but helping him with the wedding wasn't that. It was...

He realized he'd called Carol without a second thought, without considering who would be better. Why was that? Maybe because of the dreams, or maybe because...

"My sister will be heartbroken." Carol sounded more cheerful than upset, then she laughed. "Well, crap. I just realized you're asking me because I'm a woman. Just to be clear, being female doesn't mean we're all born with an innate ability to plan a wedding."

"Sure you are. It comes with having breasts."

"You're the most annoying man on the planet."

"So that's a yes?"

She sighed. "Yes, Mathias, I will help you plan the wedding. I assume it's in town?"

"At Weddings Out of the Box."

"Perfect! Pallas will make sure we don't mess up."

"I'll let you know when we have our first meeting. And thanks, Carol."

"You're welcome."

She hung up. He did the same and left his phone on the desk before walking back to the glass piece he'd been working on. The small giraffe was maybe eight inches tall. The features were all there, but the little statue was static. He wanted movement and didn't know how to make that happen.

Nick walked into the studio. "Hey. Didn't you have a call with Maya?"

"She wants me to help with her wedding."

Nick grinned. "Better you than me."

"Apparently. Obviously I'm the one she trusts."

"Or she figures you're the soft touch."

"Either way, I'm the good brother."

Mathias studied the giraffe before tossing it into the recycling bin where it shattered into dozens of pieces.

"You gotta stop doing that," Nick told him. "It was good."

"Not good enough. If it's not perfect, it can't live."

"Can't or won't?" Nick asked.

Mathias ignored the question.

"What about those?" His brother pointed to the shelves filled with imperfect pieces. Plates that weren't exactly round or vases that sloped on one side. "They're still alive."

"Not alive, just not worth destroying." They were pedestrian and didn't matter. The everyday stuff was simply how he made his living. It wasn't art.

Natalie came into the studio with Sophie on her leash. "I have to go run some errands," she said, crossing to him. "You're going to have to deal with your dog."

"She's not my dog," Mathias muttered, only to have Sophie shoot him a wounded look. As if she'd understood what he was saying.

He took the leash. Sophie turned her back to him. He sighed. Why was this happening to him? First the dog and now a wedding. It wasn't fair.

"Fine," he grumbled. "I'm sorry. You're a good girl."

Sophie still kept her back to him.

Giving in to the inevitable, Mathias opened one of his desk drawers and pulled out a bag of dog treats. Sophie spun to face him, her ears forward, her tail going about eighty miles an hour.

"Apparently you're forgiven," Nick pointed out. "It's good to see you finally in a relationship."

CHAPTER FIVE

The Sweet Dreams Inn off of Eternal Drive was the stuff of nightmares—at least for Ulrich. His plan had been to leave Happily Inc after he concluded his business with Violet Lund—thief and swindler—return to Los Angeles and catch a flight back to England. Only nothing had gone according to plan.

His meeting with the surprisingly attractive and very animated woman had left him feeling both awkward and confused. She had been able to produce a bill of sale for the buttons his grandmother had sent, and buttons were not what had been stolen from the house. Was she not the thief and if not her, then who?

Ulrich had driven to LA only to reschedule his flight and return to Happily Inc. The Sweet Dreams Inn had been the first hotel he'd seen, so he'd pulled in. Too late he'd discovered it was a *themed* hotel with each of the rooms representing something ridiculous. For reasons not completely clear to him, he'd agreed to a couple of nights in the Drive-In Room, which was how he found himself with a mattress fit into a red, 1959 Cadillac convertible, a television the size of a movie screen and a sitting room decorated like a concession stand. Even he had to admit the car was beautiful—with big fins and white-walled tires. Still, it wasn't where one expected to sleep. Regardless of the strange surroundings, the Wi-Fi was excellent and the kitchen delivered meals to his room.

Ulrich had spent nearly a day researching Violet Lund and antique buttons only to come to the conclusion that it was more than possible that she had been telling the truth. There was money to be made in the world of buttons. Even more troubling, it seemed Miss Violet Lund was nothing more than a very honest shopkeeper.

She had no criminal record, no trouble with the IRS, not even a ticket. He'd used several online sites to investigate her and she'd come back annoyingly normal and law-abiding. How could he have been so wrong?

He was never wrong—he made it a point to be sure of things. He'd only been seriously fooled once in his life and that had been by his ex-wife, Penelope. In that case, the deception had been deliberate—at least on her part. Thinking about that didn't help him at all, and he mentally turned his back on his former wife. The bigger question was what to do about Violet. He'd slept on the information, then had woken up in the morning with no clear idea of what to do next.

After showering, he ordered breakfast and knew he had to come up with a plan—only he had no idea what it would be. He opened another file on his computer and reviewed the list of missing items provided to him by his housekeeper and his own investigation.

The trouble had started three months ago when Ulrich had ordered a complete inventory of the house, including the attics. The project had taken over a month and they'd discovered some truly wonderful pieces. But many things had also been missing.

The public rooms were closely monitored and protected,

and the guests who stayed in the hotel wing didn't have access to the private residence without an escort. The previous inventory had been conducted by his father, nearly five years before. Ulrich had no way of knowing what had been taken when. Or so he'd thought.

His grandmother's new secretary had offered a possible explanation when she'd told him about the packages being sent to one Violet Lund in Happily Inc, California. He'd kept watch and had seen the last one mailed himself. He'd guessed on the delivery date and when it had aligned with his trip to Los Angeles, he'd decided to make a slight detour to confront the thief. All for naught.

His cell phone rang. He glanced at his watch and calculated the time difference, then answered the call.

"Please tell me you're having tea. Good, English tea. What they serve here is dreadful."

His grandmother laughed. "Poor Ulrich, lost in America. I wish I could say the adventure will do you good, but we both know that's not the case. How is Los Angeles? Is it sunny this morning? Are you staying by the ocean? I have to say, the Pacific is my favorite of all the oceans."

Ulrich briefly thought about not telling his grandmother where he was, then dismissed the idea. He was a man of his word and as such, truthful in all things. At least when it came to those he loved. As that list seemed to begin and end with his grandmother—in terms of people and not places—he had to come clean.

"I'm not in Los Angeles. I'm in Happily Inc."

"What on earth are you doing—" His grandmother went silent, then sighed. "You're there to see Violet? I can't imagine why."

"I thought she was stealing."

"Ulrich! No. You couldn't. How do you even know I have business with her?"

"I saw the packages."

His grandmother sniffed. "You mean that horrible woman you made me hire has been spying on me. I'm getting rid of her, Ulrich. You may be the duke but I'm your grandmother and I won't be told what to do by you or anyone. I've disliked her from the start. You convinced me I was being unfair, but I know the only reason she took the position was to be in proximity to you. I'm sure she was hoping you would fall madly in love with her."

Ulrich thought about the twentysomething woman who served as his grandmother's secretary. He honestly couldn't even remember the color of her eyes. Nothing about her was memorable. The same could not be said for the very fiery Violet, he thought. Her green eyes had flashed with annoyance, then anger, then disdain. She'd been so beautiful, so *alive*. He'd always preferred quiet, plain women, but there was something about her riot of red curls and the way she'd moved.

"Ulrich?"

"Yes, Grandmother. You're quite correct. You are more than capable of hiring or firing any one of your staff. And I apologize for listening to your secretary when she told me about the packages being mailed."

"As you should."

He smiled. Despite her stern words, her tone had already softened.

"If you are purchasing buttons yourself and then selling them to Violet, what about the other items that have gone missing?"

His grandmother sighed. "That is a more complicated question than one would think."

"I have little to occupy my day, so take your time."

"Fine. If you must know, I sold several of the paintings. I didn't mean to, but each one was admired by one of our guests. They were lesser works and I had them appraised. I know the price was fair. It was three years ago, when we had the trouble with the roof and the plumbing at the same time."

Ulrich turned away from his computer and shook his head. "The money you said you'd been saving for an emergency?" he asked quietly.

"Yes. It was from the paintings."

Her supposed emergency fund—nearly a hundred thousand pounds—had come in handy. While Battenberg Park had been in his family for nearly five hundred years, history came at a price. There was always something to be repaired or replaced. A wet and cold summer had meant a reduction in crops and had kept away the tourists. That, combined with a long-needed roof replacement and some plumbing issues had meant every spare penny had gone back into the house.

The following year had been better and the year after, better still. The coffers were, if not full, then comfortably plump. Technically the estate was never without the possibility of cash. There was always something around that could be sold, but Ulrich wanted to maintain as much of his heritage as possible. Not that he had heirs, but one day, with luck, the family line would be safe for another generation or two.

"Several of the crystal pieces were broken," his grandmother continued. "I knew you would be upset, so I didn't tell you."

He started to ask how that could have happened, then realized the answer. A school for the disabled operated quite near the estate. His grandmother made it a point to hire staff from the school. A few of the students lacked physical mobility and dexterity. It was not impossible to imagine a crystal vase, or five, tumbling to the ground.

He rubbed his forehead. "And the rest of it?"

"A few were donated to worthy causes to help them raise

money, there was a small fire in one of the storage sheds while you were traveling to—"

"A fire? You didn't want to mention a fire?"

"You were on your honeymoon. I knew you would have returned. It seemed easier to handle things myself. Which I did. My point is, you were wrong about Violet. I buy buttons for her when I find them. Nothing else."

"So it appears."

He made a mental note to have a more thorough conversation with his grandmother when he returned home. He could only imagine what else she'd kept from him in the name of handling things herself.

"I'm sorry," she told him, her voice oddly contrite. "I know how much Battenberg Park means to you. I didn't want to upset you, but it seems my good intentions have had unforeseen consequences."

"You have no idea."

He hadn't meant to say that out loud but apparently he had because his grandmother's voice sharpened.

"What does that mean? You haven't already spoken to Violet, have you? Oh, Ulrich. She's lovely and I adore her. If you've offended her or hurt her feelings…"

"I'll make it right." He didn't want to, but he had no choice. It was a matter of honor. "I have a teleconference later this morning but I will go see her in the afternoon."

"And apologize."

He sighed. "Yes."

"With great sincerity?"

"I promise."

"Good. She's very charming, Ulrich. I think you'll like her if you give her a chance. You've met her, you know. Years ago."

"So she informed me."

At his house, apparently, although he had no recollection of the event.

"Then I'll leave you to it. I love you, Ulrich. Be a good boy."

He smiled. "I will. I love you as well, Grandmother. Goodbye."

He hung up, then set his cell phone on the desk. He would speak to Violet that afternoon, as he'd said, then drive back to Los Angeles in the morning and get a return flight to London. There was nothing to keep him here. At home there was work to be done. Always work. As for someone special—he'd long since given up on that, but it was time to get on with finding a wife and producing heirs. That was as much his responsibility as the roof or the glazing. And he'd never been a man who shirked what needed to be done.

Carol couldn't remember how the standing date with her friends had begun. Perhaps it had existed before she and Violet had moved to Happily Inc and they'd simply been invited to join in. Regardless, it was one of her favorite times—enjoying a couple of hours with the women in her life.

The hosting duties rotated and whoever served as host chose either lunch or dinner and provided the entrée and drinks. Everyone else brought something and a good time was had by all.

If the weather cooperated, Carol always picked lunch when it was her turn. Her friends joined her out by the largest grove of trees on the faux savanna. Her father and uncle set out a big table and chairs for them. Carol had a camp stove where she heated the chicken she'd cooked that morning and would warm the tortillas. The other ingredients for the taco bar were ready in plastic containers and she'd made a sparkling pink non-alcoholic punch to add a festive touch.

"Hi!" Silver Tesdal called as she walked along the path.

The tall, leggy platinum blonde carried a shopping bag in one hand. "I always feel as if I need a passport when I come here. I love it!"

They hugged, then Silver set down her bag. "I have the strangest dessert ever, but I think it's a real find. We'll have to see."

Carol eyed the plain white bag. "Now I'm curious."

"As you should be."

Before Carol could ask more, the other women arrived. Her sister, Violet, Natalie Kaleta from the gallery, Pallas Saunders who owned Weddings Out of the Box, and Wynn Beauchene, owner of the town's graphic design and print store.

Violet, who knew about the tacos, had brought chips, dip and guacamole. The other women contributed a green salad and cookies. Carol reached for the champagne glasses she'd carted along, then nodded at Pallas who was doing her best not to grin too broadly.

"Show them," Carol told her friend.

Pallas laughed, then held out her left hand. A diamond solitaire sparkled on her ring finger.

Violet, Silver and Wynn shrieked, then lunged for their friend and started a group hug. Carol was waved in and they all hung on in celebration.

"How long?" Violet demanded when they'd released each other. "When did he propose?"

"Saturday at the under-the-sea wedding."

Silver looked from the pink, bubbly drink to Carol. "You knew."

Carol raised a shoulder. "I helped Nick pick out the ring. He had it narrowed down to three and texted me pictures from the jewelry store." She'd been surprised Nick would ask her opinion but then had guessed he'd asked Mathias to name a woman who could be trusted not to spill the secret.

She smiled at Pallas. "So if you don't like it, it's my fault."

Pallas clutched her left hand to her chest. "What's not to like? It's beautiful."

Carol passed out the drinks and they all toasted their friend, then sat down to lunch. She quickly heated tortillas for everyone and they served themselves from the taco bar and salad, then took their seats.

"So what's new?" Pallas asked. "I've been in an engagement fog. What have I missed?"

"Violet barely escaped being arrested by a hunky English guy," Silver offered.

Violet rolled her eyes. "He had no authority to arrest me. Being a jerk is a form of free speech, so he did that instead." She explained about the button mix-up.

"Did he apologize?" Natalie asked. "He needs to say he's sorry."

"Hardly. I'm sure he left town the same day. Good riddance."

Carol thought about the accusations. Despite her sister's defiance, she had to have been scared at the time. Or at least uncomfortable.

"I can't believe he came all this way to confront you about the buttons."

"Me, either." Violet picked up her taco. "I'm sure he had business somewhere in the country. Maybe he was lining up tea franchises or something. And that's enough about my crazy Englishman," Violet said firmly. She turned to Pallas. "So, you're putting on a Mitchell wedding."

Pallas groaned. "Don't remind me. I'm so nervous. I've never met Nick's parents and this isn't exactly how I'd choose to do it. At a wedding that I'm planning. What if something goes wrong? They'll hate me forever."

"Nothing's going to go wrong," Natalie said soothingly. "You always do a great job."

As she spoke, she reached into her large tote bag and pulled out a square piece of purple paper. Her fingers moved quickly and in a matter of seconds, she'd created a small bird. When Pallas picked it up, the wings seemed to flutter.

Carol had no idea how Natalie did that. She took origami from fun to extraordinary. She created all kinds of creatures, made mobiles and origami sculpture. Her job at the gallery was more about paying for her art than because she enjoyed answering the phone.

Everyone had a talent but her, Carol thought wistfully. Violet with her buttons and eye for fashion, Natalie with her mixed-media pieces. Wynn designed posters and banners and everything that could be printed. Pallas created beautiful weddings. Even Silver, who owned a trailer that had been converted to a traveling bar called AlcoHaul made mixology magic at weddings and other events. All Carol did was take care of a bunch of animals. They were special and she was, well, not.

"Nick's father is a famous artist," Pallas said, setting the paper bird on her palm. "Everything I've heard says he's really difficult. What if he hates me?"

"He's not going to hate you," Silver told her. "You're too likable."

"I wish." Pallas turned to Carol. "Mathias told me he'd asked you to help him with the planning. You're going to do it, right?"

Violet stared at her sister. "You're helping plan the wedding?"

"Mathias asked me to, so I agreed. He says he wants a female point of view, but he has Pallas and Maya for that. I think of myself more as his emotional support animal."

Everyone laughed, then went back for seconds on the tacos. When they were done eating, Silver pulled a tall bakery box out of her bag.

"Okay, I know this is really strange, but it's cool, too. Tell me what you think."

She opened the box from the bottom, pulling off the top and exposing what looked like several pink flowers in a flowerpot. Only the flowers were made from meringue, as were the leaves, and the so-called dirt was actually mini dark chocolate chips.

"The flowerpot is cake," Silver explained. "The fondant icing can be in any color so it coordinates. The same with the flower meringue."

Carol had never seen anything like it. Judging from everyone else's look of surprise, they hadn't, either.

"You could put these on the table," Pallas breathed. "They'd be decorations *and* dessert. Tell me you have contact information."

Silver pulled a business card out of her jeans pocket and handed it over. "Now let's find out how great this cake tastes."

She picked up a knife. Carol reached for small plates only to see movement out of the corner of her eye. She turned and saw a tail-wagging beagle racing toward them.

"Sophie," she called as she rose and walked toward the bounding dog. "What are you doing out here?"

Sophie rushed toward her, then stopped at her feet. Carol crouched down and petted her. "Are you all by yourself? Where's Mathias?" She scanned the area but didn't see him anywhere. How on earth had Sophie ended up here?

"Did she escape?" Natalie asked with a sigh. "She's good at that. Yesterday I couldn't find her for nearly an hour. It turned out she'd crawled into an empty cabinet in the lunchroom and was curled up there, sleeping."

"I don't know where she came from," Carol admitted. "Our fencing is designed to keep our grazing animals in, not small dogs out." Sophie could have easily slipped through the slats or ducked under one of the gates. The bigger question was how she got out of Mathias's place. That had to have been her starting point. There was no way she could have made it all the way here from town.

"Come sit by me," Carol told the beagle as she returned to her chair.

Sophie followed her happily, then flopped at her feet. Carol kept her in place with bits of chicken and cheese. She kept trying Mathias on his cell only to be sent directly to voice mail.

Lunch broke up about twenty minutes later. They all helped with cleanup. Carol herded Sophie to her car, then stored the extra food in her trunk. No way she could trust the dog in the same space as leftovers. She doubted there was a plastic container made that was Sophie-proof.

"We'll stop by my place first," she told her canine passenger as they started down the road. "I need to put the rest of the lunch away, then we'll head over to Mathias's place and figure out how you got out. After that I have a meeting."

Actually a teleconference with Maya to help plan her wedding.

"Let's see, if you're Elaine's little girl and Maya is marrying one of her sons, then she's your what? Aunt-in-law? Sister-in-law?"

Sophie barked and Carol laughed. "Yes, family relationships are complicated."

So were boy-girl ones, she thought as she drove toward her house. If only Mathias were slightly less attractive. Or not so interested in sexy bridesmaids. If only she were special enough to capture his attention with wild plumage or gorgeous fur.

She paused, realizing she'd slipped into an animal metaphor, which was okay, as long both she and Mathias were animals in that metaphor. Because if she walked in wearing feathers or some kind of animal skin she was pretty sure he wouldn't think she was much more than frighteningly insane. Still, it would be nice to be one of those sultry, sophisticated types he seemed to favor instead of just herself.

She pulled into her driveway and quickly unloaded the left-overs, then continued her journey to his place. Sophie jumped out of the car and led the way to the front door.

Carol knocked but there was no answer. She tried the knob and it turned easily, so she let the dog in and followed Sophie.

"Mathias, it's Carol. I brought your dog back."

There was no answer, but that was hardly a surprise. The house was huge and Mathias could be anywhere.

Sophie barked, then started down the hall. Carol went with her, through the kitchen and out toward the sunroom where she knew he often sketched.

Sure enough he sat at a big drafting table by the window overlooking the animal preserve.

She took a moment to study his broad shoulders and short, dark hair. He had a pad of paper in front of him. His hand moved, creating more quickly than the eye could follow.

"Hey, Sophie," he said absently, reaching down to rub her ears. "You just wake up?"

"No, she just got home."

Mathias turned to stare at her. "Carol. Hi. Did I know you were stopping by?"

"I'm not stopping by. I'm returning your dog. She was out on the savanna."

He dropped the pencil and frowned. "She couldn't be. She's been here with me. We came back here and I let her out to do her thing, then closed the back door." The frown deepened as he stood. "I know I made sure the door latched."

They walked to the back of the house where a door stood open. Mathias closed it and checked the lock, then turned to Sophie.

"Now you're scaring me."

She wagged her tail.

"Maybe she's like those dinosaurs in *Jurassic Park*," Carol teased. "She's learning how to open doors."

"This dog is going to take over the world." He glanced at his watch. "Come on. We have a meeting at Weddings Out of the Box. I'll drive."

Because they were going together? Maybe on the way he would turn to her and express his undying lust. They could pull to the side of the road and...

Carol held in a groan. The side of the road? That wasn't exactly romantic. She couldn't even fantasize creatively.

"I have no idea why you want me at the meeting," she said as he clipped a leash onto Sophie's collar and led the way to his car. "You're creative enough for ten people. As for the female point of view, Pallas and Violet will both be there. You really don't need me."

Mathias held open the passenger door. For a second, when their eyes met, she would have sworn she saw...something. A flash of...

No, she told herself firmly. That was just wishful thinking. Mathias was a charming, sexy lover of one-night stands with beautiful, sexy, out-of-town bridesmaids. To believe anything else was to be a fool.

"You'll be the voice of reason," he told her.

"Great. I'm the stern, maiden aunt. How wonderful."

She snapped her seat belt into place, then patted her lap for Sophie to sit on her. The beagle obliged, then gave her a quick kiss on the cheek, as if saying she was liked. Not exactly a declaration a girl could dream about, but at least beagle love didn't ever break your heart.

CHAPTER SIX

"I'm the mature voice of reason," Carol said drily as she sat next to Violet in Pallas's office at Weddings Out of the Box. "I'm not sure why anyone thinks that's necessary. I'm here to help with Maya and Del's wedding, but now I have a purpose."

"Because you didn't before?" Violet asked with a laugh.

Violet had come prepared with pen and paper. Unlike her sister, Violet was in on the meeting to offer creative suggestions. Pallas was terrified at the thought of putting on a wedding for her soon-to-be in-laws—especially on short notice. While she was happy to support her friend, Violet honestly didn't get the problem. Pallas had organized dozens and dozens of weddings and they'd all been lovely events. There was no reason to think Maya's was going to be different.

Mathias, brother of the groom, was also in on the planning meeting. Pallas typed on her computer and seconds later a pretty, green-eyed blonde appeared on the screen.

"Hi, everyone," she said with a wave.

Pallas made introductions. Maya greeted them all, then said, "Mathias, Del says hi."

"Hi back." Mathias leaned toward her. "If he's so interested in brotherly love, why isn't he part of the meeting?"

"Because it's six thirty in the morning and he was up late with clients." Maya held up a cup of coffee. "Besides, I have a lot more opinions about our wedding than he does." She wrinkled her nose. "So far his contribution consists of 'I want cake.'"

"There's going to be cake," Pallas assured her. "Not to worry. Do you have the information I sent you?"

"I do and I've looked over it." Maya shuffled several pieces of paper. "You're very thorough, which I appreciate. I know there isn't much time."

Pallas flinched, as if the reminder of putting together a wedding in three weeks was physically painful. Violet wanted to be supportive, but it was tough not to laugh. Pallas always did this—she got so invested in her clients' events that she suffered way more than they did.

"We can do this," Violet said soothingly. "It's going to be great. Pallas mentioned you already have your dress, right?"

"I do." Maya held up a picture of a mermaid-style lace-covered gown with a sweetheart neckline. It was elegant and beautiful.

Pallas typed on her tablet. "Having the dress is huge. With that and the venue, we should be fine. Do you have a theme in mind?"

Maya's eyebrows drew together. "What do you mean?"

"I sent ideas in the materials." Pallas held up a brochure. "That's what we do here. Themed weddings. Cowboy weddings, Roman weddings, under-the-sea weddings."

"Maybe something from *Lord of the Rings*," Mathias offered.

Carol poked him in the arm. "You're supposed to be helping."

"I think Del would look great dressed up as a hobbit."

"Let's stay focused," Pallas murmured. "Maya, what were you thinking?"

"I don't know. Something pretty. Elegant. I don't want anything with hobbits. Can't we just do a regular wedding?"

Pallas bit her lower lip. "That's a fairly broad category."

A statement that probably had Maya confused. Violet would guess the bride was picturing a regular kind of wedding, but the venue she'd chosen specialized in everything from pirate weddings to black-and-white Regency extravaganzas. Pallas would automatically be thinking how to make things unique while Maya seemed to want conventional. It would have made more sense for Maya and Del to go to a more traditional venue in town. She wondered if they'd chosen Weddings Out of the Box because Nick was engaged to Pallas. Or maybe the tight time frame was the driver. Pallas had a spot because of a cancellation—it was possible no one else in town could have fit them in.

"I have an idea," Violet said as she smiled at Maya. "Tell me what you think about this. An elegant princess wedding. Simple, beautiful, classic. As if Grace Kelly were getting married today."

"I like that," Maya said immediately. "I like that a lot."

Pallas visibly relaxed. "Me, too. I can picture exactly what I'd suggest." She reached for a huge three-ring binder.

"I just picked up some new linens," she said, flipping through the pages. "Here they are." She held up a picture of a sheer table runner edged with lace.

"Those are beautiful," Maya breathed, leaning close to her computer screen. "I love them."

"Me, too. Great. There's so much we can do. I'm thinking a lot of glass on the table. Maybe mirrors under clear bowls of flowers, with short, pillar candles in glass holders. Or maybe we'll alternate clear bowls and silver bowls."

Carol leaned close to Violet and lowered her voice. "Look at you, solving the problem."

"I defined the wedding, nothing more." Although Violet had to admit, she was feeling a little smug. "Pallas is used to making weddings about something." She used her fingers to make air quotes. "Pretty is going to freak her out."

Maya and Pallas were talking about fifty miles an hour. Carol shook her head. "I so could be cleaning stalls."

Mathias leaned close. "You have to be the only woman on the planet who would rather clean up after cows than talk weddings."

Violet guessed he meant the words to be teasing, but she saw her sister flush and wondered if Carol had taken it wrong. Before she could say anything, she felt an uncomfortable sensation, as if she were being watched. She glanced up and saw Ulrich standing in the hallway. He didn't speak but when their eyes locked, he nodded politely.

"What on earth," she began, then stopped as everyone turned to look at her. She felt herself flush, which she hated and was so Ulrich's fault. "Um, excuse me," she said as she came to her feet and walked into the hallway.

She stopped in front of him and put her hands on her hips. "What are you doing here?"

"I came by to have a word."

Her attention split neatly in two. Part of her brain—the sensible part—was annoyed and wanted to tell him she had a whole bunch of words she could use and none of them would be approved for listening by anyone under the age of eighteen or with delicate sensibilities. The other part of her paused to notice how dreamy he looked with his chiseled features and dark blond hair. Oh, the suit was nice, too. Tailored, probably custom from that fancy street in London.

Her sensible half won. "What are you doing here?" she demanded. "And I don't mean on the planet or even in this country. What are you doing here, in my friend's business? Are you following me? Stalking me? Last time you threatened me with all kinds of scary law enforcement. Now it's my turn. Explain yourself or I'll be on with 9-1-1 in a heartbeat."

Ulrich's stern mouth turned up at the left corner, as if he were trying not to smile. "I went to your shop. You'd left a note on the door saying where you were. I will admit, despite Americans claiming to speak English, we do occasionally have a bit of verbal confusion. Did I misunderstand?"

Damn him! Violet really wanted to stomp her foot, but knew that would only hand him more of a win. She settled on tossing her head.

"That note wasn't meant for you," she said as icily as she could, then remembered everyone in the room just behind her.

They were all watching intently, even Maya, who looked wide-eyed with interest.

"This is fun," the bride-to-be said and waved. "Hi. I'm in China."

Ulrich smiled. "Lovely to meet you."

"Thank you."

Violet grabbed his arm, which could have been a mistake. Her fingers closed around very impressive biceps. Ulrich might wear a suit, but he wasn't a guy who sat around all day.

"Let's take this down the hall and let them get back to their meeting," she said.

"As you wish."

Her body tightened as she recognized the line from the classic old movie *The Princess Bride*. Only Ulrich wouldn't know anything about that. He was simply being polite to annoy her—she was sure of it.

She carefully closed the door before moving a few feet toward the stairs. She crossed her arms and glared at Ulrich.

"Yes?"

"I would like to apologize for what I said to you the other day. I was wrong to assume the worst about you. Upon further investigation, I have discovered you are exactly who you claimed to be. The mistake is mine and I take complete responsibility for it."

Violet was careful to keep her mouth from dropping open. As apologies went, it was pretty good. Quick, to the point, with no waffling. If only the man delivering it weren't so annoying. Or handsome.

"Great. Apology accepted. Now if that's all..."

"It's not." His steady gaze locked with hers. "I'm not just saying the words, Violet. I mean it."

When had she gone from Miss Lund to Violet? Miss Lund was safer. Miss Lund was stern and strong. Violet was more likely to be overwhelmed by a combination of English accent and sexy smile.

"I believe you. Thank you for the message." She looked pointedly at the closed door. "I have to get back in there."

"Of course. There's just one more thing."

"There always is," she muttered.

He ignored that. "Would you do me the honor of having dinner with me tonight? If you won't accept for my sake, then please do so for the sake of my grandmother who speaks very highly of you."

Another nicely delivered little speech. He must have taken a class. And while she was tempted, she wasn't foolish. Or forgiving of the fact that he'd spoiled a perfectly good memory of a fourteen-year-old girl being swept off her feet by a handsome almost-duke.

"Thank you. You're very kind, but I'm busy tonight." A lie, but one she was willing to live with. "I would suggest tomorrow, but I'm sure you have to get back to whatever airport you flew in to. Your estate awaits."

His gaze remained steady. "It does," he said slowly. "How-

ever, this dinner is important to me. I'll still be in town tomorrow. Shall we say six at the Mountain Top Grill?"

Drat and double drat. She couldn't even blame anyone but
herself—still, who would have thought he would be willing
to stay in Happily Inc to have dinner with her? Or not—the
man could have business somewhere nearby. Or simply be
handling things via email and conference calls. He wasn't staying just for her. If she thought anything else, she was foolish.
Or if he was, he was because of his grandmother. Not her.

"Six," she agreed reluctantly.

"Of course. I'll see you then."

He turned and walked away. Violet watched him go and did
her best to quell a sudden sense of foreboding. It was dinner.
Just dinner. Whatever crush she'd maintained all these years
had been on a different man. Or so she hoped.

Carol straddled Mathias, her thighs nestled against his hips.
They were both naked and it was all he could do to keep
from touching her full breasts as she raised her arms, locking
her hands behind her head. As she moved, her breasts shifted
and bounced, making his erection harder and more painful.
She smiled at him.

"Take me," she whispered as she leaned close. "Take me
hard and fast until we're both—"

What? Both what?

"Carol? Carol?"

Instead of answering she laughed and licked her lips, as if
taunting him. Mathias reached for her, only to come awake—
drenched in sweat and sporting the world's hardest, most
painful boner.

"Dammit all to hell," he muttered as he threw off the covers. He continued swearing for several more seconds, then
had to push Sophie away as she rolled over to investigate the
cause of his bad mood.

"Not your problem," he muttered as he stood. He was aroused and uncomfortable. The sex dreams with Carol were getting worse, he thought grimly. More detailed and not the least bit satisfying. Those damned images would stay with him all day. There was only one solution to the problem.

He left Sophie snoring gently in his bed, and walked into the bathroom. Five minutes later he was in the shower, the hot water pounding his body. Talk about humiliating, he thought as he grasped his erection and began to move his hand up and down his shaft.

It didn't take long. The relief was medicinal at best, but at least the immediate problem was solved. As for what to do about Carol—there was an issue that had no resolution.

By the time he was showered, shaved and dressed, it was nearly daylight. Sophie reluctantly got up and he took her for an early walk. They had breakfast before driving to the studio.

Mathias had an order for custom light pendants. He began by matching the colors his client had sent him, then began the slow process of creating a perfectly formed pendant to their exact measurements.

Ronan strolled in about three in the afternoon. They hadn't seen each other since Elaine's visit, but having Ronan disappear was hardly news. Mathias had just finished the second pendant and left it to cool. His brother wandered over to study the two pieces.

While each pendant contained the same colors and had the same pattern, they weren't identical. Mathias had reversed the swirl so they were more of a mirror image. He planned to create the third one to match the first so there would be added vertical interest when they were hanging next to each other.

"Nice," Ronan said. "You were precise. I like the details."

Mathias gauged his brother's mood, based on the handful of words. For once Ronan wasn't being a jerk, which was a pleasant change.

Ever since their father had blurted out the truth and screwed up their lives five years ago, Ronan had been distant. Before that, they'd been a team. They'd grown up as twins—or so they'd thought. Not anymore. Now Ronan was the half brother. Ceallach's son, but not Elaine's child.

After their father's mild heart attack, he'd been hospitalized for observation. Ceallach had requested the "twins" come see him. When they'd arrived, he told them about his affair and how Ronan was only half brother with the rest of his sons.

Mathias hadn't been able to take it in—he'd been devastated and had started to lash out at their bastard of a father. But Ronan had only listened in silence. Partway through Mathias's rant, Ronan had walked out without saying a word. Mathias had followed. When Ronan had said he had to leave their home in Fool's Gold, Mathias had gone with him. He'd known things would be different for a while, but he'd never thought all this time would pass and Ronan would still think of himself as anything other than a member of the family.

There were moments when Mathias wanted to remind Ronan that he'd had to deal, as well. He'd always thought they would return to being a team—if not twins, then at least close brothers. But Ronan had stayed distant to the point of doing much of his work at his own studio up in the mountains.

Whenever Mathias was asked why he didn't want to fall in love and settle down, he used his father as an excuse. Ceallach was a jerk and what if Mathias was one, too? But the truth was far different. His inability to trust in love had little to do with his father and everything to do with his brother.

He and Ronan had been a *team*. They'd been a unit that had faced the world together. It was always supposed to be like that—only Ronan had changed the rules. Mathias knew in his gut that if he hadn't gone with his brother, Ronan would have simply disappeared. All this time later Mathias couldn't let go enough not to give a damn but he also couldn't forgive.

Ronan crossed to his desk. On the way he passed the large recycling container filled with broken bits of glass. He picked up a piece easily identifiable as the head and neck of a giraffe. On that one, Mathias had been close.

Ronan looked from the glass to him and back. "You're being too hard on yourself."

Mathias shrugged. "It has to be perfect."

"Now you sound like him."

"Dad being an egomaniac and an asshole doesn't mean he's always wrong."

"What about those?" His brother pointed to the stack of imperfect dishes, bowls and mugs on shelves.

"They don't matter," Mathias admitted.

Ronan didn't look convinced. "People line up in the street on the day those pieces go on sale."

"Nobody's life is changed by a plate."

"Nobody's life is changed by much of anything we can make in this studio."

Before Mathias could respond, his brother walked away. Something Ronan had been doing a lot these days. No—he'd been doing it since their encounter with their father. Everything had changed and Mathias didn't know how to make things go back to the way they'd been.

He checked on his two pendants, then ripped off his protective goggles. There was no way he would get more work done today, he thought grimly. Not with how he was feeling now. He went into Natalie's office. Sophie jumped to her feet, her tail wagging.

"Come on," he told her. "I'll take you for a walk. That will make us both feel better."

And if it didn't, at least he'd taken the moral high ground—walking a dog rather than destroying more innocent glass.

★ ★ ★

Ulrich had no idea if Violet would show for dinner or not. He told himself that regardless of the outcome, he'd done what he could and would be able to look his grandmother in the eye with a clear conscience. He'd apologized and had attempted to make amends. How Violet responded to that was beyond his control. Although as the time ticked closer to six, he found himself hoping she *would* show up. For his grandmother's sake, he added hastily. Because it would be easier on him if he was able to give a few details about their dinner. Not because he was looking forward to spending time in Violet's company.

If only he hadn't been wrong, he thought grimly. If only his grandmother's secretary hadn't mentioned the outgoing packages. If only the inventory hadn't turned up so many discrepancies. Whatever circumstances had conspired, he'd ended up here—at a restaurant in Happily Inc, California, waiting on a woman who might or might not show up for their...appointment.

Not date. Never a date. This was practically a business meeting. They were here to clear the air, nothing more. Which all sounded great but didn't explain the sudden rush of anticipation that kicked him in the gut when he saw a tall redhead walk into the foyer.

Had she been beautiful two days ago and had he just not noticed, or had she done whatever it was women did to make themselves alluring? She still had thick, glossy curls that tumbled down her back. Her eyes had always been wide and green. But her skin seemed more luminous and her dress—a simple black number that emphasized her curves—was pure magic.

He moved toward her and held out his hand. In part to be polite but mostly to feel her skin against his own. He wanted to know if there would be a reaction when they touched. If the attraction would die as quickly as it had formed or if it would explode into—

"Ulrich," she said, putting her hand in his.

The heat was immediate, as was a sinking sense of having been played by fate. His relationship with his ex-wife had been based on their being a sensible match. Since the divorce, he'd avoided entanglements of any kind, so it had been years since he'd experienced the dark, sensual, visceral burn of desperately wanting any one woman.

"Miss Lund."

She raised her eyebrows as she released his hand. "Come now, Ulrich. We're not auditioning for a drawing room comedy. You can call me Violet. It's so much nicer than the other names you've been using in your mind."

"I have no idea what you're talking about. I only thought gracious, lovely things about you."

She stepped close and lowered her voice. "You go to hell for lying, same as stealing."

Her tone was teasing, her breath warm on his neck.

"I have every confidence the good Lord wants me with him when I die."

She rolled her eyes. "Of course you do."

The hostess appeared and told them their table was ready. They were shown to a quiet booth against the far wall. The restaurant was more crowded than he would have expected for a weeknight and he was pleased he'd thought to make a reservation.

Violet sat across from him. She ignored the menu, instead focusing her considerable attention on him.

"This is awkward."

"A little," he conceded. "I appreciate you joining me. It seemed the least I could do."

"Plus, your grandmother made you."

"She wanted me to make sure we repaired our relationship.

The decision to invite you to dinner was mine." He cleared his throat. "I do want to apologize again for what I said."

"I wish you wouldn't. You were wrong. I personally get to revel in your wrongness and now you're buying me a nice dinner. It's fine. You can stop apologizing."

"You're very straightforward."

"No more than most women I know." She flashed him a smile. "I suspect it's an American thing. We're not really into subtle."

"I admire your sensibilities." And other things about her, he thought, doing his best not to let his gaze stray to the edge of her breasts exposed by the vee of her dress. "And your graciousness, under the circumstances."

"So what happened?" she asked. "How did I get to be the bad guy?"

He explained about the household inventory and the mysterious packages, carefully leaving out any mention of his grandmother's secretary. While he doubted the other woman had been trying to trap him into falling in love with her, she'd acted against his grandmother's best wishes and that was unforgivable.

When he'd finished, Violet opened her mouth, then closed it. "You take an inventory?" She held up her hand. "I'm sorry. Of course you have to. The house is like a million years old and there are beautiful things everywhere. It's just so different from anything I've experienced. My bonding story is I check to see if I need paper towels before I go to the grocery store. Other than that, I live my personal life inventory free. I do inventory my buttons, but that's different."

"I check for paper towels, as well. We have so much in common."

She laughed, as he'd hoped she would. The clear, happy sound tugged at something deep inside of him. A dark, lonely place that had avoided the light of day for too long.

"Your grandmother is lucky to have you," she said.

"I'm lucky, as well. She's my entire family. I would do anything for her."

Their server came to take their drink orders. Violet ordered a cosmopolitan while he chose a single malt Scotch.

"I'm sorry about your father," Violet said when their server had left. "Your grandmother told me she was devastated by the loss. You must have been, as well."

"I was. He'd been ill for a while, but one never expects the end when it happens. I'd been training for the job for years, but still found it difficult to be half as excellent as he had been."

"I doubt that." She smiled at him. "You're very good at what you do."

If only they were talking about sex, but they weren't. At least *she* wasn't. "You have no way of knowing that."

"Your grandmother tells me things in her letters. She worried that the responsibility was too much for you." She hesitated. "She was afraid it was impacting your marriage." She cleared her throat. "I'm not prying or asking, I'm just sharing."

"My father's death was hard on everyone, but not the reason for my divorce." If only it had been—the blame would have been easier to deal with. As it was, he'd never been sure what he was supposed to say.

She reached for her small handbag and pulled out a thick piece of paper. "I want to show you something, although now that I think about it, I should probably have waited for you to have your cocktail first." She smiled. "You know, to dull the edges."

"Now I'm curious."

She turned over the paper and he saw it was a photograph of a young woman standing in front of Battenberg Park. She had frizzy red hair, blotchy skin and the gawky, awkward stance of someone not comfortable in her own skin. Braces

showed through her tentative smile. She was, by all definitions, not pretty, and he had absolutely no recollection of her.

"This is you?"

She nodded. "During my unfortunate phase. I was fourteen."

"You were lovely."

"More lies. Shame on you." She took back the picture.
"My mother and I attended a summer party at your house.
To my mind, it was nearly a ball. You danced with me and
kissed me on the cheek, then whispered that one day I would
be a beauty." She glanced at him, then away. "You were very
charming and that night I fell madly in love with you...in a
very shallow, young teen sort of way."

He was torn between being pleased he'd acted in a way
that would have made his father proud of him and regret that
even her words couldn't produce a memory. There had been
many parties in the summer, many young ladies with whom
he'd danced.

"I was right," he said instead. "About you growing into a
beauty. I'm nearly always right."

She laughed. Their server returned with their drinks and
they touched them together in a toast.

"Where are you staying?" she asked when she'd taken a sip
of her cosmopolitan.

"The Sweet Dreams Inn." He did his best not to shudder.
"I'm in the Drive-in Room. My bed is an old Cadillac and
my television is the size of a drive-in screen."

"The *Pride and Prejudice* room wasn't available?"

"I didn't ask. And please, do not compare me to Mr. Darcy."

"Does it happen too much or do you dislike falling short?"

He held in a smile. "You're very hard on me."

"I think you've earned it, but as it's obviously too much
for you, I'll stop now."

"You're so generous."

"I know." She sighed. "It's a burden." She leaned toward him. "What do you know about our town?"

"This one?" He looked around at the restaurant. "It caters to weddings, which seems strange. But from the little I've read, it's a wedding destination town."

"It is. In the 1950s, the town was dying. Seriously, there was no industry and people were leaving. The man who owned the main bank, a man with seven daughters, by the way, knew that if the town died, he would lose everything, so he decided to take a really big gamble. He started telling a story about how the town was founded. That during the Gold Rush, a stagecoach full of mail-order brides, destined for the gold fields, was stranded in town. By the time the parts arrived to fix their stagecoach, they'd all fallen madly in love and made their homes here. Everyone liked the story, the name of the town was changed and the rest is history."

He'd heard a few things about the town's past, but hadn't paid much attention. "None of it is real? He made up the past completely?"

"Every word. A couple of big name stars got married here and ever since, we've been a wedding destination town. There's a sleep center outside of town and a handful of businesses that don't support the wedding industry, but the rest of us live in service of brides."

"You know there is generally a groom when there's a marriage."

She waved her hand. "No one cares about him. It's the bride's day. Oh, you could do theme weddings at Battenberg Park. Something with a *Pride and Prejudice* flair."

He groaned. "Stop, I beg you. Why are American women mesmerized with that book?"

"It's not the book."

"You're right, of course. It's Mr. Darcy. How I dislike that man. I had several meetings with a production company in

Los Angeles and all the women were obsessed with him. I doubt Jane Austen knew what she was creating."

"Probably not and I would guess that's for the best." She lowered her voice. "I suspect our obsession, as you call it, isn't proper."

She was delightful, Ulrich thought. Bright, funny, sexy as hell. There was a vitality he found appealing. Violet Lund was so much more than he'd expected. Accusing her of stealing might have been the smartest thing he'd ever done.

CHAPTER SEVEN

Carol waited until the night staff arrived to pack up for the day. She'd already inventoried the delivery of marionberry leaf-eater biscuits that had arrived. They were ridiculously expensive, but Millie loved them, so they were ordered. If the giraffe didn't have friends at the moment, she should at least have a happy tummy.

After turning off her computer, Carol got into her car and headed home. The late afternoon was perfect—warm and sunny. It would cool down that evening and by dawn it would be (relatively) cold—fall had arrived in the desert. To her mind, it was one of the most beautiful seasons, not that she had many complaints about the weather in Happily Inc. Yes, summer could be a little toasty, but it was a small price to pay for how great it was the rest of the year.

She drove along the road, only to slow when she saw a familiar man walking a happy, tail-wagging beagle. The man had a way about him, she thought with resignation as he approached the car.

"The cows settled for the night?" he asked.

"They are. Want a ride home?"

"It defeats the purpose of taking my loaner dog for a walk."

"Is that a no?"

"Just an observation."

He got in, then patted his lap. Sophie jumped in and scrambled up on him so that she could see out the front windshield. Mathias snapped his seat belt in place, put one protective arm around the dog and smiled at Carol.

"We're ready."

The smile hit her like a hoof to the belly with an uncomfortable combination of surprise and impact. No, no, no, she told herself firmly. Thinking Mathias was hunky was one thing—it was more of an intellectual exercise—like appreciating great art. But going further—stepping into that crazy *I want him* world was not allowed. Not only would it be a complete disaster, she would have to deal with the aftermath for the rest of her life. They were neighbors. She could see his house from her house. The town was small, their lives entwined and no. Just plain no.

She continued down the road, all the while explaining to her wayward emotions that being stupid wasn't an option. After a couple of minutes, she realized her normally highly verbal passenger hadn't said a word.

"What's wrong?"

"Nothing."

She glanced at him. "There's something. Are you not feeling well?"

"I'm fine. Just crap at the studio. I've been working on a project and it's not going well. The last couple of days have been a challenge."

"What does that mean? I'm the least artistic person on the planet so I have no frame of reference."

"I can see what I want to create in my head but I can't make it happen."

"In glass?"

"Yes."

"So not dishes."

"No." He shifted Sophie so she was leaning against him. "However, it is glass, so when I screw up, I can smash it to bits. I've been doing a lot of that."

"While we lesser mortals have to live with our mistakes."

"It's good to be me."

She pulled into his driveway. Mathias turned to her.

"Want to come in for a drink, maybe stay for dinner?"

Before she could express surprise, he added, "I'd like the company."

Meaning what? He wanted to be with her or he didn't want to be alone? Why were men so complicated?

"Um, sure." She turned off the engine and got her bag, then followed him around to the back door. He pushed it open. Sophie led the way inside, then waited for her leash to be unsnapped. She made a beeline for the sofa in the family room, jumped up and settled right in the middle.

"I see you've made it clear who's in charge," Carol murmured as she set her bag on the end table.

"Like you'd make her sleep on the floor."

"Probably not. She seems really comfortable. You two must be getting along."

"She's not so bad." As they spoke, he walked into the kitchen and pulled out a blender. "Margaritas okay?"

She'd been thinking more of a glass of wine, but sure. "Sounds good."

She watched as he poured ingredients into the blender, then hit the switch. When the mixture resembled a thick, icy temptation, he filled a good-sized glass and handed it to her, then got a beer out of the refrigerator for himself.

"You didn't have to do this for me," she said.

"It was easy."

They settled on opposite sides of Sophie. Carol sipped her

drink and found it went down way too easily. Oh, well—her house wasn't all that far away. If she overindulged, she would simply walk home and retrieve her car in the morning.

"What's going on?" she asked. "You seem, I don't know, restless, I guess." A thought occurred that stuck her like a pin, but still forced her to say, "Is the sexy bridesmaid pool too small these days?"

"I'm giving up bridesmaids."

"No, you're not."

"No, I'm not. But I haven't been looking lately."

"Why not?" Because as much as she would want his decision to be about her, she knew it wasn't.

"Like I said, I'm working on something and it's not coming out right. I'm frustrated by that. I can see it in my head and when I'm creating it, for a second, I know it's okay. Then it all falls apart."

"I have no idea what it's like to be talented," she admitted. "I can offer sympathy, but no real course of action. I'm sorry."

"Don't be. You're nice to listen."

Nice? She held in a sigh. That was her. The nice girl. Not special, not dangerous, just pleasant. She was like having oatmeal for breakfast. A sensible choice but hardly one that got your blood racing.

"Tell me about Millie," he said before taking a long swallow of his beer. "How's she doing?"

"She's healthy, but still lonely."

"And the fund?"

She sighed. "Growing slowly. The donation cans I've placed around town fill up steadily, but they're not going to get us there. My dad and uncle's donation is great, but there's still a long way to go. I've been researching different ways to raise money that get me more than a car wash or bake sale. I need to figure out some kind of fund-raiser."

"Your goal is half a million dollars?"

He sounded more curious than appalled, which she appreciated. A couple of people had expressed amazement that she would ever consider "wasting" that much on a few giraffes.

"Yes. Some of that covers purchasing the other animals, plus transportation and the new barns."

"That has to be complicated. Do you call UPS?"

"Actually FedEx has a wild animal division who does this kind of thing all the time."

He stared at her. "Moves giraffes?"

"Other animals, too. How do you think zoos do their animal exchanges?"

"In the back of a pickup in the dark of night?"

She laughed. "Nope. They're delivered."

"Nice. Okay, so we have the purchase price, transportation, the barns. You're going to need more giraffe chow."

"We are. The plans for the barn are already approved. The structure's pretty simple, so once we have the money, it will only take a few weeks to build. The different giraffes will have to be kept separate as they get to know each other. Just because they're giraffes doesn't mean they're going to instinctively bond."

"Still no boy giraffe on the horizon?"

"Not at the moment. If I get the herd established and the girls are happy, and there's extra money, then I'll look around for a male. Before I did that, I'd have to get the girls on birth control. We'd want them to breed, but on our terms, not theirs."

He laughed. "Giraffe birth control? I don't want to know what that entails."

"I'll admit it's not my area of expertise, but I can do the research."

He finished his beer, collected her half-empty glass and his bottle, went into the kitchen and freshened both, then returned to the sofa.

"What if your dad and uncle had settled somewhere else? You might not have Millie at all."

She'd never thought of that but he was right. Happily Inc had been very welcoming to the animal preserve. "I'm glad we could be here for her."

"She's glad, too." He studied her.

"What?"

"I'm picturing you in South Africa. You'd look good there. I'm less sure Violet would fit in."

Carol told herself he hadn't actually complimented her and not to read too much into his words.

"Violet would think of reasons why she had to go back home, during our summers, while I was looking for excuses to stay. I loved the animals, the work, the people. I learned a lot and always had an interesting topic for the 'what I did on my summer vacation' essay. I hated going back to New York for the school year."

"I can't see you living in the city."

"I wasn't very good at it. We were close to Central Park, so that helped. I could be outside and pretend I was somewhere else."

"By the time you were fifteen, you knew you wanted to work with animals?"

"I did. When I was around that age, my dad and uncle inherited enough money to buy the landfill here. They'd been talking about wanting to do something different with waste management and recycling and they finally had the opportunity. My dad also wanted an animal preserve, which is where I came in."

"Where did he get the animals?"

"From all over. A few came from other private preserves that had overpopulation issues. Millie's owner died and no one wanted her. That kind of thing. It's shockingly easy to find animals like ours. Most people aren't the least bit able to care for them, but my dad and uncle know what they're doing."

"As do you."

"Thank you."

They spent the next couple of hours talking about the animal preserve and town and what it was like to have a steady flow of wedding parties to deal with every weekend. She wasn't sure how many margaritas she drank or how many beers he'd had and the chips and dip he'd put out didn't do much to counteract the alcohol. It got dark outside and he flipped on a couple of lamps.

"I hope things work out for Millie," he said. "Animals are better than people. With them you know what you're getting. Put a lion and a gazelle in the same space and the outcome is clear. Humans are different. They play games."

"Okay. That was an interesting transition. Want to explain it?"

"No. It's nothing. Just some stuff happening with my brother. It's different now, you know. Not like it was."

"That would be one of the definitions of different." She stared at him, trying to figure out why he was acting so unlike himself. "Is this your third beer of the day?"

He held up the bottle. "Yup. Of course there were the couple of shots of tequila I had earlier. Like I said, a few bad nights, followed by bad days have an effect on a guy."

She angled toward him. "Mathias, what's going on?"

"A lot of crap. People who are supposed to love you betray you. Did you know that? You should be careful."

Huh? "Are we talking about women? Do you mean an old girlfriend?"

"What? No. I was thinking about my dad. He's a real bastard. And my mom. She's the saint who loves him more than anyone. Isn't that always the way? When you see male genius, there's probably a good woman in the background. History never remembers her. Only with him, we knew what we were getting, but with her…"

He shook his head. "He cheated on her and she forgave him. He ignores her for days at a time and she's fine with it. Why does she do that? Why doesn't she demand more? Only she wouldn't. She tells us to be patient, too. To understand. And then there's Ronan. With him, what I understand is—"

He took a couple of long swallows. "Hell, it doesn't matter."

She set down her margarita and slid onto the coffee table so she could sit facing him. "Now you're starting to worry me."

"I'm fine."

"You're drunk."

"Only a little. Okay, a lot. Probably because I haven't eaten today."

She stared into his dark eyes. Funny how until now she'd always seen the front he wore so comfortably. She'd never gotten that his father had somehow damaged him. That he wasn't as perfect or confident as he wanted everyone to believe. He was just a regular guy, trying to get through the day. Only this day had turned out to be harder than most and she had no idea why.

"How can I help?" she asked.

His expression sharpened and eyes darkened with an emotion she couldn't read.

"Don't go there," he warned her. "Trust me, you won't like it."

"I should get you something to eat. You'll feel better."

"That won't help at all."

She ignored that and stood. He rose as well—to get out of her way, she thought. Or maybe to stop her. What she didn't expect was for him to pull her hard against him and kiss her as if she were the one thing he'd been waiting for. Which was totally ridiculous and not the least bit relevant. Not when his lips were hot and demanding against hers and every part of her began to cheer.

★ ★ ★

Violet was more relaxed than she'd expected. Ulrich was actually a nice guy, not to mention easy on the eyes. He handed her one of the menus and they discussed the selections. At first she wasn't sure why he seemed to be so very interested in her choices, but when their server came by to take their order, Ulrich surprised her by ordering for her.

"The lady will have the house salad," he began.

It was all she could do not to sigh. *The lady will have...* She knew it was just the accent, but still, the words sounded so sexy. Plus, being taken care of like that was sweet.

"We'd like some time between the courses," he added when he was finished.

"Of course." The server collected the menus and left.

Ulrich picked up his Scotch. "How did you get into the button business?"

"It was that fateful summer in England," she admitted. "Hanging out in your attic. Your grandmother showed me some old clothes and told me I could pick out something to take home as a souvenir. I couldn't decide, then I found a box of old buttons. I asked for those. Your grandmother sent me home with three boxes. I was in heaven."

She laughed. "I know it sounds crazy, but I really enjoyed sorting them and I started to do some research. A friend's mom saw some of them and asked to buy a set for a dress. That was exciting. I was living in New York so I went to all the antique shops I could and looked for buttons. For a while I thought about going to design school and while I was touring one, I talked to someone who told me there was a whole button market. One thing led to another and here I am."

"Running a button empire."

"If only." She grinned. "I do enjoy it. I also do some tailoring and custom work for wedding parties. I can modify a wedding gown or the bridesmaid dresses. A few months ago,

I worked on a wedding set in a computer game world. It was great fun. I found these amazing buttons for the dress."

She thought of how everything had turned out. "My friend Pallas is engaged to this guy. Nick is a gifted artist. He actually painted the wedding gown." She shuddered. "The outcome was amazing, but it still breaks my heart to think about him taking paint to the lace."

"Because it simply isn't done?"

"Exactly. I'm so glad you get that."

"I'm English. I was born to be proper."

"I suspect you have your moments."

His eyes locked with hers. Tension seemed to build between them—the kind of tension that stole her breath and made her want to be reckless. Her fourteen-year-old self was thrilled at the prospect.

She sighed. "You're a dangerous man."

"Me?"

"Oh, yeah. I know it's the accent. I wonder if that's because we used to be a colony. Liking an English accent is in our DNA or something. Maybe the groundwater. Anyway, you could read the phone book and it would be appealing. Does it work that way back home?"

"Sadly, there I do not have the pleasure of being exotic."

She wanted to say he could stay here a few weeks and soak up the worship, but knew the statement would come out wrong. Or worse, sound as if she were... What? Interested in him? She was, in an I-know-you're-leaving-tomorrow-so-it's-safe-to-flirt-tonight kind of way.

For a second she thought about how things were going to end that evening. Could she suggest that they go back to his place? She liked him. She found him attractive and she would be delighted to take things to the next level. But her next level and sex weren't exactly the same. She'd never had a one-night stand and guessed that she never would. She wasn't the type. She wanted to be *the one*, which was the opposite of hooking up. And while that hadn't happened yet, it was important that she keep hoping. Sleeping with a guy for one night violated that dream in a way she didn't like.

Not that, you know, Ulrich was asking.

"You're thinking about something," he murmured.

"That I am. So, you're going to have to get married and have heirs, aren't you?"

He nearly choked. "That's direct."

And a neat change of subject, she thought smugly. "I know. It's an American thing again. So, is there a future duchess waiting at home?"

"Not at this time. There is, however, pressure."

"Sure. Your grand estate had needs."

"Don't remind me. It was difficult enough the first time." He glanced at her. "Getting married, I mean."

"I didn't think you were talking about the heir producing."

"Excellent."

She smiled. "Why was it difficult? You have commitment issues? Too many fish in the sea?"

"It was more about finding the right fish. Penelope and I were very much alike. Family and duty mattered. We were friends and thought that was enough."

They hadn't been in love? How sad. Violet wanted to be in love and she wanted to be loved in return. Otherwise, why get married? Of course she didn't have a five-hundred-year-old inheritance to steward into the next century.

"I'm sorry it wasn't," she said quietly.

"I am, as well." Ulrich finished his drink, then looked at her. "She left me for someone."

"Oh. I didn't know. Your grandmother wouldn't have mentioned that to me."

"You're right. She wouldn't." He paused. "It was a woman. When I asked Penelope why she hadn't told me the truth from the beginning, she said she'd been hoping she was wrong. That I would change her mind." His smile was self-deprecating. "I like to think I'm rather good, but no one is that good."

Violet honestly had no idea what to say. "I'm sorry."

"Me, too." One shoulder rose and lowered. "I've heard she's in a relationship now and is very happy. I wish her the best."

"You're a good man."

"Thank you. I try. Now we shall change the subject to something slightly more interesting. I'd like to hear about the wedding you're currently working on."

"It's normal. Completely and totally regular. No under-the-sea, no aliens, no cowboys."

"How disappointing."

"Tell me about it."

The evening flew by. Violet found herself more charmed with each passing minute. Ulrich had her laughing as he told her about his trip to Hollywood and she talked about her summers in South Africa and how she was so not the outdoor type. By the time she and Ulrich finished their coffees, she found herself wondering if it was possible to fall for someone in a matter of hours.

Not that she had. She was caught up in a very fun, very unreal set of circumstances. Her reaction to Ulrich was partly the wine, partly the fact that he was leaving and partly all the daydreams she'd had about the young man who had taken the time to make her younger self feel special for a moment or two. It wasn't real. Come tomorrow, he would fly home and she would return to her regularly scheduled life. All she had to do was get through the next few minutes without making a fool of herself.

They tussled briefly over the bill. Okay, she offered to pay half and he gave her a withering look followed by, "That is simply not how things are done. I invited you, Violet. The pleasure is mine."

As they walked to the front of the restaurant, he placed his hand on the small of her back. She felt the warmth of each finger, the pressure of his palm and did her best not to purr like some lonely cat. When they reached her car, she gave herself a quick "say goodbye and get out of here" lecture, in a futile attempt to keep herself from acting foolishly. Or worse, to avoid throwing herself at him. After all, they were in a parking lot and while it was dark, they were hardly anywhere private. Even more significant, she had no idea what he thought of her. She tried to be strong but the fear of rejection always made her feel small. Still, she had to say something only she had no idea what it was supposed to—

He drew her close and kissed her. The unexpected action stole her breath—or maybe it was simply the proximity of the man.

His mouth was firm yet gentle. One hand settled on her hip while the other tangled in her hair. She rested her fingers on his strong, broad shoulders. He smelled good, he kissed better and after maybe eight seconds, she knew she was a total goner.

Figuring some version of *what the hell*, she wrapped her arms around his neck, leaned into him and parted her lips. He didn't hesitate—not for a second. His tongue swept inside, then swept her away. Heat grew, as did need. Wanting whimpered. Oh, to be that girl, she thought regretfully.

Ulrich drew back and looked at her. "You are an unexpected treat, Violet Lund."

"As are you."

He smiled and stroked her cheek. "At the risk of saying the wrong thing, would you like to come back to my hotel room?"

She thought about how it would be between them. Both naked, his dark blue eyes blazing with passion. He would feel good inside of her—she just knew it. She could ask him to talk in that sexy voice of his as he touched her everywhere. There were so many reasons to say yes.

"I want to," she admitted. "But you're leaving and I'm not that girl."

His expression never changed. He kissed her again—lightly this time. "You not being that girl is part of your charm. Thank you for a wonderful evening. One I shall never forget."

The perfect words. She hoped there was a touch of regret in his voice. Maybe more than a touch.

He stepped back, brought her hand to his mouth and kissed her skin. Then he opened her car door for her and waited until she was safely inside before stepping back and waving. She drove away with the thought that doing the right thing had never felt so incredibly sucky in her whole life.

Mathias's mouth claimed Carol's with an intensity that stole her breath. His hands moved up and down her back and her sides, arousing with every touch, confusing her and exciting her at the same time. She didn't know what was happening or what he was thinking or what she was thinking, she only knew that she never wanted him to stop.

"Carol," he breathed, then eased her sideways so they weren't trapped by the sofa and coffee table anymore. "Carol. You have to say this is okay. Please."

His voice was thick, his tone pleading. The passion was clear in the way he claimed her mouth over and over again. She could barely manage a quick "Yes" between kisses. When his tongue skimmed her bottom lip, she parted for him and then groaned when he swept inside.

Heat poured through her. Hunger stole her breath and any chance at rational thought. When he grabbed her hands and put them on his chest, she allowed herself the thrill of touching him. His shoulders, his back, his arms. He felt good. He felt right. She wanted him, wanted whatever this was.

When his hands reached for her T-shirt, she only had a moment to think that she was wearing her work clothes and probably smelled of hay and gazelle feed. But before she could figure out how to offer an apology or ask for a second to shower, her shirt was off and his hands were touching her breasts over her bra.

At the first stroke of his skilled fingers, she knew that showers and eau du gazelle didn't really matter. Then her bra went flying and his mouth was on her tight nipple and she couldn't care about anything except what he was doing to her body.

He kissed her everywhere. Somehow her clothes disappeared and she was naked. He hadn't done more than take off his shoes, but before she could complain, he was pushing her onto the club chair across from the sofa and dropping to his knees. Then he parted her and leaned over to kiss her so intimately, so deeply, that she nearly came right there.

He found her clit on the first try and sucked it gently. He inserted a finger inside of her, pushing in all the way, then withdrawing. At the same time, he circled her swollen center, finding the perfect steady rhythm that had her gasping, straining and hoping he never, ever stopped.

It didn't take her long. About thirty seconds in she drew her knees up and pushed down on his finger. A minute in, she was panting and pleading and five seconds after that, it happened.

She came with a cry that was ripped from the very soul of her. Pleasure filled her as her muscles rippled and released. Mathias kept touching her, kept moving in and out, drawing every ounce of it from her, then slowing so the sensations lingered. Only then did he sit back and smile at her.

"That's my girl."

She stared at him, both satiated and in shock. "I can't believe that just happened." She was naked. In his living room. There was a dog on the sofa, although Sophie had snored through the entire, ah, event. What on earth?

He reached for his jeans and pulled a condom out of his wallet, then stretched out on the carpet and smiled. "Any chance you'd consider being on top?"

Seven simple words. Seven words that chased away any thought of being confused or embarrassed. Seven words that made everything right.

"I just might."

"Good, because I've had this recurring fantasy about you."

"It's not that...what?" Fantasy about her? Had he really said that?

He winked at her, then closed his eyes. "This is going to be good."

She smiled, then waited for him to start undressing. Or say something else. Or look at her. Only he didn't do any of those things...he just breathed heavily. Too heavily. The deep breathing became a snore nearly as loud as Sophie's.

Carol sat there, naked, sexually satisfied and totally humiliated. She didn't even have to ask what had happened. It was obvious. More than obvious. She'd had the best sex ever and Mathias had passed out.

Was that just exactly her life?

CHAPTER EIGHT

Mathias woke with the mother of all hangovers and a beagle licking his face. The previous evening was mostly a blur. He knew Carol had stopped by and they'd talked. At some point, he'd fallen asleep in the living room—hopefully after she'd left. Near dawn, he'd made his way to his bed. He remembered that much, as well as having to push Sophie aside so he could squeeze under the covers. But the rest of it...not so much with the memories.

He got up and winced as bright sunlight burned through his eyes. Note to self, he thought grimly. No more drinking when he was feeling stupid about his lack of talent. It only led to disaster and pushed him a little too close to the Ceallach side of the road. Staying sane meant being his own man.

He let Sophie out and started coffee. While his Keurig worked its magic, he scanned the living room, but nothing was out of place. In fact all the glasses from the previous night were neatly placed in the dishwasher and the salsa and chips had been put away. Had he done that? Had Carol? Jeez, he really hoped he'd stayed awake long enough to escort her to the door. He had, hadn't he?

Sophie bounced back into the kitchen, her tail wagging. He fed her before retreating to the healing warmth of a hot shower. As he stripped down he remembered the incredible sex dream he'd had, then groaned. Once again Carol had dominated his night. Damn, everything about touching her, kissing her, pleasing her, had been so real. So vivid. If only, he thought with a sigh. But his luck wasn't that good.

Once he was showered, shaved and dressed, he made his bed and took his second cup of coffee out onto the back patio. Through some quirk of geography or weather, there was still mist clinging to the ground of the animal preserve. The wisps of fog made him think of fairies or maybe just trolls.

Before he could decide which was more likely in Happily Inc, a couple of gazelles raced into view. They tore across the damp grass with the energy of schoolchildren being released for the day. He sat down and reached for his sketch pad. As he picked up a pencil, something nibbled at the back of his mind. Something about the previous night. Had he said something? What was it he couldn't remember?

Before he could pursue the lack of thought, Millie stepped into view. She moved more slowly than the gazelles, as if each step required planning. Or maybe she was just sad. He wished there was a way to let her know that Carol was working the problem. That as soon as there was money a herd would be purchased and—

Carol joined Millie. It was something she did nearly every morning. Only this time was different. Mathias wasn't sure how he knew that, but as he watched, every part of him went on alert. Something had changed. Something had happened or was going to happen or—

Carol spoke. Mathias saw her lips move. Millie bent down just as Carol looked up. Sunlight broke through the mist and in that moment, the giraffe and the woman nearly touched.

The image was perfect—all lines and curves. Friendship,

maybe love, surrounded them. Carol's chin was raised, Millie's neck arched. There were trees behind them, a hint of mist and the light from the sun. Everything was exactly as it should be, he thought as he drew frantically. This was what he'd been waiting for and now he knew exactly what he had to do.

He finished the drawing, then went inside and made copies of it before heading to the studio. After dropping Sophie off with Natalie, he began the painstaking process of turning glass into magic.

It took hours. Nick joined him and together they heated, formed, rolled and discarded different pieces. Finally, as the sun headed toward the western horizon, Mathias set a ten-inch giraffe on his desk and studied it.

There weren't as many details as he would like, but that would come with size and practice. Still, progress had been made. The piece looked like Millie. Even more important, there was a sense of movement, as if the giraffe would take the next step any second.

"Damn," Nick breathed. "You nailed it. What's next?"

"I do it again, only bigger." The final piece would be maybe three feet high, he thought absently, turning the glass around on his desk. Millie leaning down and Carol looking up. Tomorrow he would make his first attempt at creating Carol out of glass. Once he had worked out the basics in the smaller piece, he would make that one larger, as well. And then...

He stood and studied the giraffe. He had no idea what happened after that, but he was okay with the uncertainty. It had been years since he'd created something other than dishes and pendant lights. Years since he'd been willing to take a chance.

The last time, he'd been all of nineteen. Mathias did his best to ignore the past, but it flooded him with detailed memories and once again he could see the swirling abstract design—part star, part wave, color pulsing in every curve. He'd stunned himself with its beauty and had sensed down to his gut it was the best thing he'd ever done.

Both Nick and Ronan had been silent—as if they had no idea what to say. Their looks of admiration and envy had been enough. He'd *known* he'd nailed it. Known this piece was going to be the one to put him on the map. He would be more than Ceallach's talented son—he would be famous in his own right.

He'd waited anxiously for his father to see what he'd done. Waited for judgment to be pronounced. Ceallach had slowly walked around the pedestal, had frowned and said nothing. Mathias had waited confidently, ready to be told he was good enough.

His father's expression had hardened into distaste. "Garbage," he'd growled, before pushing the pedestal and causing the huge, glorious swirling, living thing to tumble to the ground and shatter into a thousand pieces.

All three brothers had stared in disbelief. Ronan had spoken first.

"You're jealous," Mathias's twin had shouted. "That's why you did it. You know he's better than you and you can't stand it."

Ceallach's next swipe of his fist had been to his son's face. Mathias had pulled Ronan back while Nick had shoved their father out of the studio. They'd stood there together, their breathing loud in the silence.

"You have to make it again," Nick said at last. "You have to show him."

"Nick's right. We'll get it out of the studio before he can destroy it. He'll be forced to admit you're the one who's going to beat him."

Mathias hadn't said anything. He'd walked out into the woods around their house and had stayed gone for two days.

When he'd returned, he'd started making dishes and bowls, mugs and basins.

He shook his head and returned to the present. The small statue of Millie still stood in the center of his desk. He touched the cool, smooth glass. No matter what, Ceallach wasn't going to take this away from him. That he knew for sure.

"What?" Violet demanded the second she sat down at the small table.

Carol sighed. Sisters—who knew they could be a problem? "Thanks for suggesting we have coffee," she said as cheerfully as she could. She motioned to the giant cinnamon roll she'd already purchased. "I was hoping we could share. Otherwise I'll eat the whole thing and wake up weighing 400 pounds."

"I don't think that's how metabolism works." Violet eyed her. "There's something. Don't think you can hide it from me." She pointed to the short line at the counter. "I'm going to get coffee and another fork. You can use that time to figure out how to either cough up the truth or lie your way out of whatever you have going on." She took a step, then stopped. "And remember, I can always tell when you're lying."

Carol wanted to say that wasn't true, only it was. She and her sister were close, which was why she'd agreed to coffee. After her unsettling evening, she'd wanted a friendly face and a bit of female support. Only she'd forgotten that although her sister loved her, she wasn't a pushover. Which meant either coming clean or making up a very believable story. While Carol knew she had many lovely qualities, she also knew that all the creativity genes had gone to Violet. So annoying.

Rather than fight the inevitable, Carol waited until her sister had taken the seat opposite.

"Fine," she said, her voice low. "I had sex with Mathias last night. Sort of."

Violet's mouth fell open, her eyes widened and she nearly

dropped her fork. "I... You... What? Mathias? But I didn't know you two were... Wait. What do you mean sort of?"

Carol took another bite of cinnamon roll. When life got confusing, sugar and fat were always a comfort.

"We're not dating, if that's what you're asking. We're friends. He's into those sexy bridesmaids and I'm..."

"Not?"

Carol smiled. "Exactly." Her smile faded. "I don't know what exactly happened."

"Oh, honey, then one of you was doing it wrong."

"You're not helping."

"Sorry. I'm confused, but I'll focus. So what happened?"

Carol explained about driving home and seeing Mathias walking Sophie. There had been the invitation to come over and margaritas and one thing had led to another...almost.

"He passed out before we could...you know."

Violet leaned close. "Seriously? You just told me you had oral sex with Mathias but you can't say intercourse?"

"That is hardly the point." She glanced over her shoulder to make sure no one had settled close to them. "I don't know what I'm supposed to say the next time I see him."

"I think mockery is in order."

"How is that helpful?"

"It's the truth. Come on, the man passed out. That's all on him, not you." Her eyes narrowed. "You're not blaming yourself, are you?"

Carol shifted in her seat. "Not exactly. It's just, I'm not like the women he sees. They're all so glamorous and beautiful."

"They're in wedding clothes. Of course they look all fancy."

Logic, Carol thought. How annoying. "Maybe if I was different he would have stayed awake."

"Only if you were coffee. Carol, you know he had way too much to drink. You didn't do anything wrong."

"I feel awful."

"Imagine how he feels. Talking about humiliating."

Carol stared at her sister. "I never thought of that. You're right. He has to be devastated. I mean, he's a guy and he just passed out. That's not good."

"See. You're the innocent party."

She liked the sound of that. Last night she'd been so shocked, she hadn't known what to do. She'd let Sophie out and had tidied up, then left. But she hadn't been able to sleep or known what to think. Even worse, she couldn't stop thinking about how great the sex had been. Imagine if they'd been able to continue!

"So what do I say when I see him?"

"Probably avoid words like loser."

"Violet!"

"Sorry. I don't know. What do you want to say?"

"I'm not sure. I haven't heard from him yet." She'd kind of thought he might text her, but so far there hadn't been a word.

"You will. I'm sure he's trying to figure out how to crawl out from under his rock. Plus he probably doesn't feel very good."

"I'm sure he'll apologize," Carol murmured. "I'll wait until that happens, then tell him it's fine."

"You sure you don't want to demand a rematch?"

Carol's stomach tightened. She would like nothing more, but sex on demand seemed way too risky. What if Mathias was regretting what had happened? What if he never wanted to see her again?

She knew she was looking for trouble, but it was difficult to be rational about the whole thing. She wasn't like Violet— she had no sense of style, no attitude. Mathias was all attitude.

"I want things to go back the way they were," she lied, hoping her sister didn't notice. "I'm sure they will."

"After he grovels."

"Yes, after that. So how was dinner with your Englishman?"

She'd thought Violet might resist changing the subject, but instead her sister slumped in her seat and sighed.

"Amazing."

"The word and the body language don't match."

"I know. We had a great time. He was funny and charming. My dance memory from all those years ago is restored."

Carol smiled. "I'm glad. So he was swoon-worthy?"

"Totally." She stabbed the cinnamon roll. "He invited me back to his hotel room."

"Did you go?" Carol asked, although she already knew the answer.

"No. I couldn't. I'm sure it would have been amazing, but he's leaving and I'm not interested in that kind of thing."

Carol studied her sister. "Your lips are saying one thing but the rest of you is saying another. Second thoughts?"

"Maybe. No. Yes." Violet sipped her coffee. "I'm not sorry I said no and I am sorry I said no. I really like him. There's something so appealing about him."

"Maybe you should plan a trip to England."

"I'm not going to go all the way over there, chasing a man. If he wanted to see me for more than a one-night stand, he would have said so. He would have stayed, or suggested we keep in touch. He did neither."

It appeared that bitch logic had it out for the Lund sisters this morning.

"I wish I knew how to make it better," Carol admitted.

"Thanks. I'll be okay. It was just dinner, right? One evening in a lifetime of evenings. It doesn't mean anything."

Which sounded great but left Carol with the nagging feeling that both of them were lying about something really important.

Carol spent the next twenty-four or so hours waiting for the text/phone call/visit that never came. Mathias had totally dropped out of sight and she honestly had no idea what to think. Embarrassment was one thing, as was regret, but this? What was the man thinking?

As her mind was more than willing to provide a hundred not-flattering-to-her scenarios to answer that question, she tried another tack. Was he sick? Injured? Had he moved to Borneo to avoid a humiliating morning after? Had it really been that awful?

She did her best not to think about what they'd done, only telling herself not to think about it was pretty much the same as thinking about it All. The. Time. It seemed there was no win in what had happened—at least not for her.

She'd nearly convinced herself that maybe she should consider a lunchtime cocktail as a distraction when her phone rang. She lunged for it, grabbed too hard so it slipped from her fingers and hit the floor of her office, then spun under the desk. She dropped to her knees and finally got hold of it and was able to see the screen even as she pushed Talk.

Mathias!

Her chest tightened, her stomach lurched and her mouth went dry, which made it hard to say, "Hello?"

"It's me. Sophie's missing. Somehow she opened the gate and got out of the backyard."

Two actual seconds passed before she was able to process what he'd said. He wasn't calling about them—he was calling about the dog. Who was missing. Her brain kicked in.

"Oh, no. Do you think she's in the preserve?"

"If I had to guess, I'd say yes. I thought I could come there and we could go out and call her. Do you think any of the animals would hurt her?"

"No. They're all grazing animals." Unless Sophie got curious and ventured too close. Then there could be some serious kicking.

She winced as she thought of the little dog being injured. "I'll grab my golf cart and head out right now." She had her

Jeep as well, but the electric golf cart would be quieter and less likely to scare any of the animals or Sophie.

"I'm at the house. Give me five minutes and I'll meet you."

"I'll be by the barn."

She hung up and called her father, then hurried to the barn. She'd barely backed the golf cart out of the bay when Mathias pulled up.

For a second all she could do was stare at him. He was so tall and handsome, she thought foolishly. So appealing with his eyes all dark with worry. What they'd done that night—

"We've got to find her," he said by way of greeting. "My mom's going to kill me if we don't and I'll feel guilty for the rest of my life."

So much for a romantic reunion. "I've already talked to my dad," she told him as he got into the seat next to her. "He and my uncle are going to drive down the main road and be on the lookout. We weren't sure how far Sophie could get on her own."

"Clear to Iowa if there's enough time."

"We'll find her." Carol headed out past the barn.

"She could be anywhere."

"Sophie wants adventure, not to run away. I'm sure she's stayed close."

She followed the main path, stopping every hundred yards so Mathias could call out. As he yelled the dog's name, Carol watched for her own charges. Quietly grazing zebras and gazelles meant a Sophie-free zone. If the animals were agitated or running, chances were they would find their beagle in close pursuit.

They went by the gazelles first. There was no sign of flapping ears or a wagging tail. The zebras were equally quiet. Even Harriet, the water buffalo, barely raised her head as they zipped by.

"I can't imagine Sophie hanging out with Millie," Carol said, "but we should check on her anyway."

She headed toward Millie's favorite midday spot only to stop when she heard a happy yip of excitement.

Mathias shot her a look of confusion. "Can Sophie even see that high? Wouldn't Millie just be weird legs to her?"

"I have no idea."

She followed the path, then stopped. Millie stood nibbling on branches Carol had hoisted into place that morning. Sophie danced between her long legs, moving perilously close to giraffe feet. Before Carol could do more than feel the cold flood of panic, Millie lowered her head so that she gently butted Sophie in a gesture that was almost maternal. The bouncing beagle swiped the side of Millie's face with a kiss.

"Holy crap," Mathias muttered. "What is she doing?"

"Making friends?"

Sophie spun toward them, barked happily and darted toward them. She jumped into the cart, landing on Mathias's lap. After planting her front paws on his chest, she licked his face, then grinned at Carol. Millie returned to her meal.

"You're a troublemaker," Mathias told the dog. "What am I going to do with you?"

Sophie sat down on his lap and leaned against him as if indicating she was ready to go. Carol used her walkie-talkie to let her dad and uncle know the little dog had been found.

"Millie could have killed her," she said. "It wouldn't have taken much for her to crush her, but she didn't. She seemed happy to have a friend."

Mathias lightly touched her hand. "You're getting her a herd."

"It's taking too long. I worry about her being happy." She shook her head. "Sorry. Not your problem."

Now that the crisis was over, the realization that she was back in Mathias's company had her wondering how to bring up what had happened...and not happened...between them.

"So you're, um, feeling better?"

He gave her a sheepish smile. "Sorry about the other night.

There's some stuff going on. I hope I didn't say anything stupid before I passed out."

She waited, but that seemed to be all he had to say. Questions formed, then faded. Weren't they going to talk about—

Her mouth dropped open. No. No! There was no way on this planet that he couldn't remember what had happened, was there?

"The whole evening is kind of blurry," he admitted, then cleared his throat. "Speaking as your neighbor and friend, I promise I won't be drinking that much again. It's not my usual practice. Like I said—too much going on."

He didn't remember. Not the evening, not the kissing, not the other kissing! How could that have happened? Only she knew the answer and it wasn't pretty. She was truly that unspecial and unmemorable.

They reached the barn. She parked the golf cart, then waited while he collected Sophie and got out.

"I'm going to take this one home and give her a stern talking-to."

"That will help," Carol muttered, still in shock.

He flashed her a slow, sexy smile that had her knees buckling. "I have hidden powers of persuasion. You'll see a changed beagle in the morning."

"You don't actually believe that, do you?"

He chuckled. "No, but I'm going to look at the gate and see how I can make it more Sophie-proof. Thanks for helping me."

"No problem. I'm glad she's okay."

Mathias waved, then walked to his car. Carol stayed where she was and told herself that later there would be cake. And some kind of pasta. Then she would give herself her own stern talking-to. The lecture would be heavy on *Mathias is not for you* with a little bit of *one day you'll find someone wonderful* thrown in for good measure.

CHAPTER NINE

Ulrich put off leaving Happily Inc as long as he could, but finally he ran out of reasons to stay. Obviously he wasn't going to see Violet again and he had no business in town, so early in the morning, he headed east, toward Los Angeles and his flight to London.

He'd assured his grandmother that the apology had been delivered and all was well with her young friend. He did not share how much he'd enjoyed Violet's company or the way her laughter had brightened a dark place deep inside of him. Being around her had made him feel alive for the first time in years. If only she'd accepted his invitation.

He shook his head as he drove toward the highway. What would that have accomplished? If leaving her had been this difficult after only a few hours in her company and a few kisses, how much harder would it have been after he'd had the pleasure of making love with her?

Still thinking about what that would have been like, he made a left only to find himself speeding toward a giraffe in the middle of road.

Ulrich slammed on the brakes, instinctively turning away

from the animal, which meant he was heading toward a ditch
and a grove of trees. Not sure which was going to be the easier
blow, he aimed between them. A plan that turned out to be
less than successful when his car hit soft dirt, came to an in-
stant stop, only to roll and roll, and then the world went dark.

Ulrich was aware of the passing of time. He'd been awake
for a while—or at least not passed out. The world seemed to
be moving with some kind of blurry not-quite-real sense of
time. Based on the bright lights and the smell, he knew he
was in hospital. He thought there might have been a car accident and for some reason there was an image of a giraffe
in his mind, but he had no real idea of what had happened.

Most of his body hurt—some places more than others. He
couldn't seem to move his left leg, which didn't bode well,
and when he tried to raise his head, the room spun. He was
hooked up to an IV, but he didn't think he'd been to surgery.
When he'd gathered enough strength, he planned on demanding answers, but for now he was going to rest.

After a while, he became aware of someone nearby. Not a
nurse. The presence was more restful and there was no pok-
ing and prodding. Despite the risk of the room spinning, he
forced himself to open his eyes and found Violet sitting by his
bed. When she saw him looking at her, she smiled, although
her expression remained concerned.

"Hey, how are you feeling? What do you remember? Want
me to call the nurse?"

She morphed into two people before settling back into one.
He closed his eyes. "No nurse."

Her warm hand reached for him and she squeezed his fingers. "Okay. I'll just sit here. How are you feeling?"

"Beat up."

"I'll bet."

"There was a car accident?"

"Yes. You drove off the road and the car rolled. The doctor said you're lucky you'd already slowed down. If you'd been going the speed limit, you could have really hurt yourself."

Considering how he felt now, he didn't want to know what actually hurting himself would be like. "My grandmother..."

"I've already called Nana Winifred. She knows you're all right." Violet hesitated. "You have a mild concussion, a lot of bruising, a sprained ankle and some cuts and lacerations. You're basically a mess, but you're going to make a full recovery."

He risked looking at her again and was pleased when she stayed just herself. "Good to know."

"You won't be able to fly for a while and you're going to need someone to look after you, so I volunteered. It was that or your grandmother was going to fly over here and take care of you herself. I didn't think you'd want that."

"Hardly."

His grandmother wouldn't do well on such a long journey and seeing him in a hospital bed would remind her of all the times her son had been bedridden.

"How long will I be in hospital?" he asked.

She smiled. "You're so very British."

"I don't understand."

"*In hospital.* We say in *the* hospital."

"That would be incorrect terminology."

She laughed. "You must be feeling better."

He wasn't, but he liked having her around. When he could see her and hear her voice, the pain wasn't so bad.

"Was there a giraffe?" he asked, hoping the question didn't mean he had to see a neurologist.

Violet surprised him by wincing. "I'm really sorry about that. Yes, there was a giraffe. Millie got out. She's never done that before. We're pretty sure it's Sophie's influence which, when you think about it, is more than a little scary. I mean

Sophie was just there yesterday and already Millie's breaking out?"

He let his eyes close again. "Who is Sophie?"

"A beagle."

Maybe he'd hit his head harder than he'd realized.

Violet leaned close. He felt her soft breath on his cheek a nanosecond before she kissed him. "Don't try to figure it out, Ulrich. I'll explain it all when you're feeling better. Get some rest. If all goes well, they're going to spring you in the morning. I'm going to leave for a couple of hours to get ready for my nursing stint, then I'll be back."

"Hurry," he murmured before he could stop himself.

"I will."

Mathias arrived at the studio at his usual time, only to discover there wasn't any parking. Every space was taken and there was a line outside the gallery. It took him a second to remember it was sale day and that brought out the shoppers.

Mathias headed around the block and found a spot, then made sure Sophie's leash was secure before letting her out of the car. He heard that somehow the crafty beagle had taught Millie to escape, causing a car accident on the road out of town.

"I'm not letting you get loose again," he told her as they walked back toward the studio.

Sophie offered a doggie grin of support and apology as she trotted along at his side. He circled around the line and went in the rear door of the studio. When he unclipped Sophie, she made a beeline for the gallery and Natalie, who not only looked after her much of the day but also kept treats in her desk. He'd barely finished his first check of the ovens before starting work when Natalie appeared with Sophie at her heels.

"I can't keep her today," she said. "I have to work one of the cash registers. Did you see the crowds?"

"I did." He glanced at Sophie. No way he would be getting much work done with her underfoot. Sophie and molten glass would not be a good mix.

"It's your own fault," Natalie added with a laugh. "If people didn't love your work, they wouldn't line up before dawn. It's not often a gifted artist has a sale. We'll have sold out by noon, I promise. Then I can take Sophie."

A couple of times a year Atsuko had a big sale of Mathias's unsuccessful pieces. Bowls and vases and plates that were irregular in some way. The color might be wrong or the shape slightly off.

The sale had started out as a joke, but it had caught on and now was a big deal. People actually lined up to get his pieces at a bargain price. Plates that normally sold for a hundred dollars apiece went for five. Thousand-dollar vases were twenty-five dollars and so on.

"I'll clean up around here," he said. "Let me know when you can take Sophie."

"I will."

Mathias walked to his desk and stared at the piles of paperwork he mostly ignored. It was going to be a long morning.

A little before ten he checked in at the gallery. There was still a huge crowd, although most of his pieces were gone. As he watched, an older woman carefully put a dollar in the Millie can, then carried her purchase out of the studio.

Mathias thought about the sad giraffe and calculated about how much he thought he would make from the day. Even if he donated every cent, it wasn't going to be enough.

He stared at the display of Ronan's glass. The flower sculptures for three hundred thousand. The starfish array for two hundred and twenty-five thousand. What were they doing, messing around with nickels and dimes?

He returned to the studio and called for Sophie. After putting on her leash, he led her to his Mercedes. They drove east, then north, up into the foothills. Ronan lived a few miles above the tree line.

When the brothers had first moved to Happily Inc they'd rented a big house together as they'd done their best to come to terms with what had happened. After a few months, Ronan had found the house in the mountains and had bought it—without saying a word. Mathias had been surprised and hurt, but he'd kept both to himself. Instead he'd purchased his place on the edge of the animal preserve.

He wasn't sure if that was when the trouble had started—when they'd stopped living together—or if it had been before when Ronan had simply left Fool's Gold, leaving Mathias to follow or not. Until his father's heart attack, he and Ronan had believed they were fraternal twins. They'd done everything together. More than once, they'd dated sisters. But everything had changed with one simple sentence.

You're my bastard from an affair.

Mathias got that Ronan had been blindsided by the information and that everything was different now. But what his brother didn't seem to understand was that everything had changed for Mathias, as well. His identity had been rocked, all his memories altered.

He and Ronan had come to Happily Inc to get away from Ceallach and to figure out who and what they were now. Mathias had assumed they would work through the problem and get on with their lives. He hadn't counted on Ronan pulling back until they were barely speaking.

Mathias parked in front of the large stone house. The place had to be at least fifty years old. It was huge, with giant windows and a massive double front door. Trees grew all around it, making the house appear to have sprung from the very earth itself.

He got out and checked Sophie's leash before letting her jump to the ground. No way he was letting her loose on the side of a mountain—he would never see her again.

After she'd sniffed, peed and sniffed again, he guided her around the back of the house to the studio. The sprawling structure had once been a barn or maybe a stable. Ronan had converted it when he'd first moved in. There were ovens and all the equipment he needed to work. Mathias wondered why he bothered to come down the mountain at all.

The door to the studio stood open. Mathias entered without knocking and found Ronan staring at a to-scale drawing on the side of the wall. It showed his latest installation—the swan to dragon morphing.

His brother didn't react to seeing him beyond a noncommittal "Hey."

"Hey, yourself." Mathias kept a firm hold on Sophie. "Carol needs money to buy Millie a herd of giraffes."

"I know."

"She needs nearly half a million dollars. It's going to take too long. Donate something so Atsuko can have a gallery event and sell it."

"Sure." He nodded toward the storage room in the back. "Take something or have Carol pick a piece herself. Take ten. I don't care."

There had been a time when Mathias had known everything his brother was thinking. Back then he would have known what was behind the offer. Was it done out of concern for Millie or lack of interest in continuing the conversation? He no longer knew. Ronan had become a stranger.

"Okay, then. I'll have her call before she stops by."

"Good. Anything else?"

There were a thousand things they had to talk about. Whatever Ceallach had said or done, they were still family. Still brothers. Shouldn't they have been able to stay close?

Mathias already knew the answer to that question. Every time he reached out to his brother, Ronan drew back just a little further. Eventually Mathias had stopped trying, afraid his brother would disappear altogether.

Mathias jerked his head at the sketch on the wall. "Let me know if you need any help with that." Because when it came to glass blowing, a second set of hands was always welcome and often needed and Ronan's interns only worked part-time.

"I will."

Mathias waited but there didn't seem to be anything else left to say.

"Thanks," he muttered, then walked out of the studio and back to his car.

Sophie trotted at his side, her expression questioning as if she wanted to know why they'd come all this way only to leave so quickly. He didn't have an answer for her or for himself, but at least the Millie problem had been solved.

Carol glanced at the suitcase and three tote bags her sister had brought over. "More proof the dinner went really well," she teased. "You're really going to stay here? Not that the room isn't lovely."

Violet rolled her eyes. "He can't stay at my place—it's upstairs, which he can't currently climb. Here, there's an elevator. Besides, I'm taking care of a sick person. You have to respect that."

"I'd respect it more if he weren't good-looking." She looked around at the oddly decorated room. Wallpaper depicted some kind of mountain range in the distance with way too many wildflowers in the foreground. The bed was four-poster, the furniture on the rustic side. She'd caught a glimpse of the bathroom and it had appeared totally normal. "Okay, I don't get it. What's the theme?"

"*Heidi.*"

Carol frowned, processing the name. "You mean the book?"

"That's the one. This is supposed to be a mountain chalet."

"I wouldn't have guessed that."

"It's not what I would have picked," Violet admitted as she looked through the totes. "But it's adjoining Ulrich's room, which makes my life easier."

"I never saw you as the private nurse type. Are you getting a uniform? Maybe one with a short skirt?"

"The man is injured."

"All the easier to seduce him."

"I'm ignoring you," Violet told her.

"Ignoring the truth doesn't make it go away."

Her sister laughed as Carol had known she would. As for taking care of Ulrich, that didn't surprise Carol, either. Violet was a good person with a big heart. No matter what she thought of Ulrich—he was alone and injured—she would be there for him. The sexy accent was only a bonus.

"You spoke to his grandmother?"

"Three times. She wants regular reports. He should be able to travel in a week or so."

"That's a long time for you to take off work."

"According to the doctor, Ulrich should be up and walking in a couple of days. Once I know he's making progress, I'll go in for a few hours at a time."

"Plus most of what you do happens over the internet and through the mail. Let me know how I can help."

"I will."

Carol knew that her sister would be bringing Ulrich back to the hotel later that morning. "Want me to pick up take-out for dinner?"

"I think we'll just order room service, but I might ask you for tomorrow."

"Just say the word."

Violet put the suitcase on the bed and pulled out several tops. She hung them in the closet. "How are things with you?" she asked when she returned to the bed. "Any word from Mathias?"

Not a question Carol wanted to answer. Which must have shown on her face because her sister dropped the blouse she was holding and stared at her.

"What?"

Crap. No, double crap. "I'm pretty sure he doesn't remember." Or he was faking not remembering, which was too humiliating to say to anyone, including Violet.

"No. Seriously? He doesn't—" Violet's expression turned sympathetic. "I'm sorry."

"Me, too. It's weird and upsetting and I don't know what to do. I can't bring it up." She shook her head. "Technically I can, but I'm not going to. This is already a personal low. I don't need to make things worse. I guess I'm going to pretend it never happened, right along with him."

She braced herself for a lecture, but Violet only hugged her.

"Can you really do that?"

"Sure. I think so. Maybe. I don't know. I'm going to try. The alternative is too awful to think about. You won't say anything, will you?"

Her sister hugged her again. "Not even for ice cream."

Carol relaxed. That was a promise she could trust.

Violet did her best not to look as awkward as she felt. It was one thing to promise to take care of Ulrich while he was recovering, but quite another to actually do it. She barely knew the man—what on earth was she doing in his hotel room? A silly question to which she knew the answer, but still. Weirdness all around.

His grandmother had insisted he be delivered back to the hotel via ambulance. The nice driver and his assistant had brought Ulrich upstairs in a wheelchair, then had got him settled in his bed. Violet was already moved into her small room next door and she had a plan for the night. Rest for her patient, a simple room service dinner, then early to bed. She would deal with everything else tomorrow.

She gave Ulrich an extra five minutes to get comfortable in his bed, then knocked once and opened the door between their two rooms.

"How are you feeling?" she asked cheerfully, hoping she didn't look as suddenly nervous as she felt. She glanced at him, found the sight of him in bed far too intimate and settled on staring at a safe spot somewhere slightly above his head.

"Foolish, mostly. You don't have to stay with me."

"That's not what your grandmother said and while you might not be afraid of her, I am. Seriously, do you doubt her ability to fly out here and whack me with her cane?"

"I have felt the power of that cane more than once. It's not something you'd enjoy. Now come and sit here so we can work out what, exactly, is our plan."

A sensible suggestion, she thought as she picked up the desk chair and carried it over to his bed. She ran her hands along the side of the red Cadillac and smiled.

"Does recovering in a car bed make you feel more or less foolish?"

"I'm not sure, but it's an excellent question. I would suppose more foolish. It's hard to look dignified in these settings."

Without thinking she let her gaze drift over his face and somehow became mesmerized by his dark blue eyes. Even pale, bruised and slightly drugged, he was one good-looking guy, she thought. And that accent!

Not anything she could dwell on right now, she reminded herself. He was her patient and while she might not be a medical professional, she did have certain responsibilities to keep things circumspect. He was already injured. She didn't want him worried she was going to throw herself at him.

"Are you still feeling dizzy?" she asked.

He hesitated just long enough for her to guess at the answer.

"It's not bad," he told her. "Better than yesterday. Not that I can convince my grandmother. I've already had to send her three selfies so she can see for herself that I'm going to be all right. I would appreciate anything you can do to reassure her."

"Of course. I'm sure we'll be talking in the next fifteen minutes." Violet thought about her conversations with Ulrich's grandmother. "She doesn't want to lose you."

"I know. She worries." He hesitated. "I don't know if she ever mentioned, my father was in a very bad car accident when he was a teenager. He never fully recovered and spent the rest of his life using crutches or a wheelchair. She was devastated by that, and later by his early death."

Violet nodded. She'd never met Ulrich's father, but had heard about him in the letters she and Nana Winifred exchanged. The older woman had been crushed when her son had died a few years ago.

"You're all she has," she said quietly. "I'll make sure I reassure her."

"Good. She's too frail to make her way here, although she would certainly make the attempt if she thought she was needed."

"Don't worry. I'm not risking the cane. All my reports will be upbeat."

Her unimpressive attempt at humor earned her a slight smile, which generated a little quiver in her stomach. Okay, she might not have caring for an English aristocrat on her schedule this week, but it was hardly difficult duty.

"I thought we'd have a quiet evening tonight," she said, changing the subject. "Dinner in, some mindless television, then an early bedtime for you. I put together a schedule for your medications. They'll be tapering off in the next couple of days, so I'll only have to disturb you for the first two nights."

He frowned a manly frown. "I can take my own pills, Violet. You don't need to get up in the middle of the night to take care of me."

"It's what I live for. Seriously, it's fine. I'll use my phone alarm. You're not going to talk me out of it, Ulrich. You were in a bad accident. Your body needs time to recover. Just say thank-you and go with it."

"Thank you."

"See how easy that was? Now let's talk dinner." She handed him the room service menu. "Your nurse said you might not have much of an appetite for a couple of days, but you do need something."

Instead of glancing at the offerings, he studied her. "I'm sorry all this was thrust upon you. You must have better things to be doing with your time."

"My life is easily transported. I have my clothes and my computer. I do most of my business through the mail and over the internet. There's a sign on my storefront explaining how to get in touch with me. If anyone needs an emergency alteration, I'm very reachable."

"You're too kind."

Drat. Kind? She wanted to be sexy or enticing. Had the man forgotten how he'd kissed her and invited her back to his room? Had he changed his mind about all that? Yes, he was injured and she wasn't expecting anything to happen between them, but a slight hint of interest or a mildly inappropriate remark would be nice.

Nursing was hard, she thought with a sigh. "All right, Your Lordship. Dinner. How about some nice soup and maybe chicken fingers?"

"I didn't know chickens had fingers."

She winced. "Now I have a visual and can never eat them again."

"My apologies. If I order them, will your world be restored?"

"I'm just not sure."

"Then I shall vow to work harder."

If only, she thought, holding in a smile. If only…

CHAPTER TEN

Mathias couldn't shake the feeling of having forgotten something important. It was there—whispering in the back of his mind, only he couldn't, for the life of him, remember what the hell it was. He wanted to say it didn't matter, only along with that nagging *what was it?* sensation was the feeling that it was important. Really important.

He returned his attention to the glass giraffe in front of him. This was the third one he'd made and he was starting to believe he was getting where he needed to go. The sense of movement had grown with each piece. This was his best one yet, and the tallest.

He liked the expression on Millie's face, the way her tail curved and the lines of her torso. She looked as if she could come to life at any moment.

He knew the next step was to start on the other half of the piece. To try to create Carol in glass. While he knew he was onto something with the image he'd sketched the other morning, he wasn't sure he could reproduce any part of the woman in a medium as static as glass. Carol was alive. She moved and talked and breathed. How could he reduce that to glass? What made the concept even more challenging was whenever he thought about how to begin, he couldn't hold a single image of her in his mind. She was always changing, shifting, morphing. First smiling, then talking, then laughing. And then it got complicated.

Lately, whenever he thought about her, he imagined her naked. A totally dumb-ass thing to do, but there it was. His guyness taking over his brain. He could practically *taste* her breasts, feeling the weight of them in his hands. That line of thought led him other places he had no business going and then he was daydreaming instead of working, and dealing with a painful erection.

He had no idea how to solve the problem. Okay, that wasn't true. He had several ideas, all of which would probably have her slapping him upside the head. Still, a guy could dream… and he did.

He lightly touched the glass statue of Millie, then surrendered to the inevitable. He couldn't avoid her—not when he had to tell her about Ronan and the donation. Better to do it now and get it over with. Then he would go home and do his damnedest to figure out what was bugging him, and how he could stop dreaming about the one woman he could never have.

Carol pulled into her driveway only to find Mathias and Sophie sitting on her porch. The beagle immediately jumped up and began wagging her tail, but Mathias's feelings were more difficult to read.

That made two of them, Carol thought as she parked her car and slowly got out. She still couldn't define all the emotions swirling around inside of her. Anger, embarrassment, anger, confusion and maybe some, you know, anger. She wanted to grab him and shake him until he either admitted he remembered but now regretted what had happened or looked at her so blankly she had to accept that he really didn't recall what had happened.

Neither scenario was especially happy, but if she had to pick, she preferred a brain freeze to revulsion.

Sophie rushed over, her leash trailing behind her. Carol crouched down to greet the happy dog.

"How's my best girl?" she asked, rubbing Sophie's face and dodging kisses.

"She knows you say that to all your animals," Mathias told her. "She's not impressed."

Sophie continued the greeting dance. Carol forgot to be mad and smiled at him. "All evidence to the contrary?"

"Yeah, there is that."

She straightened and tried to find her inner rage, but it seemed to have faded. Ah, the power of the beagle. Or maybe it was looking at Mathias. Just the sight of him was enough to right her world which was, considering their last encounter and his complete lack of reaction, incredibly frustrating.

"So how are—"

Things. She'd been going to say how are *things.* Only she couldn't speak, couldn't do anything but stare when she caught sight of the glass piece sitting next to Mathias on her small porch.

The statue was maybe two feet tall. Slim and delicate, the image of Millie was so perfect, so lifelike, that she half expected it to start walking. Despite the lack of color of the glass, Mathias had captured the giraffe's features—her wide eyes, the tilt of her head, the long, elegant lines of her neck. While there weren't any markings, there were still darker areas indicating the pattern of her coat. No, that wasn't right—the glass was clear, so were the markings etched?

She moved toward it and put out a hand, then pulled it back. Mathias gave her a lopsided smile.

"It's yours, Carol. You can pick it up and everything."

She stared at him. "Mine?"

"I made it for you. I've been working on this idea." He shook his head. "That doesn't matter. Yes, this is for you. I know how you feel about Millie and I thought you'd like to have it."

She carefully touched the cool glass, half expecting it to move, as Millie would. Everything about the piece was perfect.

"I don't understand," she breathed. "I didn't know you could—" She pressed her lips together. "You never make things like this."

"I make what I make because I want to," he told her. "Not because I don't know how to do anything else."

But why? The question went unasked. She didn't want to make him feel bad or say the wrong thing, yet what was he doing, making plates and vases when he could create something so amazing?

He stood and called for Sophie, then pointed to the door. "I'd like to talk to you about something if you have a second."

What? Had he remembered? Decided to come clean about faking not remembering? Was he going to tell her he was sorry, that it had been awful? Was the giraffe a mercy gift?

She picked up the piece of glass and handed it to him, then dug her keys out of her bag and opened the door. She would wait, she told herself. Let him say what he wanted to say before jumping to conclusions.

They went inside. Sophie sniffed around her living room, as if making sure no other dog had challenged her favorite guest-dog status, then made herself at home in an armchair. Carol took back the giraffe and placed it in the center of her small kitchen table where it would catch the light. She thought briefly about offering Mathias a drink, but the last time they'd had liquor, things had gone weird, so maybe not.

She returned to the living room and sat at one end of the sofa. He remained standing.

"It's about Millie," he began, shoving his hands into his jeans pockets, then pulling them out.

"Do you want it back?" she asked. He'd said it was for her. Did he not mean for her to keep it?

"Not that one. The real Millie. I talked to Ronan. He's going to donate a piece. Atsuko will hold a private event at the gallery. She'll put out the word to collectors and make a night of it. The proceeds will go to Millie's fund. It should be enough to buy the herd and get them here."

He kept talking, but she couldn't hear anything else. Not after those simple words—*The proceeds will go to Millie's fund. It should be enough to buy the herd.*

She thought about her solitary giraffe who had no friends and how much better it would be when Millie was part of a family. She thought about the fund-raisers she'd been researching and how far she and Millie still had to go. It could have taken years, but here in one moment, with a few words, Mathias had changed everything.

She stood, then sat back down as her shaking legs refused to support her. "What? Mathias, are you sure?"

"That you can get that much? Yeah. Ronan's work goes for a lot. He wants you to pick something out. Ask him which ones are the most rare. Those will go for the most."

She blinked away tears. "No, I mean are you sure he'll do this?"

"Yeah, he will."

The truth slammed into her. "Because you asked him to," she whispered, more to herself than him. "This is you, not him."

"It's his piece that will bring in the money you need." His dark gaze settled on her face. "I should have thought of this a long time ago. It's those damn cans. I'm tired of seeing them everywhere."

She stood and crossed to him. There were no words, nothing she could say to express her gratitude. Still, she had to try.

"Thank you," she said and instinctively reached for him.

In that moment, she wasn't sure if she was going to hug him, kiss him or burst into tears. Before she could decide, he moved back and half turned away from her.

"You don't have to thank me," he said quickly. "I like watching Millie in the morning. It will be better when she has her herd."

The words were friendly enough, the body language less so. She couldn't fool herself any longer—he wasn't interested in her that way. He never had been. Whatever had happened that night had been the result of too much alcohol. He was pretending to forget because if he admitted what happened, they would have to talk about it. He would be forced to answer questions and he didn't want to hurt her feelings.

Humiliation over that night combined with happiness about the money for Millie. Maybe he'd really wanted to help or maybe he'd asked Ronan out of sex guilt. She didn't want it to be the latter, but either way, she wasn't going to say no. Not when giraffe happiness was on the line. As for her own battered feelings, she would deal with them when she was alone.

"Thank you," she said again, careful to move away so he wouldn't worry that she would attack him again. "You're doing an amazing thing."

"It's Ronan, not me."

"It's you, but I'll be sure to thank him, as well."

They looked at each other, then away. Silence settled between them, creating an uncomfortable pause.

"I should get home so I can feed Sophie," he told her. "Get in touch with Ronan. He's expecting to hear from you. And Atsuko. She said she can pull this together pretty fast."

"I will. You were great. Millie and I appreciate all that you've done."

"No big deal."

He walked to the door and whistled for Sophie. The beagle raced after him, her tail wagging.

Carol let them out, walked to the kitchen table and stared at the giraffe statue. It was still amazing and beautiful and practically alive. A gift from Mathias—perhaps a subconscious way for him to apologize for not wanting to have sex with her again. Not that he'd had sex the first time.

Her eyes burned, but she refused to give in to anything but happy emotions. Millie was getting a herd. That was what mattered. As for Mathias—he'd never been for her. She'd been silly to think otherwise.

She dug out her cell phone and pushed a couple of buttons. When her father answered, she drew in a breath. "Dad, you'll never guess what just happened. It's about Millie. She's getting her herd."

Carol was used to being around stylish women. Her sister dressed really well and had a talent for taking an outfit from ordinary to amazing with a bit of ribbon and a couple of buttons. But when compared to the woman who ran the gallery, Violet was just an amateur, while Atsuko was a grand master.

The fifty-something gallery owner favored Asian inspired outfits. Today's magazine-worthy ensemble featured slim black pants and a deep red embroidered jacket with a mandarin collar. Her hair was sleek, her makeup perfect. Normally Carol was completely comfortable with her sensible work look, but in the gallery and around Atsuko, she felt the tiniest bit frumpy.

"I'm so sorry," Atsuko told her. "I'm an idiot. I should have thought of approaching Ronan myself months ago. It's the perfect solution."

"For me. I'm less sure about how Ronan feels." Not that she was going to push her luck by asking. Mathias had gotten his brother to agree to the donation. She was going to take it and run, so to speak. If Mathias was acting out of sexual regret guilt, that was perfectly fine with her.

Okay, not *fine*, exactly. In truth, she was still humiliated by the thought, but she would get over it. At least Millie would live a happy life. That was far more important than any shame Carol might be dealing with.

"Ronan has an entire storeroom of pieces I've tried to talk him into selling." Atsuko smiled. "I'm glad one of us was able to get him to sell one of them. The collectors are going to be salivating. I've spoken to your father and we're going to coordinate publicity. As soon as you decide which one you want, I'll get it photographed and put out the word. We're going to have a lovely event."

Carol was less sure about picking out a piece of art but she figured she would simply ask Ronan his opinion. While she'd never had much contact with him beyond casual hellos, Nick and Mathias were both nice guys. Ronan couldn't be all that different than his brothers.

"I'm so excited," Atsuko continued. "This is going to be an evening to remember."

"I hope so. Thank you for hosting the event. I really appreciate it."

"I'm happy to help."

Carol thanked her again and left. She would have to get with Ronan in the next day or so and arrange to pick out the piece of glass. She'd heard he had a big studio up in the mountains where he lived, so she guessed she would be heading there. First, though, she should take a few pictures of Millie so she could show Ronan who he was really helping.

She headed to the animal preserve, stopping by the office

to check in with her dad. Ed was sitting at his computer. He looked up and saw her, then stood and crossed to her.

"There's my girl," he said, hugging her tight. "Congratulations on scoring the money."

"It hasn't happened yet," she said.

"But it will. I've already been in touch with Atsuko and she's confident we can get at least three hundred thousand for the piece. She's going to waive her commission and donate the food and drinks. That means we get all the money free and clear." He led her to his desk and showed her the spreadsheet he'd printed out.

"Your uncle and I have been working the numbers. We already have the expanded barn permit and the money to start building. We'll be ready to welcome the giraffes we buy."

The barns would be sturdy, temperature controlled, with lots of light. Each stall would lead to a fenced-in outdoor area, allowing the new residents to get used to sights and sounds. It also meant the new giraffes could see each other without interacting physically. Later, the stalls could be used if one of the giraffes needed medical attention.

Her father tapped the spreadsheet. "Ted and I have been in touch with a few private sanctuaries who have a surplus giraffe population. Plus there's one lady in Texas who has a giraffe she wants to sell." He shook his head. "Who keeps a giraffe in their backyard? Anyway, we have a lot of possibilities. Transportation is going to be a challenge, but we'll work it out. And we're hoping there's enough money left over to pay for a vet."

An ongoing problem, Carol thought. With their growing animal population, they had to deal with how to care for them. She could handle the day-to-day issues and she had several resources in retired zoo workers who gave her plenty of advice, but medical treatment was specialized.

So far they'd been able to contract the medical help they

needed, paying a zoo for veterinary care, but that was only a short-term solution.

"We're going to have to hire someone," she said. "But that's not going to be easy."

"Ted and I were talking about an alternative. What if we found a vet who was interested in moving to exotic animal care? We could pay for their training with the understanding they would come work for us when they were ready. There would have to be a contract—they'd work here so many years in exchange for us training them."

"I like that idea."

"Us, too," her dad said, putting his arm around her. "You did good, Carol. We're proud of you."

"I didn't do anything, Dad. Ronan is the one who agreed to donate a piece. It's a huge thing and it's all him."

And Mathias, she thought, who'd convinced his brother. Possibly because he felt guilty about their night together, which wasn't something she was going to discuss with her father. Or with Mathias, apparently. He'd made it clear he didn't want to talk about it. Which left her wondering what, if anything, was going on between them.

Ulrich found himself in the uncomfortable position of missing a woman he barely knew. All right, he knew her reasonably well—they'd spent the last twenty-four hours together—but still. It wasn't as if they'd been dating or anything. He shouldn't mind she was gone.

Only he found that he did mind. He missed having Violet breeze in and out of his room. He missed the sound of her tapping on her computer keyboard when he was trying to sleep, and her fussing as she made sure he took his pills. She was nothing he'd imagined—she was smart, funny, kind and beautiful.

Having her hover over him while he was in bed was a

particular kind of torture. Thank goodness his various aches and pains and the medications he was still on were enough to keep his, ah, interest in check. Otherwise he would have been embarrassing them both with an obvious reaction to her presence.

He glanced at the clock in the Cadillac dashboard and saw nearly two hours had passed. Surely she would be returning soon. She'd said she was having lunch with her friends, then stopping by her apartment before hurrying back. She had said hurry, had she not? What if he needed her?

He knew he was being ridiculous. No doubt from the bump on his head. He was perfectly capable of spending a few hours by himself. As a rule, he enjoyed his own company. He liked solitude and not having to deal with any problems or concerns for just a few minutes. Now he had entire days of it. He should enjoy his recovery as much as he could—he would be back home soon enough.

Not that he didn't want to go. Of course he did. Battenberg Park meant everything to him, as did his grandmother. It was just…there was something about Violet.

He spent the next thirty minutes trying to convince himself he was wrong—that she was completely ordinary. Then he heard her let herself into her room and every part of him went on alert. It was as if he could breathe easier now that she'd returned.

She knocked on the half-open door that separated their rooms, and called out.

"Hi, hi. It's me." She walked in and immediately put her hands on her hips. "You're not in bed!"

How he wanted her to mean that other than how she did. If only she were scolding him for not being ready for her arrival in a dozen delicious ways. Instead he was confident she was referring to the fact that she was concerned he'd sat up too long. Which he probably had. He made a mental note not to mention the fact that he'd done a little pacing to pass the time.

"How was your lunch?" he asked.

"You've been sitting up the whole time, haven't you?"

He hesitated a second before admitting. "Perhaps."

"Get in bed," she said, pointing. "Now."

She looked ready to take him on, he thought as he allowed himself a moment to enjoy the temper snapping in her green eyes and the firm set of her mouth. A mouth that haunted him through the night.

"Yes, miss."

He rose, pleased he was steady on his feet, then walked over to the bed. He was dressed in a T-shirt and sweatpants. He stretched out on top of the covers, then rolled on his side so he was facing her.

"Better?"

"Much."

"Good." He flashed her a smile. "Now please, tell me about your lunch."

Her stern expression immediately softened. She reached for the desk chair and dragged it over to the bed. "Were you lonely by yourself? You haven't been spending time with anyone but me, have you? I'm sorry. I should have thought of that."

He almost told her he didn't need much company beyond her, but didn't want to her to read too much into his words.

"I'm interested in your life here," he said instead. "What is this town like? Should I judge it by my room?"

She looked around at the Cadillac-slash-bed and the drive-in size television mounted on the wall.

"Let's not," she said with a laugh. "Did you eat the lunch I had delivered?"

"Every bite. You're quite the taskmaster."

"I'm bossy. You can say it. You wouldn't be the first person to mention it. I can't help it—I promised your grandmother I would take good care of you, so I'm going to do that. Oh, wait. I brought you something."

She got up and walked into her room, then returned a few seconds later with a tote. She sat down and handed him a clear plastic bag filled with decorated cookies.

"We sometimes sample at our lunch."

He sat up and opened the bag. Inside were heart-shaped cookies—one decorated like a bride, the other a groom.

"Someone getting married?" he asked before taking a bite.

"Actually, yes. Pallas is engaged, but these are from my friend Silver. She got them from a caterer..." Violet grinned. "You look confused. I know it's a lot of names."

She stood up and moved the chair away, then dropped to the floor and sat cross-legged. "Okay, my friend Pallas owns a wedding destination business called Weddings Out of the Box. Couples come from all over to have her design custom weddings. You can have a princess wedding or a cowboy wedding or a Roman wedding."

He shuddered. "In costume?"

"You're horrified."

"Yes. A wedding should be dignified."

"Not everyone agrees with you. Silver owns a traveling bar. She converted an old trailer and takes it to various venues around town. She decorates it in the theme of whatever the wedding is. She does parties, too."

"You have interesting friends."

"I do. There's Wynn who owns a graphics company, and Natalie who is an artist and part-time gallery manager. Oh, that reminds me." She pulled something else from her tote and handed it to him.

He stared at what looked like a folded piece of light brown paper with one end sticking out.

"Pull on that," she said with a smile.

He sat up and did as she suggested. The paper unfolded to become a tiny owl with outstretched wings. As he tugged on the paper again, the wings moved.

He'd seen origami before, but nothing like this. "Astonishing."

"I know, right? Natalie is so talented. She works with paper. She does these paintings that are incredible and the origami is stunning. She's been working on mobiles—you know, like you hang over a baby's crib? Anyway, they're beautiful."

"Please tell her thank you from me."

"I will. Let's see, that's everyone except Carol." Her expression turned impish. "I'm not sure I should talk about her. She's my sister and I don't want you saying anything bad about her."

"Why would I do that?"

"She runs the local animal preserve. Millie is one of her charges."

"Millie?" Then he understood the reference. "You're talking about the giraffe who tried to kill me."

"I'm not sure that was her actual goal, but yes. That's her."

"I shall not hold Carol's profession against her. She is, after all, your family."

"You're so magnanimous. It must be the duke thing."

He chuckled. Very few people he knew would refer to his title as "the duke thing." Part of it was Violet was American. Over here titles were a charming British oddity—not much more interesting than how he pronounced "schedule." He liked that. Her casual acceptance made him feel as if he were just the same as everyone else. That there wasn't an estate awaiting his return, or hundreds of people who were successful or not, depending on the decisions he made.

"Your friends sound very nice," he told her.

"They are. I'm lucky."

She was. She had a sister. He'd always wanted siblings, but his mother had died shortly after he'd been born and his father had never remarried. He'd hoped to have children of his own. Penelope had agreed they should start right away. Only she'd put off getting pregnant and then their marriage had ended.

Violet stood. "I stopped by my place and picked up a few things, including a movie I think you'll like."

She pulled a DVD from the bag and held it out to him. He looked at the man in Regency dress, the woman holding an *I heart Mr. Darcy* tote and the large estate in the background and groaned.

"I'm already injured. Why do you wish to punish me further?"

"For sport," she said with a laugh.

She put the DVD of *Austenland* into the player, then started back for the sofa. Without thinking, he moved over and patted the space beside him.

"It's the best view. I promise I shall behave as honorably as Mr. Darcy."

She hesitated only a second before toeing off her shoes and sliding in next to him.

He was immediately aware of her closeness, the warmth of her and the sweet scent that was, he would guess, a combination of lotions and the woman herself. So much for being able to concentrate on the movie.

She reached for the remote and pushed the start button. "You're going to love this," she promised, then shifted slightly so she could rest her head on his shoulder.

He put his arm around her and rested his chin on her head. "You're right," he murmured. "I am."

CHAPTER ELEVEN

Carol stared at the note on her front door. Even though it was just a handful of words, everything about it was confusing.

Join us for dinner?

She recognized the writing and even if she didn't, the scrawled *Man and his dog* under the question made it clear enough. Mathias was inviting her to dinner. But why?

He'd just rejected her. Okay, not her, exactly, but her hug, which was really the same thing. He'd made it more than clear he didn't want anything to do with her, at least not physically. So what was up with the invitation?

She stood on her porch for several more seconds while she debated possibilities. She could ignore it and pretend she never saw it, but that would be cowardly. Plus what if Mathias came to investigate and found her sulking on her sofa and holding a pint of Ben & Jerry's? She could text him and say she was too busy, only he might ask what she was doing instead and she honestly couldn't think of a convincing lie. Or she could simply suck it up and deal with him for the evening. They were neighbors. It wasn't as if he were moving away anytime soon. She would see him and wouldn't it be easier if she wasn't overly worried about said run-ins?

All of which was crap, she thought as she stuffed the note into her jeans pocket and walked back to her car. She was going because in her heart of hearts, she really liked being around Mathias. The man got to her. There, she'd said it. Or at least thought it. She was weak.

However, she would *not* under any circumstances, throw herself at him again. Or drink alcohol. Although *her* margarita hadn't been the problem. It had been his whatever he'd been drinking before she'd arrived. Regardless, she would enjoy the evening with her friend, not stress herself emotionally and their practically brother-sister relationship would be restored.

That decided, she made the short drive between their houses. Sophie greeted her with a happy dance before she could even exit her car. Mathias followed, looking all tall and manly in jeans and a dark blue T-shirt. He gave her a slow, sexy smile. One she was sure he didn't actually mean. He just radiated hotness. It was like having perfect pitch—a person simply couldn't help himself.

"Hey," he said. "You got my note. I'm glad. I stopped and got ribs and some salads on my way home. And I talked to your dad."

"About?" she asked, following him into the house.

"The giraffes. He and your uncle had just started working on the best routes to get Millie's herd here. He said you'd stopped by earlier. The barn construction starts Monday. Did he mention we've settled on three giraffes, not counting Millie?"

"No, he didn't." She set her purse on the kitchen counter, then watched as he poured her a glass of white wine. He opened a beer for himself and led the way into the family room.

"Based on the cost of the giraffes, their care and feeding

and transportation expenses, three makes the most sense. Plus any more would mean too much work for you."

She'd seen her father yesterday. When had all this happened?

She settled on the sofa because there was no way she could sit in one of the chairs. Especially not *the* chair, where they'd done it. Or rather he'd done it to her and she'd had the best orgasm of her life. Nope, no chair for her.

Sophie jumped up next to her and snuggled close. Carol began to pat her as Mathias took the non-sex chair and rested his forearms on his knees as he leaned toward her.

"My brothers and I can be real competitive, so we're each taking a giraffe," he said. "For the trip. We're mapping out a route from where they are now to here. The first one who gets a giraffe to Happily Inc wins." He grinned. "It's really complicated. There are permits required and we're crossing state lines. No bridges, no overpasses, which means a lot of back roads."

"How on earth do you do that? Don't tell me there's a Google app for giraffe transportation."

"Not yet, but there's a lot of information. Plus you can call people. I had to ask about a bridge in this one town in Texas and the guy at the gas station went out and measured for me. He was really interested in what we're doing."

He sipped his beer. "So I was thinking, you should get in touch with some local media. They'd find the story appealing and it would help raise awareness for the foundation. You're going to need ongoing donations for taking care of the giraffes, and the other cows." The grin returned, then faded. "Plus the whole vet training."

OMG! How much time had he spent with her father? "Is there anything you and Ed didn't discuss?"

"I'm not sure. Probably not. My point is you can use this to your advantage. Fill the bank with lots of coin and save the world. Anyway, Nick and Ronan are in. They're planning their routes. Once we have them done, we figured we'd hire some college students to drive them, just to confirm no one has to ask a giraffe to bend her head to fit under something."

"I appreciate the enthusiasm, but I'll admit, I find it confusing. Why are you doing this?"

His eyebrows drew together. "Why not?"

"You're busy with your own life."

He straightened and waved her comment away. "This is fun. I mean, come on. How often do you get to call total strangers and ask them to measure a bridge because of a giraffe?"

"Practically never."

"See? It's great. Maybe I'll create a line of giraffe-inspired dishes. The pattern's kind of dense, so maybe just for a border." He pulled open a drawer in the end table and pulled out a pad of paper and a pen. Seconds later, he was sketching away, as if they hadn't been talking.

"You're so weird," she muttered and stood. Sophie got up and followed her, tail wagging.

"And you are the most cheerful dog," Carol told her and opened the back door.

They went out together. Sophie made a beeline for the lawn where she sniffed and sniffed before settling on the right spot for a bathroom break. Carol looked over the vast expanse of the animal preserve and tried to imagine what it would look like when Millie had her herd.

It would take time for everyone to settle. Each of the giraffes would have to get used to new surroundings. She would keep them on their regular diet for a few months before slowly transitioning them to what she fed them here. Speaking of feeding them, she would have to talk to the supplier where she got her food now. Every day she hoisted tree branches to Millie height so the giraffe could eat away, as if she were in the wild. More giraffes meant more food to be ordered.

They didn't just need a full-time vet, she realized. She would need an assistant, maybe two. The new giraffes would require monitoring, especially when they started meeting each other. She had the rest of her animals to care for, as well.

A quality problem, she told herself.

When Sophie had finished investigating the backyard, they went back inside. Mathias had moved to the kitchen table. He had several sheets of paper scattered around him. Each was a variation on a giraffe print, some with a border, some not. She wondered how often he was like this—losing himself in his work. She supposed it could get really annoying over time, but she was new enough to the process to find his intensity charming. Of course she found everything about him charming, so that was hardly news.

She went into the kitchen and read the instructions for heating the ribs, then started the oven. She set the dining room table and put the ribs on a cookie sheet, then waited for Mathias to surface.

But while she was willing to be patient, Sophie was not. The little dog walked up to him, put her paws on his thigh, shoved her head under his arm and barked. Mathias blinked.

"What?" He looked around at the papers on the table, Carol standing in his kitchen and the dog licking his arm. "Oh, sorry. I got involved in my work."

"I could see."

"What time is it? You could have told me to quit being an ass. It's just dishes."

"It's not just dishes, it's what you do. Has Sophie been fed?"

"Yes. Did she try to tell you otherwise?" He shook his head. "You always do that and I never fall for it."

Sophie swiped his chin with her tongue, as if pointing out a dog had to try.

"Do you want to work more or are you ready for dinner?" Carol asked.

"I'm starving."

She put the ribs in the oven and set the timer for twenty minutes. "It won't be long now."

They worked together to finish setting the table. Carol was still on her first glass of wine and noticed he hadn't gotten a second beer. Apparently they were going to stay sober for their meal—a good thing considering what they'd done the last time they'd been together in his house.

For a second she thought about just asking what had happened. Did he honest to God not remember? Only she couldn't. The humiliation would be too much. Not knowing and wondering were better than finding out she was little more than someone he pitied...or worse, regretted.

They sat down at the table. Sophie got into her bed, but kept her gaze firmly on them, as if vowing to take care of anything that dropped.

"How are you doing with your temporary pet?" Carol asked as Mathias slid ribs onto her plate.

"We're working it out as we go." He glanced at the beagle curled up in one of her many beds. "Don't tell my mom, but she's growing on me. She's sweet natured and wouldn't hurt a fly, but she has a knack for trouble. Yesterday I couldn't find her anywhere. I was convinced she'd gotten out again, although all the doors were closed and the gate was locked."

"Where was she?"

"In the dishwasher. Somehow she'd gotten it open and had crawled into the bottom shelf."

"You're going to be lonely when she goes back to Fool's Gold with your mom."

"Maybe."

"A man and his dog," she teased. "You could get a Yorkie. All that fluffy hair and those big brown eyes. Just your type."

He reached for a rib. "Very funny. Why don't you have a dog?"

"I'm gone a lot and taking a pet to work isn't a good idea with what I do. While the animals at the preserve fall into the 'will work for food' category, they're still not domesticated."

"You seem like the pet type," he told her. "Big house, husband, kids, a dog and two cats." His brows drew together. "Hey, why aren't you married?"

She willed herself not to blush or outwardly react to his question. She was twenty-eight and not in a relationship. As far as everyone in town was concerned, she'd never been in a relationship. No guy had ever appeared and she hadn't been seen on a date.

"Why aren't you?" she countered.

"I asked first."

"Fine. No one has asked."

He continued to study her, as if waiting for more. She groaned.

"It's not that interesting."

"It is to me. Tell me."

She put down her rib and wiped her fingers on a napkin. "There have been men," she said slowly. "I've had a couple of long-distance relationships. There was a guy I knew in South Africa. We met over the summer and were going to be attending the same college. By the second week of the semester, he'd realized there were hundreds of other women on campus and seemed to be on his way to dating each one of them."

"He's a jerk and you're lucky he's out of your life."

"Thanks. I believe you, but it hurt at the time."

"Want me to get one of my brothers to beat him up?"

"You wouldn't do it yourself?"

"I'm a lover, not a fighter."

He winked as he spoke and flashed her that smile of his. The combination had her stomach dancing and her girl parts sighing as every bit of her remembered how great a lover he'd been. Yes, that was the story of her life—the best sex ever had been on a night when the guy passed out before, ah, finishing. She was totally and completely pathetic.

"After the college guy?" he prompted.

"I met an environmental activist at a rally."

"Another long-distance relationship?"

"Yes. We were on our way to getting engaged. Then he called and told me he'd gotten his research assistant pregnant. They haven't all cheated," she added quickly. "I don't have a thing for guys who stray. But in the end, they've all left." She hesitated, the truth so close, she could touch it. Self-preservation insisted she not actually say what it was, but somehow the words just spilled out.

"I'm not special enough."

Mathias stared at her. "That's crap. Of course you are. You're plenty special. You just picked wrong."

"And that's better? You don't know what you're talking about and I think we should change the subject."

Which should have been the end of it, only it wasn't because she felt awful inside. Uncomfortable and exposed and like she needed to get away. She pushed back from the table.

"I need to go."

"Carol." Mathias rose with her. "What's wrong? Tell me. Are you mad at me? Did I say something?"

He looked so sincere, she thought grimly. So concerned.

"I can't," she told him. "I don't know what this game is and I can't play it anymore. Just leave me alone."

She started for the door.

Mathias had no idea what had just happened. One minute they'd been talking and now Carol was leaving.

He jogged after her. "Wait. Dammit, Carol, talk to me. You're not making any sense."

She spun to face him. "I'm not? That's crazy. You're the one playing games. Don't go blaming this on me."

She glared at him with obvious fury, but behind the mad was a vulnerability that hit him like a gut punch. She'd been hurt and based on how she was acting, he'd been the perpetrator. Only that didn't make any sense, either. What could he have done?

"Tell me. Tell me what's wrong."

She grabbed him by the front of his shirt and moved her hands and arms. "Dammit."

"What are you doing?" he asked, more bewildered by the second.

"Trying to shake some sense into you." Her eyes filled with tears as she dropped her arms to her side. "Let me go, Mathias. You don't want me."

The combination of her pain and the words ripped through him. He *had* hurt her. He'd done something awful. But what?

Memories whispered in the back of his mind, but he couldn't bring them into focus. Something was wrong, *he* was wrong, but why and how? He had no idea what she was talking about or what had happened, so he did the only thing that made sense.

He put his hands on her waist, drew her close and pressed his mouth to hers.

The second their lips touched, his mind exploded. Memories blew up in his mind, giant screens filled with images of him touching Carol, of her naked and him touching and tasting and pleasuring her until she screamed her release.

It hadn't been a dream!

He stepped back and stared at her. "We had sex?"

Color stained her cheeks and she turned away. "I have to go."

"No. You are not walking away from this." He swore as he tried to understand what had happened. He'd been upset, he'd been drunk. They had more to drink and then they'd...

"I passed out," he said more to himself than her. "After I, ah…and before…" He thought about waking up and trying to remember what had happened. "You cleaned up the glasses. You left. Why didn't you wake me? Why didn't you say something the next day?"

She spun back to glare at him. "Why didn't you? How do you think it made me feel to know what we'd done and you didn't even remember? You passed out. Is that better or worse than not remembering? What you said before, about me being special? Thanks for proving the point that I'm not."

Before he could figure out what he was supposed to say to that, she grabbed her bag and walked out. Mathias started to go after her, then stopped. Maybe they both needed a little space and time. In the morning, everything would be better. Or at least more clear. It had to be because he had no damned idea what he was supposed to do now.

CHAPTER TWELVE

In the morning, nothing was better. While Sophie had had a good night—snoring and dreaming her doggie dreams—Mathias had spent most of his time staring at the ceiling. More things made sense to him now. The clarity of that last sex dream. No wonder there were incredible details of taste and touch and sound. He'd lived it.

He didn't mind that he'd missed out on his end of things. He'd been with Carol and was sure everything would have been great. At least he'd pleased her. Or had he? Was he remembering her cries correctly?

By his third cup of coffee, he'd begun to question himself. Maybe he'd only imagined the feel of her coming as he'd loved her with his tongue, his fingers pushed deep inside of her. Maybe he hadn't actually felt the ripple of her body convulsing around him, which was a problem because he needed it to have been good for her. Needed it a lot.

He walked to the window and stared out over the preserve. There was only one solution. A do-over.

While he was sure Carol would refuse his request, he would have to convince her. Them making love again was the only way to repair the rift between them. Surely she would see that. It made sense, it assured they were both satisfied and, well, he wanted to.

He'd imagined being with her so many times, he couldn't believe he'd passed out in the middle of making love with her. Worse, that he'd forgotten. No wonder she'd been acting strangely for the last week or so. And now he knew what had been nagging in the back of his mind. So they would make love again and everything would go back to where it was supposed to be. It was the most sensible plan—he was confident she would see it his way.

He showered and took Sophie on a long walk while he decided what he was going to say. When they got back to the house, he and the dog got in his car and they drove to the preserve. He found Carol in her office.

She looked up at him as he entered. There were shadows under her eyes and a sad set to her beautiful mouth. Remorse gripped him—he was responsible for what she was feeling. He was the problem and he had to be the solution.

"Morning," he began.

She rose and shook her head. "Whatever it is, I don't want to hear it."

Sophie crossed to her. Carol dropped down to cuddle with the dog. Sophie eyed him as if pointing out *this* was the way to solve every problem. Doggie hugs and a quick kiss on the cheek.

She might have a point.

"I'm sorry," he said. "About last night, about what happened before. Or didn't happen."

"I don't want to talk about it."

"We have to."

She rose and shook her head. "We don't. Not at all. It's in the past, let's just leave it there."

"I hurt you."

"Not on purpose. I'm fine."

"Let me make it up to you," he said, holding her gaze. "A do-over. I want to show you what it can be like with me."

She stared at him, her expression unreadable, then her mouth twisted and she walked around him toward the door.

When she reached the hallway, she glanced back at him. "No. Just no. I should have realized your ego was what mattered the most, so let me reassure you, the earth moved. It was fantastic and you have nothing to prove. Happy?"

Before he could answer, she was gone.

He picked up Sophie's leash and led the dog back to the car. In theory Carol had told him exactly what he needed to hear. He should be fine. He should feel better. Only he didn't. He felt small and scummy and like the biggest jerk on the planet. Funny how until Carol, women had all been so damned easy.

Violet studied the picture she'd downloaded, then looked back at the small dress. The lace was nearly a perfect match. Now she just had to sew a row of satin-covered buttons down the back and she would be done.

"You look intense."

She glanced up and saw Ulrich standing in the doorway between their respective rooms. He still wore sweatpants and a T-shirt, which looked oddly regal on him. He'd showered and shaved, so the sexy, scruffy look was gone. In its place were the *young duke works from home* clean lines and strong jaw.

He was dreamy, she thought, doing her best to not sigh out loud. Funny and sweet and smart and those blue eyes of his...

"Violet?"

"Huh? Oh. Sorry. I was lost in thought."

His mouth turned up at the corners. "Were you? It was difficult to tell." His gaze dropped to the dress. "For a very small flower girl?"

She grinned and held up the garment. "Not exactly. It's for a dog. A beagle, to be exact."

"Someone wants a dog in their wedding?"

"It's a long story." She glanced at the clock and was surprised to see it was nearly one. "We need to order lunch. You must be starved. Do you know what you want?"

"Sandwiches are on their way," he told her. "Any minute."

"Oh. What did you order me?"

"What you said you wanted yesterday, then changed your mind about and were disappointed. Chicken salad, no nuts on toasted white bread."

Which *had* been what she'd originally wanted. "You remembered all that?"

One shoulder rose and lowered.

She wanted to believe the information was significant. That his remembering was because he cared, only she knew better. Or at least she knew enough not to fool herself. Ulrich was used to taking care of a huge estate and running multiple businesses—having him remember her sandwich order was simply his impressive mind at work.

As if on cue, someone knocked on Ulrich's door. He let in the server, who then set up their lunch at the table by the window. Violet took a seat. Ulrich sat across from her, then glanced out at the view.

"I know the mountains are there," he told her, "yet they continue to surprise me. The peaks are so sharp. Nothing like the rolling hills back home."

"There are mountains in Scotland, aren't there?" she asked.

"Yes, but that's hardly the same as the English countryside."

She grinned. "Your Grace, I had no idea you were such a nationalist."

He chuckled. "I'm not. A couple of hundred years ago, I would have been."

"Or off with your head?"

"I believe the monarchy ceased using beheading as a way to keep the nobility in line long before that."

"I'm sure you're right. I'm a sucker for all things Elizabethan when head chopping still occurred."

"We are a savage people."

"Not anymore. Now you're refined."

"On the outside."

Meaning what? There were hidden depths to him? Did any of those depths have a soft spot for her?

As that was a dangerous train of thought and a worse line of conversation, she made a deliberate attempt to change the subject. "Is the Wi-Fi fast enough for you to handle your email?"

"It is. I'm nearly caught up. All is well at Battenberg Park." He picked up his sandwich. "And by that I mean there have only been four minor crises since I left."

"Plumbing? Electrical or guests?"

"Not electrical. Plumbing is a constant problem in a house that old and water damage is the devil to stay on top of. We had a group of schoolchildren come through yesterday and a lamp was broken."

She winced. "You have insurance, don't you?"

"We do, but many of the items in the house can't be replaced and getting them repaired is challenging. We are constantly balancing giving our guests a true feel for what life was like in a house like ours and not having antiques stolen or broken or damaged."

"So people come through for day tours of the house and grounds?" she asked.

"Yes. We also have a conference center and a hotel."

She tried to hold in a smile. "But no theme rooms."

He sighed. "Alas, no. Perhaps I should learn from *Austenland* and embrace all things Mr. Darcy."

For a second she imagined Ulrich in Regency dress. The picture was delightful and sexy. *Allow me to express how ar-*

dently I admire and love you. Violet was sure she had the line from *Pride and Prejudice* wrong, but she was close enough to get a little shiver.

"You would hate playing Mr. Darcy," she said, forcing herself back to the present. "You much prefer being yourself."

"That is true, but I didn't hate the movie as much I would have expected."

"It was charming," she told him. "You laughed."

"I did laugh."

His gaze seemed to linger on her face. Violet felt the intensity of his attention down to her toes which curled ever so slightly.

"I'm sure that a lot of older homes are exploiting all things *Pride and Prejudice*, not to mention *Downton Abbey*."

"They are," he said. "Tourists flock to them."

"And when word gets out about your TV series, they'll flock to you, as well."

"It's not my series," he assured her quickly. "We're simply the vessel." His mouth twitched. "A well-paid vessel. The influx of tourists will be welcome."

"And endured," she added, her voice teasing.

"That, too." He picked up his sandwich. "Do you have any plans to visit my grandmother?"

Violet's mind spun in fifteen directions. Was he really asking about Nana Winifred? Was she ridiculous to hope he was secretly trying to find out if he would see her again? Did he like her?

"We haven't talked about it, but I always enjoy her company."

"You should plan a trip. I could show you the estate. Perhaps we could spend a few days together in London." He offered her a smile. "As my way of thanking you for taking such good care of me."

She laughed. "How could I turn down a chance to hang out in the Drive-in Room?"

"I know it's been a treat for me, as well."

Their gazes locked again. Something warm seemed to grow in Ulrich's eyes. Violet knew she was being foolish, but couldn't help saying, "A trip to see your grandmother sounds like something I should do. Sooner rather than later."

"I agree."

Carol had a long, serious talk with herself. She knew she'd totally overreacted to what had happened between her and Mathias. Finding out he hadn't remembered about that night had been both good and bad. On the one hand, at least she knew he hadn't been ignoring her. On the other hand, seriously? He'd forgotten *that*? Talk about unfair.

She'd been nearly on her way to dealing when he'd shown up with his ridiculous do-over suggestion. The man was a moron. Worse, he was breaking her heart. She didn't want some weird, awkward "Hey, I owe you" encounter. She wanted what every woman wanted—to know that the man who was standing in front of her was totally and completely swept away. That he was weak with longing and found her the sexiest, most appealing woman on the planet. Instead he was offering her the sexual equivalent of "You got lunch last time, it's my turn to buy."

Not that she was going to try to explain that to him. There was no way—not without revealing too much and she didn't want to risk that.

If only she could ignore him for the rest of her life. Or not see him. Only that wasn't an option. Not only were they neighbors, their lives here intertwined. Exhibit A—she was on her way to a teleconference about Maya and Del's wedding. Backing out wasn't an option and she knew for a fact Mathias would be there.

Life certainly had a sense of humor.

She parked by Weddings Out of the Box. She'd deliberately come a little late, hoping not to get trapped in the conference room alone with Mathias. For once, her timing was perfect. Mathias's car was already in place, as was her sister's. As Carol got out, Silver pulled up next to her and they walked in together.

"I love brides who want to have fun," Silver said as they headed for the conference room. "Maya's pretty much given me free rein. I've come up with a couple of really great signature drinks."

"Mojitos?" Carol asked, her voice teasing.

Silver shuddered. "No and no. Signature drinks can't be labor intensive. Not unless you can do all the heavy prep in advance. No one wants to stand in line for twenty minutes just to get a drink. No mojitos. Don't even think the word."

"Sometimes you're really bossy."

"I know. I can't help it." She linked arms with Carol. "You love me anyway."

"I do."

They went into the conference room and saw that Pallas had already started the call. Maya waved at them.

"Hey, you two."

"Hi back."

Carol and Silver took their seats. Carol smiled at everyone, careful to keep her gaze moving so it didn't linger on Mathias, even though lingering on him made so much sense.

She couldn't decide if fate was on her side or not. Mathias gave her an absent smile, as if their most recent encounter hadn't happened at all. Which was good, right? They weren't alone and if he acted strangely, people would notice. So his disinterested nod was perfect and there was no reason to feel slighted or hurt.

She held in a groan. There were days when she had to question her emotional sanity.

"Shall we get started?" Pallas asked, pulling out her tablet. "Maya, I want to go over our progress since our last call. First, the flowers."

The meeting went quickly. All the details were reviewed. Silver made her drink suggestions and then confirmed the catering menu. Violet opened a garment bag to show Maya the work she'd done on her veil.

"That picture you sent was perfect," Violet said. "I matched the beading." She waved at Carol. "Come, model."

Everyone turned to look at her. Carol felt herself flush as she stood and walked over to her sister. Violet set the veil on her hair.

The tulle was anchored with a mini tiara that fit snugly. The edges of the veil had been decorated with tiny beads in a swirling pattern. Violet pulled the shorter piece down over Carol's face and angled her sister toward the camera.

"What do you think?"

"It's beautiful," Maya breathed. "Exactly what I wanted. Carol, how does it feel?"

"Tight," Carol admitted. "I have no idea if my head is bigger or smaller than yours, but you'll want to put it on the day before the ceremony to see if it needs to be adjusted. Otherwise, you could walk down the aisle with a headache."

"I'll make a note," Pallas said as she tapped on her tablet.

Violet removed the veil. "I won't make you try on this," she teased as she held up a small dress.

Maya clapped her hands together. "I can't believe you did that."

"It was easy."

Carol took her seat while Violet showed the dress from all angles. As she'd gotten the measurements, she knew who the dress was for.

"Buttering up your future mother-in-law?" Mathias asked drily. "Smart lady."

"I adore Sophie," Maya told him. "And Elaine is my friend. I don't have to butter her up." She grinned. "Think of the pictures."

Carol caught Pallas's slight shake of her head.

"It's not going to be like the zebras," Carol assured her. "Sophie is mostly behaved."

"I've hired a dog sitter," Mathias added. "After the ceremony Sophie will be taken back to my place for an evening of dog play and treats."

"That's so nice," Maya told him.

"My gift to the bride and groom. That dog could destroy a wedding reception in five seconds flat."

Carol couldn't help adding, "He's right. She's sweet, but has a nose for trouble. Plus, she'd totally eat all the food."

"I'll make a note that Sophie's leaving," Pallas said as she entered the information.

Carol leaned close and lowered her voice. "Relieved about the dog sitter?"

"You have no idea," Pallas whispered back.

They went through the rest of the list.

"I can't believe I'll be seeing you all in person for our next meeting," Maya said with a laugh. "I'm very excited."

"Us, too," Pallas told her. "If that's everything, we'll let you go."

Carol was about to grab her purse and bolt when Maya said, "Carol, can you stay for a second? I want to talk to you about something."

"Sure."

Trapped like a rat, she thought, hoping Maya didn't also ask Mathias to stay. But the other woman only waved goodbye to everyone as they filed out of the room.

When they were alone, Maya leaned close to the camera.

"I heard about your Millie project and that Ronan is donating a piece to help raise the money."

"I'm heading out to his place tomorrow to choose one. I have no idea what I'm supposed to look for."

"He's brilliant. I don't think you can go wrong with anything he does." Maya tilted her head. "When Del and I are in Happily Inc, we'd like to do a video about Millie and your quest to raise money for her herd. I don't know if Mathias mentioned it, but we own a video production company. This is what we do, all over the world. We'd make something short you could use on your website. I've been emailing with your dad and he has some great ideas for where we could set up our shots. You've been really sweet to help with the wedding and this is my way of saying thank-you."

"You don't have to do that," Carol said automatically.

"I want to. Del and I love our work. It won't take long and we'll have time."

"Thank you. That would be wonderful. We need to beef up our website so we can continue to raise money to support the preserve. A video from you and Del would really help."

"Good. We're looking forward to seeing you and Millie in person in a week."

"Us, too."

They ended the call. Carol sat alone in the conference room as she tried to figure out what had just happened. She hadn't done much of anything to help with the wedding, so why would Maya want to thank her in such an extraordinary way? Did Mathias have something to do with it?

There was only one way to get an answer and right now speaking to him was impossible. She had no idea what she thought or felt, let alone what to say. The man made her insane.

The only solution seemed to be not to think about him. An impossible task considering he pretty much haunted her thoughts nearly every second of every day.

CHAPTER THIRTEEN

Carol stopped by the studio before heading up the mountain. She'd seen Mathias's car still parked in his driveway, so knew he was home and it was safe. Okay, not safe, exactly. Just that she wouldn't run into him—something she couldn't deal with right now.

She pulled into the studio's parking lot, then went around back where Natalie had told her she would be working.

The huge open art studio was nearly the size of a warehouse. There were high ceilings, lots of light, and several separate workstations. Mathias and Ronan took the far end— massive, dangerous-looking ovens dominated the space. Nick's area was more in the middle. He mostly worked with wood— creating carvings that were so lifelike as to breathe. Natalie had claimed a small corner close to the double doors.

Carol walked in and found her friend sitting at a large drafting table. Natalie created beautiful mixed-media artwork, but instead of using acrylic or oil, she used scraps of paper and found objects.

Natalie looked up. Carol waved and walked over to sit in the spare chair by the table. She saw several small origami animals standing together. They were all in shades of dark pink and purple.

"Adorable," Carol said as she studied a three-inch-high penguin. "Who are they for?"

Natalie seemed to hesitate for a second, then pushed up her glasses and smiled. "I have a friend with a nine-year-old daughter. She's into pink and purple these days and adores animals."

"They're wonderful. She'll love them." Carol wondered who Natalie knew with a girl. None of their friends had daughters. Maybe it was someone she'd known from before she moved to Happily Inc.

"Thanks. So today's the big day. You're driving up the mountain."

Carol wrinkled her nose. "I'm not going on a pilgrimage. I'm just picking out a piece of artwork for an auction. Which is why I wanted to stop by. You're an artist with a great eye— any advice?"

"Anything of Ronan's will sell for big money. He's so gifted." Natalie sighed. "I wish I were that talented."

"You are! Look at the beautiful paintings you create."

"Thank you for being my friend, but let's get real. My stuff sells for maybe three hundred dollars. Ronan's can go for three hundred thousand dollars. We're not in the same league."

"Beauty and creativity aren't about money."

"Maybe not but money helps pay the bills." Natalie laughed. "It's okay. Ronan's used to others envying his talent, if not his brooding personality." She reached across the table and picked up a small owl, then placed it in Carol's hand.

"At the risk of mixing my metaphors, not to mention my animals, choose wisely, young grasshopper."

"That's not especially helpful."

"Sorry. Ask Ronan what will sell for the most. No one knows what his buyers like better than he does."

"Isn't that insulting and crass? Shouldn't I love the art for the sake of it?"

"Not when you're trying to get the most money out of the sale."

"Thanks," Carol murmured, secretly wishing she was dealing with Mathias instead. They might be in an awkward phase of their relationship, but he was always easy to talk to. Even when he was making her crazy, she was comfortable around him. Ronan was a lot more mysterious.

"Wish me luck," she said as she rose.

"You'll do fine."

Carol followed the directions Mathias had given her. Ronan's house was several miles off the main highway. As the roads got steeper and steeper, she was grateful for the relatively warm weather and dry conditions. She would not want to make this journey when it was raining. As for snow—she didn't think he lived high enough for that to ever be a real problem.

At about a thousand feet, desert gave way to lowland scrubs and small trees. At two thousand feet, she entered actual forest, no doubt watered by the huge underground aquifer that allowed the town to flourish.

She turned onto a private road and drove until she saw a huge stone house. The structure seemed to have grown out of the mountainside—no doubt because of a great architect, she thought as she walked to the front door. There were lots of windows and trees everywhere. She would guess the back of the house had amazing views of the whole valley.

Ronan opened the door before she could knock.

Like his brothers, he dressed casually in jeans and a T-shirt. His coloring was lighter than theirs, but she recognized the smile.

"Hey, Carol. Thanks for coming up here to pick your piece.

I would have brought a few down for you to choose from, but I didn't know what you were looking for."

"I'm happy to make the trip," she said as he led the way through the house. "You're being so generous."

"I'm glad to help. I only wish we'd thought of this a few weeks ago. It would have saved you setting up all those little change collection cans around town."

She had a brief impression of tall ceilings and large rooms before they walked out back. A covered pathway led to a studio. They entered a large foyer. She caught a glimpse a work space similar to the one back in town but instead of going in there, Ronan pushed open another door.

"I've been building the Millie fund for a while now, but it's been slow going," Carol said. "Being able to auction something like—"

Ronan flipped on a light. Carol hadn't known what to expect. Storeroom in her mind meant shelves with things like paper towels and canned goods. This room was filled with tables covered with the most exquisite glass artwork. There were vases with flowers, abstract swirls, fish and horses and a few dancers. Everywhere she looked, she saw something more beautiful, more amazing.

Some were colorless, others vibrated with color. A few stood on the floor and soared nearly to the ceiling. Others were so small, she could hold them in the palm of her hand. She saw a collection of miniature animals that had an almost angled shape to them. It took her a second to realize they were glass interpretations of Natalie's origami.

"Anything interesting?" he asked.

Carol turned in a slow circle, then stopped in front of Ronan. "I couldn't begin to choose. Everything is too wonderful." She thought about what Natalie had said. "Would it be too weird to ask you to pick for me?"

Instead of answering, Ronan walked over to a table and

pointed to a tall statue of a crane about to take flight. The wings were spread, the head raised. She could practically feel the breeze generated by the movement.

"This one. It will have international appeal and will bring a higher price."

Words designed to get her heart beating faster, she thought, but she couldn't get past the magic inherent in his work.

"How do you do it?" she asked softly as she gently stroked one of the legs. "How do you make it move even while I know it's not alive? Mathias did the same thing with the little Millie statue. It's uncanny."

"Mathias showed you the giraffe he's been working on?"

She turned back to Ronan. "He gave me one."

Something flickered in his eyes and for a second she would have sworn he was going to smile. His expression returned to careful neutrality. "Creating the illusion of movement is a lot about technique and some about talent. I won't bore you with the details. So this one?"

She nodded. "Thank you so much for your generosity. This is the most amazing gift." She swallowed against sudden and unexpected tears. "Millie's been lonely and I've been worried about her. This is going to allow us to get her a herd so she can have friends again."

Ronan took a step back. "Ah, yeah, it's fine. I'm glad she's going to be happy. I'll let Atsuko know which one you've chosen and get her some pictures."

"Thank you." She hesitated. "Do you need some kind of tax receipt? We have a nonprofit. It's registered with the state and everything."

This time the smile was fully formed. "Your dad already took care of it."

"Oh, great."

Ronan walked her back to her car. "You know your way down the mountain?"

"Yes."

He stopped by her Jeep. "Carol, did you know that Ceallach is coming to Del and Maya's wedding?"

The change in subject surprised her. "Sure. Your mom and dad are traveling. That's why Mathias has Sophie. They're going to be here at the end of the month."

Ronan stared at something in the distance. "Make sure Mathias has put the pieces together on that. Having Dad around is going to be hard on him."

"Won't it be hard on all of you?"

"Yes, but we're not targets. The parents will be staying with him."

She stared at Ronan. "What do you mean about him being a target?"

He met her gaze. "Those bowls and dishes he makes? They're not him. He's hiding—something he would never admit, even to himself." Ronan hesitated, as if deciding how much to say. "He has more talent than all of us. He was always going to be the famous one, not me. Then something happened and he couldn't risk it anymore. Ceallach wouldn't let him. No." He shook his head.

"That's not right. Ceallach tried to destroy that part of him. He has to find his way back to who he was or he's never going to be whole."

She couldn't believe what he was saying. Or that he was saying it to her. "I don't understand. If you're worried, you should talk to him."

"I can't. Not anymore. But you can. You should."

"Why me?" She had no idea how to define her relationship with Mathias, but talking about him being broken by his father was so far out of her purview. She would have no idea where to start. "I'm not family. I'm just a friend." And not the least bit special.

"You need to let him know you've got his back. He'll want to know that, so he can get through the visit."

"Why me?"

"Because he gave you Millie."

"The glass piece or the herd?"

The smile returned. "Both."

He opened her car door, as if they were done talking. As Carol couldn't think of a single thing to say or ask, she thanked him again for the contribution and left. When she reached her office at the animal preserve, she still had no idea what on earth Ronan had been talking about...or what she was supposed to do to help.

Carol told herself that her frustration and concern were about the complex zoning regulations in the state of California, but she had a bad feeling she was lying to herself. While there were unexpected roadblocks, so to speak, they weren't the reason she couldn't stay focused on her work. Instead she had something else...or someone else...on her mind.

She wasted an entire morning trying to get the right people on the phone, then went out to hang with Millie. Walking with the beautifully gangly giraffe often put things in perspective. But this time, Millie didn't seem to be working her magic. Or maybe the problem was Ronan's words had been too powerful.

She couldn't forget what he'd said about Ceallach and Mathias and their troubled relationship. Was Mathias's father the real reason he created dishes instead of art? She knew that Mathias and his father didn't get along, but now she wondered if the rift went much deeper than she'd ever realized.

Mathias was always so upbeat and charming. Of course he had issues—everyone did. But she sensed what Ronan had been talking about went deeper and did a lot more damage than the usual "My parents never understood me" of most people's youth.

She decided she needed a distraction and drove into town. Maybe a quick visit with her sister would help. But instead of driving to Violet's store, or the hotel where she was spending most of her days while Ulrich recovered, Carol found herself at the art studio where Mathias worked.

Theirs were the only two cars, which meant he was probably alone—if she didn't count Sophie. And for all her quirks, the little beagle seemed to be trustworthy. Carol told herself she was a fool, then got out of her Jeep and walked into the studio.

Sophie jumped up from her dog bed and raced over for a greeting. Mathias sat at his desk, several large pieces of paper in front of him. Carol moved closer, hoping to see a sketch of some other Millie-inspired art but he seemed to be working on a design for a vase.

He glanced up and smiled at her. "Hi. You're a surprise."

Good or bad? Not that she would ask. When it came to Mathias, she was chronically lacking in courage. Why was that? Yes, he was good-looking and funny and successful and a bit of a man whore, but so what? She was...

When nothing came to mind, Carol decided to deal with that problem later.

"I'm having zoning issues," she said, picking the first topic that came to mind. "I don't suppose you know anyone in government who could help me?"

He leaned back in his chair and chuckled. "As a matter of fact, I do." He waved her into the visitor's seat. "Mayor Marsha, California's longest serving mayor. In Fool's Gold," he added.

"I knew she wasn't the mayor of Happily Inc and while I appreciate the offer, I'm not sure a small-town mayor is the answer."

"Have a little faith." His tone was teasing. "Mayor Marsha knows all and is friends with everyone. I wouldn't be surprised if she could get the president on the phone. Let me know what you need and I'll see what I can do."

"Thank you," she said, trying not to sound doubtful.

"You'll see and you'll be impressed."

She already was, but that had nothing to do with his governmental connections.

"I went to see Ronan," she said. "He helped me pick out a piece."

"Which one did you get?"

She described the crane.

"That's a good one," Mathias told her. "He hasn't done many birds and it will appeal to a lot of international buyers."

"That's what he said. Why?"

"Cranes are considered good luck in many cultures, which means corporate and hotel buyers will be interested, along with individual collectors."

"A whole world I knew nothing about."

"What I know about cows wouldn't fill a Post-it."

"You're doing all this work for Millie, yet you continue to insult her. We're all confused."

"Teasing is a sign of affection. I thought you knew that." One corner of his mouth turned up. "I've always had a thing for leggy, brown-eyed girls. I thought you knew that, too."

In her head, Carol knew he was referring to the giraffe. But in her swooning heart, she had other hopes and dreams. She was a brown-eyed girl, too, and while no one would call her leggy...

Such foolishness, she told herself, then squashed the cringeworthy feelings by remembering what Ronan had told her.

She picked up a pencil, then put it down. "I need to ask you something."

"Sure. What?"

She hesitated. "I guess it's not a question so much as a..." She looked at him. "Ronan said your dad would be at the wedding."

Nothing about Mathias's expression changed. "That would be my guess, too, what with Del getting married. Mom mentioned they were going to be here to reclaim Sophie and they're staying with me."

The beagle raised her head and wagged her tail when she heard her name.

"He thought that might be a problem for you."

Emotions flashed through his eyes, but they were gone before Carol could figure out what they were. She knew he had to be feeling something, but what? Annoyance? Anger? Concern?

"My dad's a difficult guy," he admitted. "Everywhere he goes, it's always about him." He flashed her a smile. "Don't worry, I'm immune to his drama."

"Were you always?"

"No. There was a time he could destroy me with a word. He ruled all of us through fear and intimidation." He shook his head. "I take that back. He ruled Nick, Ronan and me that way, but he pretty much ignored Del and Aidan."

"The non-artists?"

"Yeah. If you couldn't create, you didn't have value."

She understood not feeling special, but her parents had always worked so hard to make her and Violet feel as if they were the most important parts of their lives.

"Why would he do that?"

"Pride, maybe. Sometimes I tell myself he's the one who was scared. Of us. Of what we could be."

He ran his fingers across the paper, outlining the shape of the bowl. "I used to do pieces like Ronan, back when I was a kid. I'd learn a new technique and stay up all night to put it into action. I wanted to be the best, to be like my dad." He glanced at her. "We all did. To hear him praise a piece was food for a month."

"Because praise was hard to come by?"

"Nearly impossible. He was a big believer in finding fault. For a while I thought it was because he wanted to make sure we were the best—like he was. But after a while I began to realize that there was some fear there, too."

"He didn't want his sons to be better than him."

His gaze settled on her face. "You're insightful today."

"I'm insightful every day."

He chuckled. "Yes, you are." The humor faded. "Dad can be difficult. In the end it was easier not to fight with him."

She thought about what Ronan had told her but didn't want to admit all that she knew. It was too much like violating Mathias's privacy or something.

"I saw what you did with the Millie piece. You should do more of that."

"Giving me career advice?" he asked, his voice teasing.

"I wouldn't do that, it's just so extraordinary. You have a gift. But what do I know—maybe working like that doesn't make you happy."

He was quiet for a second before saying, "It's complicated."

She was sure that was true. All families were complex, but his more than most. There was the fact that his father was a world-famous artist, his relationships with his brothers, especially Ronan not being his twin anymore. She didn't know the whole story, but she'd gotten bits and pieces of it when Natalie and Pallas discussed the Mitchells at their girlfriend get-togethers.

"Hey," he said as he grabbed her hand. "Quit worrying about me. I'm fine."

His fingertips grazed her palm. She felt the light touch all the way down to her toes, which wasn't nearly as interesting as the tingling that started low in her belly. A kind of swirling, moving heat eased through her until she would have sworn the room temperature had just climbed about fifty degrees. Her throat went dry, her heart started to pound and all she could think was how much she—

"Well, damn," he muttered before standing, then pulling her to her feet. Before she could figure out what he was doing, he'd drawn her close and settled his mouth on hers.

He tasted faintly of coffee and mint. His lips were firm, but not demanding, as if he had all the time in the world. As if he liked this part a lot.

She rested her hands on his broad shoulders and felt the warmth of his skin through his shirt. He was strong and steady, she thought. Funny, kind. Look how he'd accepted Sophie into his life, even though he hadn't wanted to. He was a good guy who kissed like a dream.

Then he moved his mouth against hers and she couldn't think anymore. She could only react, tilting her head slightly and parting her lips.

His tongue slipped inside and stroked hers. Fire shot through her at the first touch, then burned hotter and brighter with every second of contact. She moved closer, wrapping her arms around his neck and pressing her body against his. He put his hands on her hips, as if encouraging her to stay. Silly man—didn't he know she had no plans to ever leave? He was—

She drew back and covered her mouth with her hand. Desire battled with worry. How much was because he wanted to and how much was because he was embarrassed about what had happened before?

"Carol?"

"I don't want to be a makeup test."

"Is that what you think?"

"I'm not sure."

"No. I don't accept that. You felt it just now, when I

touched your hand. That's why I kissed you. There isn't another reason."

He reached for her hand again and pressed it against his groin. She felt the hard ridge of his erection and her doubts faded. She looked at him and smiled.

"Oh."

"Yes, oh," he teased, as he drew her close. "Now where were we?"

Sophie raised her head and barked. She scrambled to her feet and ran toward the door. A second too late, Carol saw she hadn't closed it completely, allowing Sophie to nose it open and disappear into the parking lot.

"Dammit," Mathias growled as he raced after her. "Sophie, get back here!"

Carol followed, terrified the little beagle would be hurt if she got onto the street. "Sophie, come back! Sophie, I'll give you a cookie."

She burst outside and then stumbled to a stop when she saw the beagle being hugged and petted by two people she'd never met before, yet were oddly familiar.

The man swept Sophie up in his arms. "How's my best girl? Come on, kisses please."

Sophie obliged with tongue swipes. The man's obvious resemblance to Mathias and Nick had her guessing this was Del Mitchell. She turned to the woman and recognized the pretty, green-eyed blonde from the teleconferences.

"Carol!" Maya practically squealed her name as she held out her arms. "In person at last. Yay!"

They hugged, then Maya introduced her to Del.

"This is the friend I was telling you about," Maya said. "She models my veils and keeps Mathias in line. Thank you so much for helping me. You don't know me from a rock and you just stepped in and started doing things."

"It was fun," Carol assured her. "A lot of my friends are in the wedding business. I enjoyed being on the inside this once."

Del put down Sophie and shook hands with Carol before pulling Mathias into a bear hug. Sophie danced around, barking her excitement.

"When did you get back?" Mathias asked as he led everyone into the studio.

"We arrived in LA yesterday," Del told him. "Spent the night by the airport before driving out here. I thought we'd head to Fool's Gold first, but Maya wants to check on the wedding details."

Maya laughed. "Yes, how terribly shocking that the bride is concerned about such an event. However do you stand me?"

"I manage." Del pulled her close and kissed her. "Still want to do it? Be shackled to me for the rest of your life?"

"As if I'd let you go now. I finally have you trained the way I like you."

The teasing was sweet but what impressed Carol was the intensity in the way they looked at each other. Their connection was tangible, as if she could reach out and touch it. They belonged together.

Maya turned to Carol. "We saw Millie on the drive in. She's so beautiful. We're really looking forward to getting some footage for you. The way she walks and those big eyes. What a sweetie."

"You're going to really like her," Carol said.

"Just stay away from the zebras." Mathias winked. "They have attitude."

Del put his arm around Maya. "You can't scare us, bro. We're experienced world travelers."

Mathias slapped him on the back. "You say that now. Let's talk when it's two hours before you walk down the aisle. Your knees will be shaking."

"Only with anticipation."

Maya rolled her eyes. "They're always like this. You haven't really lived until you've been in a room with all five Mitchell brothers."

"I'm looking forward to it," Carol admitted.

Del glanced at Mathias. "You still okay with us staying with you?"

Carol blinked in surprise. Despite the big house and friendly personality, Mathias had always been a little on the solitary side. When he spent time with his bridesmaids, he went to their hotel room. When he hung out with his brothers, it was always somewhere that wasn't his place. To the best of her knowledge, she was the only person who regularly visited him. Until now.

She looked at him and raised her eyebrows. "You're going to be busy."

"It's no big deal. I asked the housekeeping service I use to spruce the guest rooms and make sure there were towels." He turned to Maya. "Do you need more than that?"

"Not at all." She laughed. "We'll be fine. Thank you for letting us stay with you until the wedding." She touched Carol's arm. "I was terrified to leave my dress in a hotel room for several days. What if Del saw it or stepped on the train?"

"I'd never do that," her fiancé protested.

"Not on purpose." Maya smiled at Mathias. "You saved me, little brother-to-be, and I'm very grateful."

"You've been traveling for a couple of days," Carol said. "You must be exhausted. Let's get you settled."

Mathias sighed. "She's prodding me. Did you see that? It was subtle, but I saw it."

"Give it up, bro," Del told him. "You'll never win." He whistled for Sophie. The dog raced toward him and jumped. Del caught her in his arms. "Come on. I'll let you drive if you promise to be careful."

Sophie barked in agreement.

Maya fell into step with Carol. "I didn't know you two were dating. Not that Mathias talks about his personal life much, but still."

"We're not," Carol said, careful to keep her voice low. "We live kind of next to each other and we're friends. He's the one who convinced Ronan to donate a piece of artwork to raise money for Millie's herd. I know all three Mitchell brothers who live here. It's a small-town thing."

She pressed her lips together when she realized she might just be talking a bit too quickly. Maya's expression was knowing but all she said was, "I'm glad you're on the team."

Carol had no idea what that meant, but decided to simply go with it. Protesting too much would only add to the confusion. If Maya said anything to Mathias, Carol was sure he would set her straight. They were friends. Neighbors. Absolutely nothing more.

CHAPTER FOURTEEN

The Boardroom had a warm and friendly feel, or maybe that was more about how Violet hovered at his side. Ulrich knew he would forever link the two in his mind. After nearly a week in his hotel room, he'd insisted on going out for the evening and Violet had suggested a few hours at The Boardroom.

There was a long bar against the far wall and lots of tables and chairs but what truly dominated the space were the floor-to-ceiling bookcases filled with boxes of board games. Some were new and some were obscure. Ulrich saw several that he'd played as a child. On the days that his father's old injuries had made it impossible for him to work, he and Ulrich had spent afternoons playing board games. Summers had meant a table in a shady part of the garden while winters had meant sitting near a warm fire.

"It's tournament night," Violet said, sounding happy. "That will be fun." She pointed to an empty table and led the way. "Now I'll get to find out how competitive you are."

"I can hold my own." If things went badly, he could always blame the concussion.

"We'll see," she said with a laugh and pulled out a chair. He sat next to her, leaving two empty seats at their table for four.

The room was filling up. The noise level rose, but not uncomfortably so. Most of the people seemed to know each other and the atmosphere was friendly and relaxing.

"Like the pub back home," he said, leaning close to Violet. "If only there were darts."

"And warm beer," she teased. "And bangers and mash."

"Someone's been on the internet."

She laughed. "Yes, someone has." She studied him. "You doing all right? There's not too much noise and the lights are okay?"

"While I appreciate the concern, I assure you that I'm perfectly fine. No headache, no pains of any kind. I'm looking forward to the evening."

"Me, too."

Her gaze seemed to linger. Or maybe that was simply wishful thinking on his part. Since his accident, despite how much time they'd spent together, he'd been unable to determine if Violet had any interest in him beyond helping out a friend. He wanted to tell himself that her attitude was her attempt to be professional as she took care of him, but he thought he might be fooling himself. Violet wasn't in the medical field. She was allowed to act as she would like—which made it very clear she wasn't all that interested in him.

Too bad. After their first dinner together, he would have sworn they had chemistry. She had reacted positively to his suggestion that she come visit Battenberg Park, but maybe that was more about seeing his grandmother rather than him.

A woman walked over and put her hands on the back of an empty chair. "Mind if I join you?" she asked, her gaze settling on him. "Or is this table royals only?"

She was attractive, with platinum blond hair and blue eyes.

"We only have to curtsy at the beginning and end of the

evening," Violet told her, then grinned. "Although Ulrich does like to be called 'Your Lordship.'"

"And here I thought Americans prided themselves on their honesty," Ulrich said as he rose and held out his hand. "Ulrich Sherwood. And it's not Your Lordship, it's Your Grace."

"Silver Tesdal," she said as she took a seat across from him. "Your Grace." She flashed him a smile. "How are you feeling? Recovering from the accident?"

"I am. Thank you."

Ulrich wasn't surprised Violet's friend knew about what had happened. He would imagine the news had spread all over the town. It was the same back home—everyone knew everyone's business. Every now and then the reality irritated, but most of the time he enjoyed being part of the community.

According to his grandmother, all was well at Battenberg Park. So much so, she seemed in no hurry to have him return. Whenever they talked, she insisted he take a few more days to recover. He'd already extended his visit much longer than expected, even taking the accident into account. At some point he was going to have to leave. The truth was—he simply didn't want to.

He told himself it was because he rarely took a vacation where he got away from all his responsibilities. Even this trip had been work-related—two days in Los Angeles to finalize the rental of the estate for the film company, then a quick trip to Happily Inc to confront Violet. Had he not had a run-in with a giraffe, he would have been home over a week ago and Violet would have been little more than a distant memory.

Perhaps he owed Millie a note of gratitude.

"Tonight is going to be fun," Silver said. "It's a Trouble tournament."

"Trouble?" Ulrich asked.

"It's a board game," Violet told him. "I love it when we play kids' games. They're the most fun. You'd be amazed at how many adults get annoyed when they're sent back to home base."

"You've played this game before," he said.

"I have and I plan to win."

Silver leaned toward him. "Watch out. She can be competitive."

A woman who look remarkably like Violet joined them. They both had red hair and similar features. The other woman was more casually dressed, but her mannerisms and smile were just like Violet's. The sister, he thought, standing up to greet her.

"You must be Carol," he said, holding out his hand. "A pleasure. I'm Ulrich Sherwood."

"Duke of Somerbrooke," Silver muttered under her breath. "He likes to be called Your Lordship."

"No, Your Grace," Violet said.

Ulrich smiled at Carol. "Or simply Ulrich."

"Don't worry. I'm used to ignoring those two," she said as she took a seat. "How are you feeling? Recovering from the accident?"

"I'm nearly good as new." His tone turned regretful. "I fear I shall have to make my way home soon."

Violet's mouth formed a straight line and she looked away for a second before she smiled at her sister. "Our plan to trap him and hold him for ransom seems to be failing."

"If you're going to let him wander the streets, then he's hardly going to feel threatened."

"I was attacked by a giraffe," Ulrich pointed out. "Very unexpected."

"Earlier this summer, we had escaped zebras," Silver told him. "We do live in a weird little town."

"But you love it," Ulrich said.

"I do."

He turned to Carol. "Violet tells me you are the local gamekeeper for the animal preserve."

"That's a fancy title, but yes. You've already met Millie." She winced. "I am sorry that she got out and caused the accident."

"It wasn't Millie's fault, it was mine. I was driving and she was not. I'm glad she was uninjured."

"She's fine and soon to have a herd."

Ulrich must have looked confused because Violet explained about Millie being alone and Carol's quest to raise the money to buy more female giraffes.

"The fund-raiser is next week," Carol said. "It's going to be quite the event." She looked at her sister. "I'm going to need a mini makeover or at least suggestions for my hair and makeup."

"Of course."

Several servers began passing out the games. Ulrich scanned the rules, which were fairly simple.

"The winner at each table moves on to the next round," Violet told him. "I'll warn you, you're playing with some very competitive women."

"Then I shall enjoy myself even more."

She leaned close. "You say that now."

Her breath whispered on his cheek. He could inhale the faint scent of her perfume—one he would always associate with her. The need to kiss her was nearly as powerful as the desire to do so much more. She was bright, charming, kind and a pleasure to be around. He didn't want to leave her and he had absolutely no reason to stay. Except...

"The fund-raiser for Millie is a week from Thursday," he said. "Would you mind if I stayed until then?"

She met his gaze. For a second, he would have sworn he heard her breath catch, then told himself wishful thinking did not make it so.

"That would be great. The evening is going to be a lot of fun. And it's for a good cause."

"Millie's herd."

"Yes."

He wanted to say something else, something significant that would help her understand his conflicted feelings. He wanted to know if she felt anything for him or if he was simply in danger of making a fool out of himself.

Silver rose. "I'm making a bar run. Who wants what?"

Ulrich rose. "Allow me. What would you ladies like?"

Silver raised her eyebrows. "Nice manners, Your Lordship."

He bowed. "My lady."

Silver sank back in her chair. "I don't know, Violet. This one might be a keeper. The house would probably look really nice on a Christmas card."

Violet flushed. "She's teasing, Ulrich. You don't have to freak out or anything."

"I'm English, Violet. We never freak out. We don't believe in it."

He took their orders and made his way to the bar. As he waited to be served, he glanced back at the table. The three women were speaking intently, their heads bent together, their voices low.

If he was lucky, they were talking about him. Perhaps Violet was admitting some fondness and her friends were telling her to go for it.

And then what, the practical side of his nature asked. Where would they go from there? His life was not movable—he belonged to Battenberg Park as much as the estate belonged to him. Violet was American. Her family and work were here, in Happily Inc. She would never consider leaving...would she?

A ridiculous question. They'd only known each other a few weeks. He'd known Penelope for years before they'd married and look what had happened there. No, this was a brief respite from his responsibilities, nothing more. He would enjoy his time with Violet and then he would go home—where he belonged.

Mathias studied the latest glass version of Carol. He was closer, but the piece still wasn't right. While the individual features looked like her, the essence of her being seemed to be missing. Although he didn't have a clue as to how he was supposed to capture essence.

His cell rang. He recognized the area code and grinned. "Hello?"

"Mathias, it's Mayor Marsha. I'm sorry I couldn't take your call earlier. I was in a meeting. How are you?"

"Very well. We're looking forward to seeing you next weekend, at the wedding."

"I wouldn't miss it. You and your brothers might have moved away from Fool's Gold, but you will always be a part of our family. I hope Sophie is staying out of trouble."

He glanced at the sleeping beagle, then wondered how on earth the mayor had known his mother had dropped off her dog in the first place. His was not to question the mighty one, he reminded himself.

"She's keeping out of trouble, but the day is young. Ask me in a few hours."

Mayor Marsha chuckled. "I remember the time she managed to find her way into the storeroom of Jo's Bar. She ate three bags of cookies and half a ham before she was discovered. Your mother was so worried about her getting sick. Sophie being Sophie was just fine. She had a little gas, but not much else."

"That's my girl."

"So tell me, Mathias, how can I help you?"

"It's about a couple of giraffes."

"For Millie? I had heard your brother donated a piece to

be auctioned off to raise the money. Moving giraffes will be a challenge, but I'm sure you have that in hand already. You'll be needing permits. Let me see what I can do."

Mathias wondered if he should have bothered calling. Maybe just thinking the request would have been enough.

"Thanks for your help," he said.

"You're more than welcome. I'll see you at the wedding. I'm driving down with Eddie and Gladys." The mayor sighed. "They took two days to pick the rooms they wanted at the Sweet Dreams Inn. I hope they don't get too wild."

Eddie and Gladys were two old ladies from Fool's Gold. They were feisty, highly verbal and known for ogling much younger men.

"Did Del invite them?" he asked, sounding doubtful.

"Maya. They're close to her. Apparently the new trend is grandmothers as flower girls. Eddie and Gladys are filling in. I try to stay ahead of trends but every now and then one gets by me. Take care, Mathias. I'll be in touch. Oh, and I'm very much looking forward to meeting Carol."

Mathias felt his mouth drop open. "How did you—? Who told you I—?" He shook his head. "Never mind. It's not important. See you soon."

"Yes, you will."

He hung up and stared at his phone. Nick and Del walked into the studio.

"Bad news?" Nick asked.

"Nope. Just Mayor Marsha being her slightly scary self. She's going to look into the permit issue so we can move giraffes across the state. Oh, she's bringing Eddie and Gladys to the wedding."

Nick grinned. "I can't wait. It's been a long time since an old lady patted my butt. I've missed it."

Del chuckled. "Me, too. The old ladies in China are much more respectful."

"Maybe they think you're ugly," Mathias teased.

"Not possible. I'm with Nick on Eddie and Gladys."

"There's something wrong with both of you," Mathias grumbled.

"Naw," Nick said. "I know a good thing when I see it. Or in this case, feel it. We should all be so feisty when we're their age." He pulled up a stool and leaned toward the glass piece. "You're nearly there."

"With luck, a couple more tries should do it."

Del joined them. "That's Carol. It looks just like her."

"Thanks."

Nick turned the statue. "You could show it at the event for Millie."

"If it's ready."

Nick looked surprised. "You'd do that? Display art? You know he's going to be there."

The "he" in question being their father. "I know."

Nick had been in the studio all those years ago when Ceallach had sent Mathias's glass work tumbling to the ground. They'd all stood in the aftermath, watching the glass shards fly across the room.

"Maybe it's time I let the past go," Mathias said. "He's just an old man. To see him as anything more important gives him too much power."

Del glanced between them. "I used to wish I was like you two—talented like Dad. When I was little, I couldn't understand why I didn't have what he had. Now, I'm grateful. It's not worth the crap."

"I agree," Mathias said slowly. "You and Aidan weren't involved." Ceallach had never much bothered with his "non-artist" sons.

"Everything comes at a price." Nick glanced at Del. "You didn't have much of a father."

"I know, but I've moved on. He might have paid attention to what you did, but he wasn't much of a father to any of us."

"When do Aidan and Shelby arrive?" Mathias asked. When it came to Ceallach, the more family around, the better. It would be easier to keep him distracted with a lot of moving parts.

"Tuesday, I think." Del shrugged. "Maya is the keeper of the calendar. I'm just the guy who gets to marry her." He grinned. "Which makes me one lucky bastard." He looked around. "Ronan doesn't work here?"

"He has a studio at his house," Nick said.

"How's he doing?" Del asked, turning his attention to Mathias. "Is he dealing yet?"

"Ronan doesn't deal. He avoids." Mathias thought of all the other things he could say. That his brother was withdrawing a little more every few weeks. That they barely talked. They didn't even fight much anymore. At least the fighting had been a connection of sorts. These days they had nothing going on between them.

He tried to see things from his brother's point of view but every time he got close, he also got mad. He was dealing with plenty, too. Ronan wasn't the only one who had stopped being a twin. He wasn't the only one who had lost something. Not that his brother would listen, he thought grimly.

"Will he be at the show?" Del asked.

"He'd better be," Mathias said. "It's his piece bringing in the big money."

"You donating anything?" Del asked Nick.

"I've done a couple of fun giraffe pieces in wood. They're mostly going to be there for atmosphere."

Mathias was sure his brother would sell everything he brought and for plenty of money. With luck Carol would have enough to support Millie and her herd in style for years.

"Want me to make some calls?" Del asked. "I still know

some famous guys in the sports world. We could try to generate some publicity."

"Good idea," Mathias told him. "The more press, the more money we'll raise."

"I'll text Jonny Blaze." Nick pulled out his phone. "I should have thought of it sooner."

"The actor?" Del asked. "You know him?"

"He moved to Fool's Gold a couple of years ago. He married Madeline Krug. You remember her."

"Not really," Del said, "but sure. Invite everyone. I'll check around for rooms."

"Eddie and Gladys are staying at the Sweet Dreams Inn," Mathias told him. "In case you want to warn anyone."

His brothers laughed.

This was good for them, he thought. He and his brothers hanging out together. Hopefully Ronan would put in an appearance and soon Aidan would join them. Everyone in one place. Mostly at his house.

He thought wistfully of the usual silence of his place, then reminded himself it was only for a few days. He would be fine.

Violet told herself not to read too much into Ulrich's decision to stay in town for a few more days. Maybe he was genuinely excited to see what happened at the auction. Maybe he'd formed a connection with Millie because of the accident. She shouldn't assume that he was staying because of her.

Oh, but how she wanted him to be.

She'd come back to her office for an afternoon of catching up while Ulrich dealt with issues back in England. They'd agreed to meet up for dinner. Now that he was fully functional, there was no reason for her to sleep next door, so she'd returned to her place. Funny how she'd gotten used to being near him and found herself already missing having him in the next room.

"Don't be ridiculous," she told herself as she sorted through the mail and bills that had piled up in the past few days. She'd been fine before and she would be fine again. Ulrich was simply a little emotional vacation from her regularly scheduled life. Yes, he was great and yes, she would miss him when he was gone, but she would go on as before.

For a second, she allowed herself the fantasy of him asking her to go back to England with him. Of him telling her he couldn't stand to be without her. He would take her in his arms and...and...

Okay, sure the sex would be easy and great all that, but then what? Would she really leave everything she knew behind and move halfway across the world for a man she barely knew? Technically she made most of her money with sales of her buttons, which she could ship from anywhere, and the internet meant staying in touch with customers and family would be relatively easy, but still. She was a self-actualized woman. She didn't need a man to be successful or complete herself. If she were to get involved with anyone, she planned on a true partnership. Could that happen with a duke who owned a five-hundred-plus-year-old estate?

Not a problem she had to solve today, she told herself.

She made quick work of her bill paying, then started opening the packages that had been delivered. There were dozens of buttons to sort—a few sets looked to be exciting finds.

She forced herself to go through everything before she started on her research. She'd just begun her first internet search when Atsuko walked into her shop.

"I'm looking for giraffe inspired buttons," the gallery owner said. "I'm going all out for the event. If you have actual giraffe buttons, that would be perfect. I have a couple of jackets in mind."

While Violet offered to change out buttons for local customers, some people preferred to do the sewing themselves.

Atsuko had a flair for the dramatic, a stunning wardrobe and mad sewing skills.

"I think I might have some giraffe shapes," Violet said, thinking about her inventory. "I know I have some buttons that could be considered giraffe inspired."

She pulled up her inventory program and searched the database. Three different buttons popped up, along with their location in her storage closet. She quickly found the boxes and set them on the counter.

The first had three giraffe-head-shaped buttons. They were carved ebony and from the mid-eighteen hundreds.

"The work is beautiful," Violet said, as she pulled on white cotton gloves, then pulled the buttons out of the box. "But they're so dark, it's difficult to see the detail."

Atsuko put on gloves as well, then picked up a button. "I don't think I have a jacket with only three buttons. And you're right about them being dark. I do have a gold jacket that might work. I'm not sure."

The second box held painted buttons. The brown and tan pattern was very giraffe-like but the buttons themselves weren't overly inspired. The third box held six amber-and-onyx buttons.

"From the seventeen hundreds," Violet said, placing one button on her palm. "Italian. They're edged in gold, so not cheap, but they're beautiful."

The work was exquisite and detailed, and the pattern matched Millie. These buttons had been a find from one of her buyers in India. The woman had sent a huge jar filled with dozens of buttons. Most had been cheap or broken, but there had been a few treasures—these six among them.

"I want them," Atsuko said firmly. "While I'm not taking a commission on Ronan's piece, it won't be the only thing sold. I plan to have a good night." She smiled. "These will bring me luck."

"They're going to look lovely," Violet told her as she put the buttons back in their box.

A happy sale, she thought as she wrote up the receipt. Her mortgage was paid for the next two months and she had money left over to buy more buttons.

Atsuko took the receipt and the box, then put both in her Prada handbag. She started for the door, only to turn back. "By the way, your English gentleman friend got in touch with me this morning. Apparently he's sending over a little something for the auction, as well. Something from his estate back home."

Ulrich hadn't mentioned anything to her. "Did he say what it was?"

"No. I was hoping you'd know."

"Sorry. I don't have a clue."

"Then we'll find out next Thursday."

Atsuko waved and left. Violet thought about asking Ulrich when she saw him, then decided she preferred to be surprised. For a second she fantasized that he'd asked his grandmother to ship over one of the family's fabulous diamond rings. He would drop to one knee and...

"You're being ridiculous," she told herself out loud. "It's something giraffe-like. Nothing more."

Oh but how she wanted it to be more. Much more.

CHAPTER FIFTEEN

Carol had always thought of herself as the more sensible of the sisters. While Violet always looked so pretty and put together with her accessorized outfits, Carol was more concerned if she could get grass stains and grazing animal poop out of her clothes.

She'd been fine with that. She loved her work and never in a million years could imagine herself happily sorting through huge jars of buttons or tying the perfect scarf for the right outfit. But surrounded by lace, tulle and a very stunning wedding gown, not to mention gorgeous shoes, she found herself wondering if she was just a tiny bit too utilitarian. Even more troubling, she felt the first *ping* of wistfulness. Until this very moment she'd never thought about being a bride.

Oh, sure, she'd thought about getting married, but that was different. That was about being in a relationship, about finding someone to love who would love her back. That was about family and future and having babies and all that kind of stuff. She was talking *wedding*.

Cakes and invitations and showers and receptions and rings

and yes, an amazing lace-covered, fitted wedding gown that made Maya look like the most beautiful woman in the world.

"There aren't enough words," Carol admitted, walking around the bride-to-be. She took a couple more pictures before carefully setting the veil in place and adjusting it. "You're stunning. Del is going to faint when he sees you."

"I hope not." Maya bit her lower lip. "I wouldn't mind him being blown away, but I'm not that excited about him fainting."

"Good point. He'll have trouble catching his breath. How about that?"

"Perfect."

They were at Mathias's house. One of the smaller spare rooms had been converted to wedding central. Maya had asked Carol to come by and help her with a few last-minute details. One of them was to take some pictures of her in the dress so she could send them to their friends in China.

Carol passed over the phone. Maya scrolled through the photographs and nodded happily. "Exactly what I wanted. Thank you so much for helping me this morning."

"Happy to do it. This is fun."

Later, when she was alone, Carol would allow herself a few minutes of wedding fantasy. Nothing overly detailed—just her in a dress and the man of her dreams waiting at the other end of the aisle. Mathias would look so—

Her brain slammed on the brakes and then quickly backed up. Mathias wasn't the man of her dreams. He couldn't be. They were friends and that was it. He wasn't a man who had romantic relationships and she wouldn't settle for anything less. As for how she felt about him…best not to go there.

Carol unfastened the long line of buttons so Maya could step out of her dress. Together they put it back on the oversize hanger, then fluffed and straightened so it hung perfectly.

A sheet was draped over the dress to protect it from accidents and prying eyes.

They went into the kitchen where Maya fixed tea, then they sat on the sofa by the window. Sophie joined them, obviously hoping for some kind of cookie. She settled next to Carol, leaning on her heavily before finally slumping down with her head on Carol's lap.

"I think I'm ready," Maya said as she passed over a cup to Carol. "Can I say that? Do I jinx myself if I do?"

"You seem really prepared. I think you're safe."

Maya flashed her a smile. "Thank you. You've been so great. I want to say I'm sorry Mathias roped you into helping, but I'm not. Every time we had a videoconference, you were so engaged while being totally calm. That helped a lot."

Carol was surprised by the assessment, but also pleased. "I was happy to help. A lot of my friends are in the wedding business." She made air quotes with one of her hands. "But I never get really involved in any of the weddings. This has been fun for me."

"Me, too. To be honest, it's hard to imagine how it's all going to come together. Pallas has been fantastic, handling the details." She sipped her tea. "This is the lull before the storm, as they say. Your fund-raising event is Thursday night, the rehearsal dinner is Friday and then the wedding is Saturday."

"When does your family arrive?" Carol asked.

Maya shook her head. "I don't really have any blood relatives. I have friends coming in from Fool's Gold. Eddie and Gladys are my stand-in grandmothers. They're going to be flower girls, which I totally love. Mayor Marsha is going to perform the ceremony. Elaine, Del's mother, and I are close, so she's going to be standing in for my mom as I get ready that morning. Other people I know are coming. It will be great."

Carol thought that it said a lot about Maya that even though she'd lost her biological family, she'd created a family of the heart for herself.

"How do you get along with Ceallach?" she asked, curious about the man who had such an influence on his sons.

Maya's expression turned cautious. "How much do you know about him?"

"As a person, not much. As someone who has met several of his sons, I can't decide if I'm going to shake his hand or slap him upside the head."

Maya relaxed. "Okay, so you know what to expect."

"Not exactly but I plan to be braced and on guard." Not for herself, she thought. But for Mathias.

"Ceallach is practically a legend," Maya told her. "He's brilliant and famous and difficult. Elaine worships him. I wouldn't want their marriage, but it works for them and I guess that's what matters. As for how he deals with his sons... Del and Aidan got ignored and the other three had too much attention. I guess it's safe to say each of them are scarred, in their own way."

Maya leaned toward Carol. "I can't figure Ceallach out. It's not just that he has to be the center of attention, it's that he needs others to be suffering. I don't know if that makes sense."

"It does."

"I've done some reading. Sometimes I wonder if there's something wrong with his brain. I don't believe that being that gifted means you have to be crazy or anything, it's more about the way he treats people, especially his sons. He has no empathy, no sense of anyone but himself." She shook her head. "Sorry, I am way out of my area of expertise here. I should simply tell you to smile and keep your distance."

"That was my plan." And to watch Mathias's back.

Sophie trotted happily at Mathias's side, stopping occasionally to sniff or mark her territory with a quick squat. When his mother had first dropped her off, he'd been convinced taking care of the dog was going to be a disaster. Instead, she'd grown on him and he had to admit, if only to himself, that he was going to miss her.

"You're not half bad," he told her.

Sophie looked up and wagged her tail, confirming what must be obvious.

"On the bright side, when you're gone, I'll get to eat my entire breakfast by myself."

She gave a low woof, as if asking why he would want to do that, when sharing with her was so much more fun.

They continued down the road. Mathias told himself they had no destination, then thought it was dumb to lie to himself. It wasn't as if he didn't already know where he was headed. Because despite everything going on, or maybe because of it, there was only one place he wanted to be.

Five minutes later, he was on Carol's front porch, ringing the doorbell. She answered a couple of seconds later.

She'd already changed from her work uniform into jeans and a T-shirt. Both were soft looking, kind of like her. She was barefoot. Unlike most of the women he knew, she didn't paint her toenails. Funny how seeing them without any color made her appear more vulnerable somehow.

"Hi," she said, stepping back to let him in. "How's it going at your place?"

"It's crowded."

She laughed. "You only have Del and Maya to deal with. Okay, and the dress, but it's pretty quiet. What are you going to do when the rest of the family arrives?"

"I have no idea." Aidan and Shelby were getting a room in town, but his parents would be staying with him. A nightmare he would deal with when it happened.

She led him out to the back patio. "You two sit here. I'll be right back."

Mathias did as she requested, taking a seat at the table. After he unclipped Sophie's leash, the beagle jumped onto the chaise and stretched out in the last rays of sunshine. Carol returned in a few minutes. She had two open beer bottles along with a bowl of chips and guacamole.

She set everything on the table before settling into the chair next to him, her foot tucked under her butt. She touched her bottle to his, then said, "What's going on?"

"I'm good. How the countdown to the event?"

"I'm nervous," she admitted. "There's a lot on the line. Atsuko is confident, so I try to be, too. She's handling everything—I just have to show up and talk about Millie." She glanced at him. "You're going to be there, aren't you?"

"With bells on."

She laughed. "Where, exactly, will those bells be?"

"You're going to have to wait and see."

He thought about the glass pieces in his studio. He'd completed the one of Millie but was still refining the Carol statue. If he got it right in time, he might bring it to the event…to continue the giraffe theme. It wouldn't be for sale.

The late afternoon was warm, the breeze light. In Fool's Gold fall would have arrived with cooler temperatures and brilliant colors.

"What are you thinking?" she asked.

"I miss the changing colors of the leaves. The desert is beautiful in its own way, but there's something to be said for the mountains."

"Regretting your move?" she asked, her tone light.

"No. Coming here was the right decision. This is home now."

"How did you decide to leave in the first place?"

"Ronan needed to get away and I needed to go with him."

"For him or for you?"

"Both."

"What was it like before?" she asked. "When you were twins?"

Her voice was kind, as was her gaze. He could feel her concern. Carol would never ask for the sake of knowing. She wasn't like that. Funny how, at the end of the day, he trusted her. Whatever was going on, he knew that she would do the right thing, be it for him or someone else she cared about. Because he knew she did care about him. They were friends.

"I don't remember not being Ronan's twin and him being mine," he admitted. "We shared everything. Mom used to talk about us sleeping in the same crib when we were babies. I always thought it was because we couldn't be separated, but looking back I'm guessing it was because when she took Ronan in, she didn't have another place to put him. She hadn't actually been expecting another baby."

"I'm still amazed she was willing to take him in the way she did. I couldn't do it."

"Not many people could. She's the complete opposite of my father. He only thinks of himself and she only thinks of him. At the risk of being too cynical, I've never believed the story about her knowing the second she saw Ronan that she had to raise him. I think it was because he was a part of my father and Ceallach has always been the center of her universe."

"But you said Ronan was her favorite. How do you explain that?"

"I can't."

All the brothers had known it. Mathias never knew how everyone else felt. Personally he hadn't minded because he'd been a part of Ronan's inner circle. The two of them against the world. Everyone else had come in second.

"We were in the same class at school, we played the same sports. When one of us got sick or injured, the other stayed home, too." He smiled. "We never liked the same type of women, though. When we were in high school, we tried dating sisters. That didn't go well."

"Then it all hit the fan," she said softly.

"It did." He still remembered the shock—not wanting to believe the words. How could Ronan not be his twin brother?

"It was hard on me," he continued, "but worse on him. I was still Elaine's son while he wasn't. We both had to deal with all the years of lies but he had to figure out who he was."

"Has he?"

"Hell if I know. These days we barely speak. He's pulling back more and more." He reached for a chip. "When we first moved here I thought we'd figure it out. We still worked together in the studio. We'd even rented a house together. Then he found that place up in the mountains and once he moved, he started withdrawing."

"I'm sorry."

"Thanks. We'll get through this."

At least he hoped they would. Bad enough to have lost his twin, but to end up losing his brother...

"What can I do to help?" she asked.

Let me take you to bed. A phrase only to be thought, not spoken, because she would think he was trying to make up for what had happened before. Even though he did want a do-over, today wasn't about that. Not that he could explain that to her.

Still, getting lost in Carol would go a long way to healing what ailed him.

"I'm good," he said instead.

"Let me know if that changes."

"I will."

"Want to stay for dinner?" she asked.

"I need to get back to Del and Maya. Want to join us?"

"Sure."

He didn't care if it was a mercy agreement—he wanted

her with him. "Weren't you over earlier today, helping her with something?"

"I dropped by at lunch and took pictures of her in her dress. It was fun. I always enjoy your view when I'm at your place. Looking down at all the little animals."

"My house is the closest one to yours and our views aren't that different."

"And yet we are worlds apart."

"I'm ignoring you," he grumbled as he grabbed more chips.

"At your own peril. I'm all that keeps you grounded in the real world."

He chuckled. "Lucky me. Now if only you had superpowers to keep my father at bay."

"Sorry. I can try to think of a few ways to distract him, if that would help."

"No, it's okay. We'll get through it."

All of them, or so he hoped. He might not enjoy dealing with his father, but he would manage to survive the visit. Ronan was less of a sure thing. His brother would be fine with Ceallach—Ronan was used to ignoring their father's pronouncements. The bigger problem would be Elaine. Ronan still hadn't come to terms with the woman he'd always thought of as his mother.

Carol reached out her hand. He took it and ignored the wanting that accompanied the warmth of her skin. He knew what she was offering and while he wanted a lot more, he was going to be happy with what he could get.

Violet and Ulrich walked along the boardwalk by the river. They'd gone out to dinner and then had decided to take a stroll before he dropped her off back at her place. The sun had set, the air was still warm and she was doing her best not to read too much into their evening, but it was difficult not to. Ulrich was just so great to be around.

"I can't believe how warm it is," he said as they passed an older couple on a bench. "Back home it would be rainy and cold."

"Isn't it like that all the time?" she asked, her voice teasing. "I had a friend visit London once in July and she said it was the coldest she'd ever been in her life."

"We do have challenging weather," he admitted. "But we more than make up for it with our culture and charming accents."

"Your accent is charming."

"As is yours."

"I don't have one," she told him. "You're simply hearing me incorrectly."

They moved closer to the river and leaned against the railing. Behind them was The Promenade and all the uptown shops. Across the river was the downtown district, such as it was.

Ulrich pointed. "The Boardroom is over there, isn't it? I'm starting to get my bearings. Your shop is by the art gallery that will host the party to raise money for more giraffes." He smiled at her. "I've made my peace with Millie, by the way. I shall not have any hard feelings about her gaining a herd."

"How very nice of you."

"I'm a very nice man."

He was, she thought wistfully. One she would miss when he was gone.

"Tell me, Violet, why aren't you married?"

The unexpected question had her blurting out the truth. "No one has asked."

"Have you wanted anyone to?"

"Not really. I have a habit of choosing safe, boring men to have a relationship with. I pick them because there's no way I can fall for them, so there's no way they can hurt me. But being with someone for the sake of having a relationship isn't

good, either. Eventually the men figure out I'm not emotionally engaged, so they end things, usually blaming me for trying to trick them."

She glanced at him and saw him watching her intently.
"There's an old saying that knowing the problem is half the
battle, but they're wrong. Knowing the problem just means
I can see it when it happens, but it doesn't seem to make me
act very differently."

Except with Ulrich. She'd fallen for him and he was neither boring nor safe. But he was leaving, which meant there
was a predefined end to whatever it was they had together.

"Do you know why you choose safe, boring men who
won't hurt you?"

She drew in a breath. "Yes. I think so. Mostly."

"If you're sure."

She laughed. "I have ideas. My parents are wonderful, loving people who told my sister and me that we were incredibly
special. The most wonderful children in the world."

"Most parents do that. At least the good ones do."

"The problem is we believed them and no one told us otherwise. Not until we got to school and found out the truth
the hard way. It was more difficult for Carol—she was older
and got the brunt of the teasing. She tried to explain it all to
me, to spare me the trauma, which helped. I kept my special-
ness a secret. Then, when I was seventeen, I was discovered."

He shifted so he was facing her. "What does that mean?"

"A famous photographer saw me walking down the street
in New York and instantly claimed me as his muse. Within
weeks I was literally everywhere—in ads, on billboards. I had
three major clothing campaigns and he put together a show
that was pictures of me."

"I had no idea."

Violet did her best to stay in the moment. Talking about
her past—at least that part of it—always upset her. "It was like

being on a scary, wonderful roller coaster," she admitted. "At first my mom wasn't sure I should get involved with him, but I convinced her it was a great opportunity. I was interested in fashion and planned to study it after high school. What better way to make contacts than be a model for this guy?"

"I take it things didn't end well."

"No. What we didn't know was he had the habit of picking a young woman to be his muse. I was just one in a long line of temporary faces in his work. Four months later, he moved on to someone else. It was only then I found out the advertising campaigns were with him, not with me. As far as the companies were concerned, we were all interchangeable. That was just his thing. My pictures disappeared from the gallery. It had never been about me at all. I wasn't famous, I was a fool."

"Not special," Ulrich said quietly.

"Exactly. One of the masses. There were no contacts, very little money and no good memories. I went to fashion school and pretended it never happened."

"On the outside. You had to deal with it on the inside."

"I did. My mother felt terrible for not figuring out what was going on. I had to fake being fine so she could feel better." She sighed. "It's not like anything really horrible happened. Not one tried to sleep with me, I was never hurt or drugged or assaulted. I had my dream shattered. It happens every day."

"Is that when you decided on safe, boring men?"

So he wasn't going to try to pretty things up? "It wasn't a conscious decision, but I would say yes. Part of living here is also about that," she added, then tried to call back the words. That truth was one she usually kept hidden.

"Things are safer in a small town?"

She nodded. "There aren't a ton of single guys in a wedding town. Not who live here permanently. And I'm not the type to pick up a groomsman for the weekend." She managed a smile. "It's okay. I'll figure it out."

"I'm sure you will." One corner of his mouth turned up. "The timing of this statement might be suspect but I'm compelled to tell you that I've become quite smitten. You are lovely and I can't stop thinking about you."

She'd expected him to say something like, "You were a fool. Did you really think you were going to be a model?" Or "Could your story be less interesting?" Smitten? *Smitten?* Who used that word? Who meant it?

Ulrich turned back to look at the river. "You don't have to say anything, Violet. Your silence speaks volumes, as they say. Not to worry. I'll be gone soon enough."

He spoke lightly, as if he was perfectly fine with his assessment of her lack of response, only that hadn't been what she meant.

She spun to face him and grabbed his arm. "No," she said quickly. "I'm not speaking with my silence. I was surprised by what you said." She smiled. "Good surprised. I mean that. I'm fairly smitten myself."

His features relaxed as he smiled back at her. "You are?"

"Yes. Unfortunately that means we find ourselves in quite a pickle."

His dark blue gaze settled on her face. "Because I'm leaving?"

"That has been made pretty clear. You're not from around here. I get that—what with the clues. Your accent, the funny clothes."

He glanced down at his jeans and long-sleeved shirt. "How are my clothes funny?"

They weren't but she liked teasing him. She had a feeling Ulrich didn't get a lot of teasing in his life these days. "They're just so British. And royal."

"I'm not royal."

"Sorry. They're so dukeish."

"As am I."

They looked at each other. She read wanting in his eyes. There were other emotions but that was the one she was going with, mostly because she liked it. But when he didn't move toward her or try to kiss her, she wondered if maybe he wouldn't…because he was leaving. Because it would be bad form or whatever it was he would say. And because he was, at heart, a gentleman. He'd asked once and she'd refused. She doubted he would ask again.

Yet another pickle, she thought, although this one had a very simple solution.

She rose on tiptoe and lightly brushed her lips against his. The sound of his inhale was audible. His body stiffened, but he didn't touch her.

"Violet," he began.

She took his hand in hers. "I'm sure."

He laced his fingers with hers. They walked back to her car and she drove to her place, then eyed the stairs up to her loft.

"You'll never make that," she said. "Let me grab a few things and I'll take us to your hotel."

Ulrich got out of the car. "I'm perfectly fine and extremely motivated. I can handle the stairs."

"But your leg—"

"Is really the least of it," he assured her. "Trust me."

He was as good as his word. He climbed the single flight easily, then waited while she opened the front door. Once they were inside, he glanced at the open space, nodded approvingly, then pulled her close.

His kiss claimed her with mastery that left her reeling. She went from interested to *take me now, big boy* in less than two seconds. As his tongue brushed against hers, his hands moved up and down her back before settling on her hips.

Heat burned. Heat and need and some whisper of emotion she dare not name. Not now...maybe not ever.

She wrapped her arms around his neck and hung on as if she would never let go. He was tall and strong. Lean, yet powerful.

They kissed for the longest time. Deep, slow kisses that seemed to tug at her soul. He could have touched her anywhere, but he didn't—not at first. Finally, when she was ready to complain that she wanted things to move just a little faster, he slid up her sides and lightly stroked her breasts.

Wanting grew as her breathing quickened. She broke the kiss to lead him to her bed at the far end of the loft. She set an unopened box of condoms on her nightstand, then unbuttoned his shirt. He unzipped her dress and let it fall to the ground.

With each article of clothing, they paused to explore, to touch, to taste. The feel of his mouth on her breasts had her moaning. The warmth of his skin against her fingers was its own form of arousal. Every touch, every kiss, every move was a promise.

She slid into bed first and he followed. He touched her everywhere before easing his fingers between her legs. He quickly found her swollen center and pleasured her until she found her release. While she was still lost in the aftermath of her orgasm, he put on a condom and eased inside of her.

She kept her eyes open, wanting to watch him—only he was watching her, as well. Even as he began to move inside of her, their gazes stayed locked, as if neither was going to be the first to look away.

The combination of what he was doing and their intense stares touched more than just her body. It was as if she and Ulrich really were becoming the same being.

He moved slowly, steadily, filling her until she couldn't help arching her back and drawing him in deeper. The tell-tale pressure began again and she knew she was close to a second orgasm. He quickened his pace, exciting her further. Her breath turned to pants as her body tensed.

"Come for me, Violet."

His voice was low and guttural. The words were just enough to push her over the edge. She cried out as her body surrendered. He groaned and pushed in deeper, before thrusting faster and faster until he, too, was lost in his release.

Later, when they lay together, a tangle of arms and legs, her head on his chest, his hand on her side, she wondered what on earth she was supposed to do now. Great sex was one thing and yes, she would think about making love with Ulrich often after he was gone. But there was no danger in that kind of longing.

The bigger problem wasn't with her body, it was with her heart. Somehow while she hadn't been paying attention, Ulrich had found his way inside the very essence of her. She'd fallen in love with him and having done so, she had no idea how she was supposed to let him go.

CHAPTER SIXTEEN

Mathias stood outside his house like a prisoner waiting for execution. He supposed there were those who would say he was being dramatic, but those people hadn't met Ceallach Mitchell. Nothing about this visit was going to go well—at least not from his perspective. He could only hope that Del and Maya had a great wedding and didn't sense any of the underlying tension.

Sophie sat at his side, her tail wagging tentatively. She knew something was going to happen and given how happy her life was, surely it would be good, but she had no frame of reference.

"Your mom's going to be here soon," he told the dog.

Her tail wagged faster as she responded to his friendly tone, but she didn't understand the words.

Del came out and joined them. "You could wait inside. We can see the car when it pulls up."

"Being outside is better."

Not that he was going to bolt, but if he had to, he was closer to his car.

"You okay?" Del asked.

"Never better."

"Does lying help?"

"It doesn't hurt."

A car rounded the bend. As it got closer, Mathias felt his gut clench, as if in anticipation of a fist. Not that Ceallach would be hitting anyone. He'd stopped doing that when his sons had gotten big enough to hit back. No, he thought grimly. Not his sons. Del.

Del had been the oldest, the first to stand between Ceallach and the younger boys. He'd been the one to tell their father to stop it. Mathias still remembered how surprised he'd been when Ceallach had listened.

"Thanks for getting between us and him," Mathias told his brother.

"No problem. I'll do it again, if necessary."

Mathias grinned. "I think we can take him ourselves now."

"Hopefully it won't come to that."

"Hopefully."

The rental car pulled into the driveway. Elaine opened the passenger door and Sophie immediately lunged toward her, tail wagging furiously. Mathias released her. The little beagle raced toward Elaine, barking, whining and writhing in total happiness. Elaine dropped to her knees and pulled Sophie close.

"I've missed you, baby girl."

Mathias had the brief thought that their lives all would have been a lot easier if their mom had shown as much enthusiasm for them when they'd been kids. Then Ceallach got out of the car and there was no way to think about anything else.

Mathias tried to see his father as a stranger would. The mighty artist was older now, thinner. There were lines by his eyes and around his mouth. He still had the carriage of a proud, powerful man, but one who was past his prime.

Nick and Maya joined them. Maya rushed toward Elaine

and they embraced. The Mitchell brothers and their father stayed carefully apart.

"Where's Ronan?" Ceallach asked.

"In town," Mathias said. He started to say Aidan would arrive in the morning, then figured there was no point. Their father wouldn't care about him.

Elaine rushed toward them, her arms open, Sophie dancing at her side. "My boys!"

The three of them hugged her. She examined them, pronounced them handsome and healthy, then ushered everyone inside. Mathias wondered if he was the only one who noticed their father hadn't greeted them beyond asking about Ronan.

Maya had gone to the store and bought different snacks, along with fixings for dinner. Mathias hadn't paid attention to the details. He'd been unable to think about much beyond his father in his house. Now he watched the man prowl around his living room, then look out at the view.

"Good energy," his father said. "You work here?"

"I have a studio in town."

"Still making crap?"

Elaine hurried to her husband's side. "Ceallach, please. For me. Maya and Del are getting married and I want to hear all about the wedding plans."

"Then talk to her about them," Ceallach said, his gaze locking with Mathias. "You could have been somebody. Instead you're a useless hack making dishes." Disdain dripped from his words.

He turned to Nick. "What about you?"

Nick glanced at Mathias and winked, then turned back to their father. "I'm doing some things with paper."

"Paper!" Ceallach's voice was a roar. "No son of mine is working with paper. The wood was bad enough. How could you?"

Nick shrugged. "You know what, Dad? It's not that hard. I could probably show you a few techniques."

Elaine shot him a warning glance, then stepped between her husband and her sons. "Mathias, why don't you show us our room so we can get settled. Maya said we were eating in tonight. That's so nice. I'll unpack, then help in the kitchen. How's that?"

Always the peacemaker, Mathias thought. Always making sure their father was fine. While she would get between Ceallach and his sons, she wouldn't stand up for her children. Not against the great and gifted artist.

Nothing had changed. He supposed at this point, it never would. His parents had a relationship that seemed to work for them. As for what he felt about his father, well, those were words he wouldn't say aloud.

He showed them to the master suite. He'd already cleared out most of his stuff. He would use the futon in his home office, then find out if he could get his mattress fumigated after they left. Or maybe he should simply replace it. There was no way he could sleep in it after his father had.

When he stepped back into the hall, Maya was waiting for him. She hugged him tight, then led him back to the living room.

"Are you okay?" she asked when they were out of earshot of the master bedroom. "I can't believe how awful that was. Del always tries to tell me what it was like, but I guess I didn't believe him." She worried her bottom lip. "Elaine should have stood up to him." She held up her hand. "I know, I know. She doesn't. She's my friend and sweet to me, but jeez. This is horrible."

Mathias hugged her, then kissed the top of her head. "Don't worry. We're all used to it. He'll be gone soon and you're going to be married to my brother." He glanced at Del and

Nick. "Hey, we're getting another sister and when you marry Pallas, that will make three."

"Pressure's on, bro," Nick drawled.

Mathias shook his head. He wasn't getting married. He knew the danger of that—of loving someone. People who were supposed to love you betrayed you. Something he'd always believed, only lately he was having trouble summoning the same energy. Maybe it was because he was getting older. Maybe it was Carol.

Carol? What did she have to do with anything? Before he could decide, Ceallach and Elaine joined them.

Maya took charge of the evening. She moved everyone outside. She and Elaine brought out trays of appetizers while Del mixed drinks and Sophie claimed her favorite chaise.

They all settled on the patio and watched Millie and the other animals make their way back to the barns. The giraffe paused and turned toward them, the sinking sun behind her.

The moment was perfectly framed in reds and oranges, the trees nearly black by contrast. Mathias felt the familiar itch to work. Some of it was that Millie inspired him and some was the need to escape his father. Whatever the reason, he rose.

"I have to get to the studio."

"No!" his mother protested. "We're all having dinner together."

"A dish crisis?" his father asked.

"Go," Nick told him.

"I don't know when I'll be back," Mathias said, then walked through the house, to his car.

He entered the studio just as the sun set and crossed to his desk. After sketching for a few minutes, he walked over to study the latest version of the glass statue of Carol, then went to work.

Eleven hours later, he stared at what he'd created and knew he'd finally gotten it right. The clear glass piece seemed to breathe. The woman looked up, one hand raised. He put the Millie piece in front of it, with the giraffe bending toward her.

"Damn. I wish I'd made that."

He turned and saw Ronan standing in the studio. Mathias accepted the high praise with a simple "Thanks."

"You work all night?"

"Yeah."

"The folks arrive?"

"Yesterday afternoon."

Ronan walked around the two pieces. "Hell of a thing, Mathias. Don't let Dad destroy this one."

"I won't."

Carol carried her to-go cup of coffee out to her Jeep. She'd barely opened the driver's door when Mathias pulled up in the driveway next to her.

As always, just knowing he was close made her heart beat a little faster. It didn't matter that it was barely after six in the morning and that she had to get to work to feed her animals. For a couple of seconds, she needed to simply know that he was there.

He got out of his car and smiled at her. "Morning."

He looked exhausted. His skin was pale and there were dark circles under his eyes.

"Were you out all night?"

"At the studio. Working."

"Did you have to or was it because your father arrived yesterday?"

He winced. "It's early, Carol. Or late, depending on how you want to look at it. Maybe you could be a bit less direct."

"Do you really think that's going to happen?"

"Not for a second."

She put her coffee in the cup holder and set her bag on

the passenger seat before straightening. "Come on. You can stay here."

He grinned. "You're finally going to sleep with me?"

Her stomach clenched and a few key parts of her body tingled in anticipation.

"No," she said firmly. "You're going to sleep here alone. My house is small but I have a guest room."

He followed her inside. "I'd sleep better in your bed."

"I doubt that."

She got him clean sheets and towels, then pushed him gently toward the guest room. "Text someone at your house and tell them where you are, then get some sleep."

Mathias turned to face her. Before she could stop him, he'd leaned in and lightly kissed her.

"Thank you."

"You're welcome."

"You're good to me."

I can't help it. Luck was on her side and she only thought the words instead of saying them. Taking care of Mathias couldn't possibly be healthy—at least not for her. But she couldn't help herself. There was something about him. Reminding herself about their disastrous sexual encounter didn't seem to make a damn bit of difference. It was as if he had a firm grip on her heart and she couldn't get him to let go. Or she didn't want him to.

As either scenario was dangerous, she backed up a few feet and did her best to smile.

"Go get some sleep. I'll be at work all day. If you wake up before I'm back, let yourself out."

His dark gaze met hers. "Thank you."

"Anytime."

She wanted to say so much more, much of it along the lines of *take me, take me now.* So she did the only sensible thing she could think of. She ran.

★ ★ ★

Violet slid the omelets onto two plates. It was day two of their little domestic arrangement and she was enjoying herself way too much. Yesterday, after a night of incredible lovemaking, she and Ulrich had spent the day together. They'd walked around town, done some grocery shopping and spent the afternoon in bed. Last night had been just as magical.

It was more than what he was doing to her body, she thought with a sigh. It was what he was doing to her emotions.

What a silly thing—a shopgirl in Happily Inc, California, falling for an English duke. Not that falling for a duke from anywhere else would be all that sensible.

She carried the plates to her small table. Ulrich had already squeezed fresh orange juice and made toast. They were both on their second cup of coffee.

"This is a lot of food," she said as she sat across from him.

"We need to keep up our strength."

She laughed. "I suppose that's true." They both picked up their forks.

She found herself watching him. In part to memorize everything about being with him, but also because she enjoyed looking at him. This morning he wore a T-shirt and sweatpants. His hair was mussed, his jaw shadowed. He looked sexy and faintly dangerous—nothing like the elegant man she'd first met.

"You were so pissed at me when you first got to town," she said conversationally.

He grimaced. "I believe I have apologized for that."

"You should do it again."

He smiled. "I'm very sorry that I misjudged you."

"You assumed really bad things about me."

"I did and it was wrong." He studied her. "Is this your way of saying you're into spanking and you want to punish me?"

"What? No. Never. Ick. Why would you ask that?"

He grinned. "Just checking. One never knows what others find erotic."

"Not that." She narrowed her gaze. "You're not spanking me, by the way. Just so we're clear."

"Good to know."

"You totally messed with my train of thought," she complained.

"Then my work here is done."

She smiled. Ulrich had a surprising sense of humor. He was smart and loyal, caring, determined and sexy. Falling for him was not her fault. How could anyone not want to be with him? Okay, maybe his lifestyle wasn't for everyone—there would be a lot of expectations and it wasn't as if his wife would ever inherit the house, but still. That was okay. Any children would be the ones—

She stared at him. "You have to have children."

Ulrich nearly choked on his juice. "Excuse me?"

"Children. You need heirs. You have to get married and get on that, Ulrich. You have a duty to your family and the estate."

"Volunteering?"

She rolled her eyes. "I'm serious. What are you going to do?" She sighed. "You're going to be sensible, aren't you? Find someone who understands your situation and wants the same things you do. Won't that be difficult? Not to love her? Or do you think you'll grow to love her?" Not that she wanted to think about Ulrich loving anyone, but this was bigger than them. She had to be realistic.

"You seem to have all the answers," he said drily. "What do you think I should do?"

"I can't decide for you. Plus, I'll admit I'm not wild about the idea of you falling madly in love with someone else at this exact moment." She realized what she'd said and flushed.

"Not that I'm implying that you, um, are more than smitten with me. I was just making, you know, a point."

He leaned toward her and took her hand. "I know exactly what you meant. For what it's worth, as you Americans say, I have no interest in falling for anyone else, Violet. I will at some point have to do my duty to God and my country but that is not for today. Today is about us. Agreed?"

She nodded, then wondered how he defined smitten. Did he like her a lot? Did he like her really a lot? Or was he possibly in love with her?

She knew there was no way she would ask, which made her pathetic, but better to wonder than find out the answer wasn't what she wanted to hear.

"I'm glad you danced with me all those summers ago," she said instead.

"As am I."

She laughed. "You don't even remember me. I was simply one in a series of duty dances. I, on the other hand, will treasure the memory forever."

"In that, sweet Violet, you are far more fortunate than I."

Mathias pulled the small statue of a glass bird out of an Amazon box. "You drove down the mountain like this?"

Ronan shrugged. "I used tissue paper."

"Not very much."

Ronan had shown up at the studio with several boxes, all filled with his artwork. He'd decided to use the fund-raiser to showcase a few more of his bird pieces. Or as Nick put it, yard sale a few dusty leftovers.

Mathias turned the smallest of the birds so it was directly under the light. He could practically feel the wind ruffling feathers as the creature took flight. Damn, his brother was good.

Nick had also set out a few of his wood carvings. There was a three-foot-tall giraffe that was a surprise to everyone.

"I worked at home," he said with a shrug of his shoulders.

"Pallas's neighbors had to love the sound of a chain saw going at all hours." Ronan crossed to the elegant carving and ran his hands down the smooth neck. "I don't know how you do this."

"I didn't plan on a giraffe, but that's what it wanted to be."

Nick had also set out a couple of plant carvings, along with a crouching cheetah.

"I sense a theme here," Ronan said. "And we'll all be represented."

Mathias glanced at his own work. The two pieces stood on a thick pedestal in the back of the studio. He hadn't yet decided whether he would show them or not. When he'd finished, he'd been sure, now he wasn't. He figured he would wait until Thursday night and make his final decision then.

The studio doors opened. In the second before the visitors appeared, Mathias felt something cold slip across the back of his neck. When Ceallach and Elaine walked in, he couldn't help thinking of the late, great Obi Wan Kenobi. *There has been a great disturbance in the Force.* Only when compared with Ceallach Mitchell ready to assess his sons' work, Darth Vader seemed kind and gentle.

"I just had to see where you worked," Elaine said cheerfully, hurrying over and hugging each of them. "So I can picture it later."

Mathias thought about pointing out that she'd been to the office to drop off Sophie and she hadn't been all that interested in touring it back then. Then he told himself not to be an asshole. His mother would do what she always did in situations like this. Dance around her husband, trying to keep the peace without actually siding with any of her children. Funny how that had always pissed him off before, yet right now he couldn't summon much beyond sympathy. She'd picked a difficult road when she'd married Ceallach. He wondered if she questioned whether or not it had been worth it.

Ceallach walked directly to Ronan's bird pieces and studied each of them. The room went quiet. It was more than the principal showing up in a classroom. This was a god come down from on high. Mere mortals who wanted to keep their lives knew to be quiet and await judgment. Only when it came to his father, Mathias had never been very good at following the rules.

"Pretty rad, huh, Dad?" he said.

Nick and Ronan both shot him a look, warning him to shut up. He ignored them.

"The way the feathers seem to flutter. You can feel the breeze. Ronan has some talent."

Ceallach walked around the pieces. Elaine hovered by Ronan, lightly touching his arm, as if wanting to reassure herself he was real. Mathias wondered if this was the first time she'd seen him since she'd arrived for the wedding. Ronan, being a total jerk, took a step away from her.

"There's too much movement," Ceallach said at last. "It's distracting."

Nick snorted. "It's glass, Dad. How can there be too much movement? Movement is life. That's what we're trying to recreate."

"Think what you want and be wrong," their father said as he crossed to Nick's carvings. "I see you're still wasting your time with wood."

"Every single day."

Ceallach circled the giraffe. "I've seen worse."

Nick put his hand to his chest. "Was that a compliment? I might faint."

Elaine's hands began to flutter, as if she wasn't sure what to do. "It is nice, isn't it? There's going to be a special event on Thursday night. To raise money for Millie." She frowned. "Or is it to get Millie a mate?"

Mathias took pity on her. "It's to buy Millie a herd, Mom. Male giraffes are solitary, but the females stay together in a loose herd. Millie's lonely, so we're raising money to buy three giraffes and have them transported to the animal preserve." He thought about mentioning the plans to hire a vet, but figured no one was that interested in the details.

"Ronan donated the large bird piece to be auctioned off," he continued. "The rest of our work is going to be on display, as well."

Elaine's gaze settled on Ronan. "That was very generous of you."

"It was Mathias's idea."

"Someone had to do something," Mathias said.

"Yes, and it's not as if you could have donated a set of dishes and raised more than a few dollars," Ceallach said, still studying Nick's work.

Elaine's gaze darted around the studio. Mathias wondered if she was looking for a distraction or an escape. She spotted his piece in the back and hurried toward it.

"Ceallach, look. This is wonderful." She paused. "Nick, you didn't make this, did you? You don't work with glass anymore and it's not Ronan's style." She turned back to Mathias. "You made this! Ceallach, you have to see this. The way the woman is looking up and the giraffe is gazing down… It's beautiful."

Mathias felt both proud and annoyed. He wasn't ready for his father's assessment—whatever Ceallach had to say, it would be biting. Telling himself he was the bigger man didn't make him feel any more comfortable with the situation.

But his father being his father didn't even glance in that direction. He explored the rest of the studio, carefully avoiding the pedestal with Mathias's statue.

Nick stepped close to Mathias. "He's jealous as hell. That's why he can't say anything."

Mathias nodded even though he wasn't sure his brother was right. Maybe he'd been fooling himself into thinking he had something. Maybe he should stick to dishes and vases. Ordinary pieces people used in their everyday lives.

"Who's in charge of the fund-raiser?" Ceallach demanded.

"Atsuko," Mathias told him. "She owns the gallery."

"I'm going to speak to her. I'll donate a piece, as well. Something the whole world will want to see. We'll raise enough for the giraffes and whatever they need."

Elaine hurried to her husband's side. "Darling, that's wonderful. With you donating, they'll get more press and the whole evening will be special." She beamed. "Isn't your father the best?"

The three brothers exchanged a look. Mathias knew they were all thinking the same thing. Ceallach didn't give a damn about the giraffes or anyone but himself. He only cared about making sure no one got more attention than him.

Being in the spotlight had always been their father's drug of choice and each of them had experienced the pain of stepping between him and that light. Punishment was swift and brutal.

Mathias started to say something but before he could speak, Ronan slipped out the studio door. Elaine saw him go, as well. Her shoulders slumped and her mouth turned down. She looked old and sad and lost. Then she drew in a breath and smiled at her husband, leaving Mathias to wonder if he'd only imagined the transformation.

CHAPTER SEVENTEEN

Carol knew she would wait as long as it took. Mathias had shown up at her door nearly an hour before. She'd let him in and they'd settled in her living room. She'd put on music and had waited for him to speak, only he hadn't. Every few minutes, he got up and paced the length of the room, then returned to the sofa.

Just when she was about to give in and ask if he was all right, he looked at her.

"Sorry."

"For what?"

"Invading your house. Being a pain. It's my family." He shook his head. "Mostly it's my father, but the rest of them aren't helping, either."

She wanted to say she was fine with whatever he needed, that knowing he saw her place as a refuge meant a lot to her. What she said instead was, "Want to talk about what happened?"

"Nothing. Everything."

She glanced at the clock. It was nearly nine. "Did you eat anything today?"

He flashed her a smile. "It's not your job to take care of me."

"We're friends. I don't see it as a job. Besides, you're dealing with a lot right now. I want to help."

"You are. Thank you." He leaned back against the sofa. "Has Atsuko called you?"

"No. Is there a problem with the auction?" Her mind whirled with possible disaster. Had someone dropped Ronan's donation, shattering it and Millie's herd into a million pieces?

"Not a problem." He glanced at her. "My father is going to donate something to the evening. Whatever it is, it will go for a lot of money and bring a lot of attention to the event. Atsuko doesn't have much time to pull it together, but if anyone can do it, she can."

Carol honestly had no idea what to say. "Wh-why?"

Mathias's mouth twisted. "You want the politically correct answer?"

"Sure."

"It's a worthy cause. He wants to help where he can. Pick your platitude."

"And the truth?"

"He doesn't want to see Ronan getting all the attention."

She angled toward him. "Seriously? But Ronan is his son."

"Glory is far more important. Ceallach came and toured the studio today. He made sure to criticize everyone's work. When he saw the bird piece he asked what it was for, then thrust himself in the middle of all of it."

He took her hand in his. "It's okay. He's always done this. When Ronan and I were in the second grade, he came to parent-teacher night. When he saw the display of our artwork, he had to immediately do a few sketches, then sign them. God forbid some kid should be center of attention when he was around."

"I don't know what to say," she admitted. "He's horrible."

"That he is. Did I tell you how we found out about Ronan being his bastard?"

"You didn't, but Pallas mentioned that he was in the hospital after a heart attack."

Mathias nodded. "He asked Ronan and me to come see him. It was still early and we had no idea how bad things were. For all we knew, he was going to die."

His hold on her hand tightened. She wasn't sure he even knew they were touching—but that was okay. She knew.

"He told us about the affair and said that Ronan was the result of that, but Elaine had taken him in. Then he said he was tired and wanted to sleep and that we should leave. Oh, and not to tell our mother. That was it. Don't tell your mother."

"What did you say?"

"Nothing. We didn't say a word. I tried to talk to Ronan a few times, but he refused. I didn't want to go to Mom. Ceallach's heart attack turned out to be mild, so life went on as it had for everyone else, but not for us."

He grimaced. "The worst part was he never said a word. Not to me and not to Ronan. He acted like it had never happened. Who does that? Why wouldn't he have checked in on us, or at least on Ronan? But he didn't and after a few weeks Ronan told me he had to leave. I couldn't let him go alone, so I went with him."

"I know he was grateful."

"I hope so. I keep thinking one day he'll just disappear and I won't be able to find him. I've tried talking to him, I've suggested he see a therapist." He rolled his eyes. "That didn't go well. The thing is, I can't figure out what I'm supposed to do or say."

"Maybe he has to work this out for himself."

"What if he doesn't? It's been five years. I don't want to lose him. I don't care if he is only my half brother. To me, he'll always be my twin."

Which made him about the best man she'd ever met, she thought with a sigh. How was she supposed to resist that?

"Enough," he said firmly. "Let's talk about you. Tell me something I don't know about your past."

"When I was eighteen and Violet was sixteen, our mother took us to get matching tattoos."

He stared at her. "No way."

"It's true. The three of us have a little butterfly on our hip."

She could practically hear the wheels turning in his brain. They'd had sex...sort of. Shouldn't he have noticed a tattoo?

"It's very small and you were pretty drunk," she said, trying to be helpful.

"Thanks for reminding me." He leaned back on the sofa and rested his forearm across his eyes. "I'm okay with Violet having the same tattoo but I'm less sure about your mother. Did you have to tell me that?"

"You wanted me to tell you something you didn't know. It wasn't as if I could talk about my three broken engagements."

The arm lifted. "Do you have three broken engagements?"

"No. Do you?"

"Nope. And I don't have a tattoo. Damn. Now I have to get one."

"Why?"

"Because I want to be one of the cool kids, too." He straightened and drew her close. "Any chance I could convince you to show me what I've been missing?"

His voice was teasing. Had she thought he was the least bit serious, she would have ripped off her clothes in a heartbeat and done her best to seduce him right there on her sofa. Which probably meant she wasn't mad at him anymore. So much for standing on principle or righteous indignation.

She leaned in and lightly brushed her mouth against his. "You have to get home."

"I could text Del and let him know I'm going to be late."

"Or you could go home."

"I could."

He stood and pulled her to her feet, then cupped her face in his hands and kissed her. His mouth lingered for a second before he drew back.

"Thank you."

"You're always welcome here, Mathias."

He looked at her and for a second she thought he was going to say something. Maybe hint at what he really felt about her or beg her to take him to her bed. Because it wouldn't take very much on the begging front to get her to change her mind.

But in the end, he simply smiled and promised to see her soon and then he was gone. Carol sagged back on the sofa and wrapped her arms around a pillow.

Doing the sensible thing, even when it was right, really sucked. In her next life, she was going to be bad all the time. Or maybe come back as a spoiled lapdog, which was pretty much the same thing.

Ulrich strolled through Happily Inc on his own. Violet had a meeting with a client—something about a bride who wanted her gown to be covered with stars. Beading and pearls wouldn't do, so Violet had been on the hunt for star-inspired buttons and was going to show her what she'd found.

He would have preferred them to spend the afternoon together. They only had a few more days until he had to fly back to England, but he of all people knew the importance of duty. He couldn't walk away from his and he had no right to get in the way of hers. So he window-shopped and enjoyed the warmth of the desert sun, all the while knowing every second that ticked by meant he was that much closer to returning home.

He didn't want to go. Barring that, he wanted to take Violet with him. The thought had haunted him for a few days now—the endless loop in his brain asking if it was possible. Could they make a relationship work? He'd made what he thought were all the right decisions with Penelope—he'd known her, had thought he understood what she wanted from him. In the end, he'd been wrong about all of it. Did it make any sense to throw caution to the wind and commit to someone he'd only known a few weeks?

A question he wasn't prepared to answer, he thought as he walked by the river. And perhaps that was the point—that there wasn't an answer at all. That he was meant to take a step of blind faith.

He found himself outside of the Willow Gallery where the fund-raiser would be held. He would attend that with Violet, then drive to Los Angeles the following morning for his flight home. She had promised to come visit him and while she might be convinced to stay for a few weeks, then what? They were an ocean and a continent apart.

He saw two men carrying a large glass statue of a bird in flight and hurried to open the gallery's rear door.

"Thanks."

"You're welcome." He nodded at the statue. "The donated bit of art to raise money for Millie?" he asked, following the men inside.

The men put down the bird. They were both about his height, with dark hair and eyes, and similar features. Brothers, he thought. As he spoke, they glanced at each other.

"Bit of art?" the first man asked with a grin. "That's one way to put it." He stared at Ulrich. "You're that English guy dating Violet. Mathias Mitchell." He stuck out his hand. "This is my brother Nick."

"Nice to meet you both. Ulrich Sherwood."

Mathias turned to his brother. "He's lying. He's some lord or earl or something. Carol told me. Carol is Violet's sister."

"Yes, we've met. She's the one with the giraffe."

"Technically it's an animal preserve. Giraffes, zebras, a few gazelles."

"There's a water buffalo," Nick added. "You'd think it was a boy, but nope. All girls. Nobody's having babies."

"Are they sure?" Ulrich asked. "Let us remember the lesson of the movie *Jurassic Park*."

Mathias grinned. "*Nature finds a way.* Great movie. Scared the crap out of me when I was a kid. I didn't sleep for a week."

Nick shook his head. "He's the baby of the family, what are you going to do? So, what brings you to Happily Inc?"

"I had business in the area," Ulrich said, avoiding mention of his first encounter with Violet where he'd accused her of stealing, if not the family jewels, then something else equally valuable.

They all walked out of the gallery and toward a large, low building with lots of windows. Their studio, Ulrich would guess. When they walked inside, he saw he'd been right.

There were large desks, cabinets and workstations, along with a huge oven and all kinds of equipment he couldn't begin to name. Even more compelling were the pieces of art scattered everywhere. There were carvings, creations done with paper instead of paint, an origami mobile and several wood carvings.

"You've been busy," he said quietly.

"Let me take you on a tour," Mathias told him. "Nick and I work here most of the time. I have a small studio at home but it's mostly for sketching. My brother Ronan has a studio at his place. He's the one who created that bit of art we were carrying."

Ulrich held in a smile. "No insult intended."

"None taken," Nick said with a grin. "But if Ronan gets riled, you're on your own."

"I shall be on my best behavior." He glanced around. "Who works with wood?"

"I do." Nick crossed to a large log mounted vertically on a stand. "Still trying to figure out what this one is supposed to be. I keep seeing some guy holding a lute, but I'm hoping I'm wrong."

As all Ulrich saw was a log, he was impressed. He looked at Mathias. "You work with glass, correct?"

"Mostly everyday stuff. Dishes, bowls." He motioned to the pieces stacked on shelves by the window.

"So Ronan made that?" he asked, pointing to the piece in the back. It was made up of two separate statues. A giraffe—Millie, he would guess—bending down to greet a woman. As he moved closer, he recognized the features. Carol, he thought. Carol and Millie together.

"I did that," Mathias admitted. "Just something I've been playing with."

Ulrich walked around the pedestal and he looked more closely. Millie seemed ready to take a step. He would swear he saw Carol breathing. There was talent in the piece, and something more. The artist who had created this loved his subjects. He wondered if Mathias knew what he was telling the world with his work.

"It's brilliant," Ulrich told him. "Will you be selling it at the event?"

"It's not for sale and I don't know if I'll display it or not."

"Someone might accidentally knock it over," Nick grumbled as he walked to the coffeepot on a table by the front door. He held up a mug. "Ulrich?"

"Yes, please. Black is fine."

"Good, because we don't have tea."

Ulrich sighed. "You Americans do love your stereotypes."

"That we do." Nick handed him the coffee, then poured a mug for himself and his brother.

Ulrich looked back at Mathias's artwork. "Why would it be damaged?"

The brothers exchanged a look. "You get along with your father?" Nick asked.

"I used to. He passed away."

"I'm sorry."

"I am, as well. He was a good man. Kind and generous." Ulrich had always aspired to be like him. When the responsibilities of the estate seemed unmanageable, he reminded himself his father had done it all with a broken body racked with pain, and he'd never once faltered.

"Our father isn't like that," Nick said. "He's a famous artist who doesn't like anyone doing better than him. Not even his sons."

"I see." Ulrich didn't know much about the art world but even he had heard of a famous glass artist with the last name of Mitchell. "It's unfortunate he can't be proud of you."

"Not his style," Mathias murmured, then sipped his coffee. "You'll meet him on Thursday."

"He's attending?"

"He's donating something, as well."

"Ah. To share in the glory?"

"Sure," Nick said. "Will you be bidding?"

Ulrich chuckled. "I'm afraid not. I have an old, drafty house with bad plumbing."

"Uh-huh. Let me guess. The drafty old house is a five-hundred-year-old estate with a couple hundred rooms."

Ulrich sipped his coffee. "Something like that. And the plumbing is awful. But I shall be hoping for a blowout in the bidding."

"Didn't Millie cause your car accident?" Mathias asked.

"I'm not one to hold a grudge." Not when the accident had resulted in him spending more time with Violet. "From what I've been told, Millie needs her herd. Here's to that happening."

He chatted with the brothers for a few more minutes before excusing himself and walking back toward Violet's store. She should be finished with her client by now and he wanted to spend every second he could with her. Despite their short time together, she'd become extremely important to him. So important, he wasn't sure how he was going to leave her. But return home he must, and therein lay the dilemma.

Carol silently yelled at herself the entire way up the mountain—worse, she knew she was right. It was a family matter—she shouldn't get involved. No good deed went unpunished. The list went on and on. Still, she was compelled. She had to do what she could, even if it went badly. Despite their cruel and disinterested father, the Mitchell brothers were all basically good guys. If the meeting went badly, she would throw herself on Ronan's mercy and beg him to forgive her. Or at least not tell anyone what she'd said.

She parked by the front door and took a second to admire the grandeur of the house. The solitude of the structure had a peaceful quality to it. Not that she was having anything close to house-envy. She liked where she lived just fine. Her view of the animal preserve was all she wanted.

She got out of her Jeep and headed up the path. The front door opened before she could knock.

"You're unexpected," Ronan said mildly.

"Did the perimeter alarms alert you to company?" she asked, only half joking.

"In a manner of speaking." He held open the door. "Come on in."

"Thanks."

Once they were in the foyer, he put his hands in his jeans front pockets. "Is this a long visit or a short visit?"

Was he asking if they could talk while standing here? She wasn't sure and while sitting down was probably a good idea; she kind of liked the idea of being able to bolt if he got mad.

"This is fine. I'll be quick."

"If you're going to ask my permission to marry my brother, I'm happy to agree. He has some quirks and a few annoying habits, but basically he's a good guy."

Carol felt herself flush. Considering her mouth also dropped open, she couldn't begin to imagine how pretty that made her look.

"I... We..."

Ronan's eyes brightened with amusement. "Not that, then. Okay, I'm intrigued. Go ahead."

She couldn't get past the marriage thing. "Why would you think I'm here about Mathias?"

"Aren't you?"

"Yes, but not because I want to marry him."

No way. They were friends. Sure, she liked him and all but that wasn't anything like being in love with him. Loving someone was different. It was big and loud and flashy. It was like a roller coaster and she'd never been a roller-coaster kind of girl. She'd never liked big parties or fancy events. She liked—

Her mind whipped all those thoughts around five or six times before settling on something that might be truth. Love wouldn't be flashy for her. It would be like her regular life. Steady, ordinary, happy. It would be kindness and affection and laughter and holy, holy crap, was she in love with Mathias? Was she?

"Carol?"

She liked being with him and talking to him. She knew she desperately wanted to make love with him, but only because it was what he wanted, too, and not out of duty. She wanted him smiling at her and teasing her about her cows and holding her tight. She wanted to be there for him, too, to be his partner and his support and what if she was in love with him?

"Carol?"

"This is all your fault!"

Ronan looked at her. "What is?"

"All of it."

All right, maybe her being in love with Mathias *wasn't* technically Ronan's fault, but he'd been the one to make her see it.

"I didn't want to know," she added, hoping she didn't sound as desperate as she felt. "This is a disaster. Why would you say that? Why?"

He took a step back and held up both his hands. "I was kidding, trying to be friendly. I thought you and Mathias were just friends and that you'd laugh."

She glared at him. "This is not a good time to develop a sense of humor!"

"It won't happen again."

"It's too late now. How could you? I don't want to be in love with him. Do you know what's going to happen now? Do you?"

The last two words came out louder than she'd wanted and Ronan flinched.

"Something that isn't good and is also my fault?" he ventured.

"You got that right. Now we both have to pretend this never happened. You are not going to say a word, do you hear me?"

"The last person I want to talk to about this is my brother."

"Not good enough. No. One. Am I clear?"

"Crystal."

She narrowed her gaze. "You've really upset me. I have to deal with this now. The auction is in two days. I don't have time to worry about being in love with your brother."

"I'm sorry."

"That's not good enough. Make it go away."

"I can't. Once you know something, you can't forget it. Trust me, I know."

Her terror and wonder and worry evaporated as she got his point. Of course Ronan would know about not being able to let something emotionally significant go. It was how he lived his life.

"It's okay," she told him, not sure if she was talking about him or herself.

"It's not, but dealing isn't an option."

Only with him, it kind of was, she thought with a sigh, which brought her right back to why she was here in the first place.

"We should go sit down," she said.

"Sure."

They went into the living room. There were two couches covered in a dark plaid. Club chairs picked up the deep green from the pattern. She sat on a sofa while he took a chair. There was a moment of uneasy silence.

"I wouldn't have picked you as a plaid man," she admitted.

"They were the floor models. It was faster to just take them than to order something."

"You're such a guy."

Humor replaced wariness. "Thanks."

"What makes you think I meant it as a compliment?"

"We both know you did. Now what's going on?"

He could work on his small-talk skills, she thought, but then she'd been the one to show up unannounced. He'd probably thought polite chitchat wasn't required.

"Your dad's in town," she began.

"That I know."

"He's having a piece shipped for the event on Thursday."

"I've heard."

"And while I appreciate the extra income and Atsuko's

thrilled about it because she'd already said she wouldn't take a commission off your piece but now she'll get one from Ceallach's, it doesn't feel right."

"Do you need money for the herd?"

"You know I do. That's the whole point of this."

"Now you'll get an extra three or four hundred thousand dollars. Go buy a hippo."

She opened her mouth to explain that they were in no way equipped to house a hippo. The water requirements alone were impractical. They lived in a desert and while there was an aquifer, she still tried to conserve wherever possible. Besides, hippos weren't the fun, dancing creatures from the movies. Hippos could be aggressive and she had no training when it came to...

Her brain kicked in. Ronan wasn't talking about hippos, he was talking about taking the money and being grateful.

"I *am* grateful," she murmured. "This isn't about me or even Millie. It's about how it makes you feel." She looked at him. "You specifically."

Nothing about his expression changed, yet in less than a heartbeat he went from semi-friendly and engaged to disconnected.

"Don't worry about me."

"I can't help it. You're Mathias's brother and you're my friend." Sort of. She thought of him as a friend, but she had no idea how he saw her. "You're being so generous. I don't want to see that repaid with something unpleasant."

"My father stealing the spotlight and making the night about him?" Ronan sounded bored. "Trust me, I've seen that one before. It's how he lives his life. I don't give a damn."

"You do give a damn. If you didn't care, you wouldn't have left Fool's Gold."

His gaze settled on her face, but he didn't speak.

"You know I'm right," she continued. "Ronan, I know

it's confusing to have your family here. You love them and want to be with them and your dad is really difficult. Plus your mom is—"

"She's not my mother."

Carol decided not to argue that point. Whatever his lack of biological connection with Elaine, the woman was still his mother in every sense of the word. She thought about pointing out that his being unable to accept that might be the heart of whatever problem he was having but doubted he would listen. Worse, he might dismiss everything she had to say and she couldn't let him do that. There was too much on the line.

"Why are you here?" Ronan asked. "It's not to talk about Elaine."

"No, it's not."

She'd hoped to come up with something really compelling and inspiring, but now that the moment had arrived, all she had was the truth.

"Please don't leave. I know this visit is hard for you, but the wedding is Saturday, then everyone will be gone and you can get back to normal."

"Why would you think I would leave?"

She twisted her hands together. "I don't know. I have a gut feeling you might and that is not going to go well. Mathias needs you. You're his twin."

He started to speak, but she cut him off with another glare. "Don't say you're not. You spent the first twenty-plus years of your life believing you were a unit. Nothing is ever going to change that. It's who each of you are. He doesn't want to leave and if you go, I'm not sure he'll follow you again. And then what? You'll both be alone. You'll lose each other and I know you don't want that."

"You don't know anything about me."

"I know enough."

"Why are you doing this? What do you get out of it?"

Finally a question she could answer without having to plan what she was going to say. "There's nothing in it for me. This is about Mathias and you. Please don't leave."

Ronan rose. She had no choice but to stand and follow him to the front door. He waited until she was on the porch to speak.

"I'll think about what you said," he told her. "But no promises."

"Thank you."

It wasn't much but at this point, she would take whatever she could get.

CHAPTER EIGHTEEN

Carol and Violet sat on a blanket in the shade of a tree. The afternoon was warm and sunny, the air still. The zebras grazed in the distance. Millie was a little closer, foraging for the occasional leaf.

"How does she get what she needs to eat?" Violet asked. "Are there enough trees for her to nibble on?"

"No. In the wild, giraffe territories can be as large as a hundred square miles, which means there's time for trees to grow back leaves before the giraffes return." She pointed to a tall pole by the grove of trees. "I hoist up branches every morning for her. We're having three more poles installed for the new giraffes. They can feed together but have their own space."

Construction would take a couple of days. The poles would be mounted in concrete to make sure they were secure enough to endure wildlife butts and brushes.

Her sister smiled at her. "Buttons are much easier."

"Yes," Carol said with a laugh. "And there's no poop to clean up."

Violet wrinkled her nose. "How often do you have to do that?"

"If we had more land, we could let it decompose into the soil, but we're all at closer quarters here. I send one of the interns out every couple of weeks." She smiled. "One of the perks of being the boss. Not that I haven't collected my share of animal poop in my day."

Violet laughed. "I swear, if I had a blog, I would so put this conversation on it. Even though it has nothing to do with anything." She flopped back on the blanket and stared at the sky. "I want to freeze this moment forever."

"Because I'm such good company?"

Her sister's mouth twisted. "You are, of course, but there's more to it than that."

"Ulrich?"

Violet sat up and seemed to be fighting tears. "I'm a mess. Everything is wonderful and he's so great and I'm happy and it's all going to end and I don't know how I'm supposed to survive that."

Carol had the brief thought that she was grateful for having to think about her sister's dilemma because it allowed her to forget her own.

"Are you in love with him?" she asked bluntly.

Violet sniffed, then nodded. "I know part of the reason is he's safe to love. If he's leaving, then he can't hurt me. Outside of his going home, of course, but that was always a given."

Carol thought about the irony of them both falling for men who were totally out of reach, but for very different reasons.

"What does he think about you?" she asked.

"I'm not sure. He likes me. I'm clear on that. We get along. I know he'll miss me. He's asked me to visit him in England."

"There you go. That's good."

"It is, but it's not love." She bit her lower lip. "I want him to be wildly and madly in love with me. I want him to sweep me off my feet."

"Didn't he break his leg?"

Violet rolled her eyes. "Figuratively, not literally, and his leg isn't broken. I want him to..."

"You want him to propose."

Violet shrieked, causing the zebras to stare at them before returning to their foraging. She covered her face and rocked back and forth, then dropped her arms to her sides.

"I *do* want that. How pathetic, right? What is it about women that we all want to get married?"

"The need to pair bond is biological," Carol said gently. "We want to be part of a community and that includes having a romantic partner and then having children. You want to belong just as much as Millie wants a herd."

"But Millie's herd isn't going to break her heart. They're going to love her back and be friends and they'll all be happy together."

"How do you know Ulrich doesn't want what you want?"

"Because there are complications. He has to live in England and I live here."

"You don't have to live here," Carol pointed out, ignoring the fierce ache in her chest at the thought of her sister moving so far away. There were airplanes, she told herself. They would still see each other. There was email and texting and Skype. Carol and Violet stayed in touch with their mother that way.

Funny how she was willing to urge her sister to follow her dream not three hours after begging Ronan to stay put. She supposed the difference was Violet was running *to* something, she was going to be happy, while Ronan would simply be running away.

"Your button business can be located anywhere. You do most of your work through the mail and online. It's not as if you have a button store people flock to."

"You're right," Violet said slowly. "I have my store, but that's mostly for the alterations and I only do that because it's fun." She shook her head. "No, it would never work. He's a duke."

"Dukes have to get married and have kids."

"To appropriate women. I'm not titled. We don't have any lineage. That kind of thing is important."

"Not to Ulrich."

"How do you know?"

"Because you love him and if that was important to him, he would be a jerk and you couldn't love a jerk."

Violet's eyes filled with tears. "I do love him, but I'm so scared."

"Have you told him how you feel?"

"No. I don't want to pressure him. I want him to…" She wiped her cheeks. "Oh, I hate to repeat myself, but yes, I do want him to sweep me off my feet. I hate being a cliché."

"You're not. You want the man you love to love you back. How is that wrong or bad? As for being swept away…that's more about him demonstrating how he feels than the grand gesture. There are birds who—"

"If you give me a bird analogy, I'll scream and that will scare Millie."

"It's a good analogy."

"I'm sure it's riveting, but no."

Carol smiled. "Fine. How about a hug?"

"That would be better."

She held on to her sister as hard as she could. "No matter what, we'll have each other," she promised.

"Thank you."

"Love sucks. It's supposed to be amazing, but it's not."

"Tell me about it."

At least Violet had a shot with Ulrich. Carol had a feeling the English duke was just as crazy about Violet as she was about him. For Carol, it was different. Mathias might not be leaving any time soon, but having him around only made things worse. If he was gone, she could pretend that it all could have worked out. As it was, she was stuck with nothing but the unvarnished truth. Mathias didn't want to love anyone...not even her.

Thursday morning Carol walked into the gallery and came to a stop in the middle of the main room. She couldn't believe how the space had been transformed. Every piece of the gallery's artwork had been removed, as had most of the display cases. A bar had been set up in one corner. There were small bistro tables scattered around the edges of the room. She knew that catering staff would circulate trays of appetizers all evening.

But that was all background noise for what was front and center: Millie. Huge pictures of the leggy giraffe hung on the walls. Some were in color and others were black and white. They were all stunning and completely new to Carol. She crossed to the closest one and saw a tag on the wall offering the photograph for five thousand dollars. Maya Farlow was the photographer.

"What do you think?"

Carol turned and saw her friend Natalie walking toward her. Natalie pushed up her red glasses and grinned.

"The pictures came out nice."

"Nice?" Carol shook her head. "No. They're incredible. When did Maya do this? She's supposed to be preparing for her wedding."

"She went out a couple of mornings ago and took the pictures. Wynn blew them up and voilà. Art." Natalie laughed. "Not to mention more money for you." Natalie linked arms with her. "Come on. I'll give you the grand tour."

They walked over to the two center displays.

"Ceallach's donation arrived late last night," Natalie said. "It's beautiful."

Carol stared at the six-foot-tall, abstract, angled glass. It was all sharp edges and needlelike points, each done in different shades of red, orange and yellow. Looking at it made her want to shiver. There was a coldness. No, she thought. It wasn't cold, it was angry.

"Is it supposed to be war or something?" she asked cautiously.

"A vengeful heart."

"That's happy," Carol murmured. "Nothing says let's raise money for giraffes like a vengeful heart."

Natalie laughed. "I know it's a little on the dark side, but Ceallach's emotion collection, as it's called, is wildly popular with collectors. Atsuko is practically levitating with happiness at being able to sell one."

"Good for her," Carol said faintly, turning from the aggressive piece.

Several feet away was Ronan's crane about to take flight. It was about half the size of his father's donation, but somehow seemed to dominate the room.

"He's amazing. So talented."

"He's okay," Natalie said, her voice teasing. "He can be a little brooding, but hey, he can afford it. Now over here, we have a very special carving from Nick."

There were actually four carvings grouped together on a table. A rush of emotion swept through Carol, making her eyes burn.

"Millie and her herd," she breathed. "It's so beautiful." And just how she pictured the giraffes—as a family.

She squeezed her friend's arm. "It's really happening."

"It is. Now over here, we have a charming collection of slightly impertinent giraffes."

Carol saw nearly a dozen charming paper giraffes on floating shelves. There was a ballerina giraffe and one that was a pirate. Business executive giraffe, a giraffe on a skateboard.

Each little caricature was about eight inches tall and fully dimensional.

She leaned close to take in all the wonderful details, then turned to her friend.

"How did you do this? They're adorable and fun and I love them."

"Thank you. It's a combination of origami and construction and a lot of glue. I had fun. They won't sell for a lot but I wanted to be a part of things."

Carol hugged her. "Thank you so much. You put in way too much time."

"It's okay. I enjoyed myself and they'll go into my catalog, so that's a win for me."

Carol knew that Natalie was trying to build the list of pieces she'd sold—her artist's catalog.

"You're wildly talented and one day you're going to be discovered," Carol told her. "Just promise you won't forget we're friends."

"That will never happen, I swear." Natalie led her to another pedestal topped with an intricately carved ebony giraffe.

"This bad boy comes all the way from England, compliments of the Duke of Somerbrooke. It's nearly three hundred years old and unique in not only the detail but its pristine condition. Notice the wood hadn't cracked at all and tail wisps are all intact." She grinned. "Why yes, I do watch way too much *Antiques Roadshow*. I can't help it. I'm addicted." She spun in a circle. "And there you have it, ladies and gentlemen. The Millie collection."

Carol honestly didn't know what to say. She was overwhelmed by the beauty around her, not to mention the money that would be raised. The giraffes had been put on reserve, the transportation arranged, the permits sent for. The mayor of Fool's Gold had given Mathias the name of someone to contact to get the last leg of the journey approved. Nearly everyone she knew and loved had participated. The evening was going to be a success.

There was only one thing missing.

She thought of the small glass giraffe Mathias had made for her. Until this second she hadn't realized how much she'd been hoping he would have made another one for the event. Perhaps it wasn't fair of her—he was an artist and maybe he couldn't produce on demand. Not something so incredible.

Her gaze moved to Ceallach's abstract piece and she wondered how much its presence had changed everything. In a room filled with promise and joy, his vengeful heart was a dark shadow sucking the life out of all it touched.

Carol worried that her curling iron was lonely and bitter and determined to punish her for lack of use. Or maybe the more realistic problem was that she got it out it all of once or twice a year, so she simply forgot how to maneuver it without burning herself.

She stood in her bathroom and carefully curled her short, red hair the way Violet had suggested. With enough product and attention, she could manage a decently fluffy style that was far more festive than her usual wash and go-ness. She'd already applied makeup—another beauty ritual she did her best to avoid. It wasn't that she didn't know *how*, it was that she rarely saw the need.

Violet was a big help, keeping her up-to-date on all the latest trends and guiding her toward the most foolproof ones. Whoever had invented crayon-like eye shadow deserved an award. No more fussing with oddly long brushes. No more shading. She simply swiped it on, smoothed it with her finger and she was done. The same with a bronzer-highlighter kit her sister had found. Two colors, two brushes and a little diagram showing her what went where. Honestly, if she didn't already love her job, she would look at starting a company called "Makeup for the beauty challenged."

She put down her curling iron and studied her hair. The curls were perky and even, her bangs straight. She reached for her can of hairspray and gave herself two coats, just to be sure, then went into her closet to finish dressing.

Atsuko had said to aim more toward cocktail party attire than anything too formal. While Carol didn't want to be the center of attention, Millie was her girl, so at some point she was going to have to speak to everyone, which meant dressing appropriately was important.

So was saying the right thing. The thought of having to address the crowd had been keeping her up for days, but again, she was the giraffe representative. She'd finally gotten her remarks down to a couple of paragraphs. She talked about Millie, then thanked everyone involved. The end.

She'd practiced enough to have her little speech memorized, but had notes, just in case her mind went blank. Which seemed fairly likely, given how nervous she was going to be.

She slipped on a simple black cocktail dress. It was sleeveless with a scooped neck and a slightly flared skirt. Growing up in New York City had meant going to lots of different events with her mother. Violet had loved dressing up, while Carol would have rather stayed home and read. Regardless of her wishes, she'd been dragged along.

Every year her mother had bought each of them a new black cocktail dress. Somewhere along the way, Carol had learned it was better to be prepared for the unexpected. While she didn't get a new dress every year, every third or fourth, she ordered a few online and kept the best one or two.

There was no way she could manage high heels, but she had a pair of classic pumps that worked in a pinch. At least she would be able to stand all night without twisting her ankle or limping.

She checked her small clutch and made sure she had her house keys and her speech. With three minutes to spare, she made her way to the front of the house.

Mathias pulled up right on time. He'd texted her earlier, offering her a ride into town. She was grateful not to have to arrive alone, but nervous about seeing him. It would be the first time they'd been alone since her emotional discovery. She was terrified that now that she knew she was in love with him, she would somehow give it away. Like as soon as she saw him, the truth would be written on her forehead or something.

Hoping fate wasn't so unsupportive, she crossed to the front door and pulled it open. Mathias was halfway up the front walk. He stopped when he saw her, giving her a chance to admire his lean, muscled body in something other than jeans.

He'd put on a black suit. The jacket had been tailored by someone who understood and admired the male form. His shirt was also black, as was his tie. He looked sexy, handsome and just a little dangerous. Fluttering started deep in her belly and worked its way out. Her chest tightened and she knew she was going to have trouble breathing.

"You're stunning," he said, moving toward her. "No one's going to notice the artwork."

"I hope you're wrong. We've already spent the money."

He chuckled, then lightly kissed her. "Nervous?"

"Desperately."

"You'll do fine."

"I have a speech prepared. It's short."

"Those are the best ones."

He put his hand on the small of her back and led her to his car. Carol exhaled with relief. He hadn't figured it out—her secret was still safe. Now all she had to do was get through the rest of the evening without tripping, spilling or making a fool of herself in any other way. Tomorrow she would figure out what to do about being in love with Mathias.

The gallery looked different with nearly a hundred people filling the space. Or maybe it was the lighting or the delicious smells of the appetizers. Or maybe it was the sudden and total terror that gripped her and promised to never let go.

Carol stood just inside the front doors. Mathias gently urged her inside, but she couldn't seem to move or breathe. No way she could do this, she thought frantically. She wasn't the right person to represent Millie to all these people. She'd never spoken to a crowd before—the closest she'd come was the other twenty-seven students in her college freshman speech class.

"You're beautiful, accomplished and this isn't about you. It's about Millie. So think of her, take a breath and smile."

Mathias's quiet words were whispered in her left ear. Until this second she would have sworn there was nothing she would rather hear from him than *I love you desperately.* But given the situation, this was even better.

She thought about the beautiful, lonely giraffe depending on her, reminded herself that as Millie's representative, she had to make Millie proud, sucked in air, then smiled.

"That's my girl."

Was she? Despite the sudden need to know, Carol reminded herself about what was important.

"Thanks," she said quietly. "The freak-out has passed. I'll do better now."

Before Mathias could respond, Atsuko descended. She wore a slim black pantsuit with gorgeous buttons that had a slight giraffe motif. Carol had a feeling Violet had done well with the sale.

"You're stunning," the gallery owner announced, sweeping in for an air kiss. "The crowd is hot. I can feel it. We're both going to make so much money tonight." She smiled. "While yours is the more worthy cause, I still have bills to pay." She turned to Mathias. "You'll keep our star circulating."

"I know the drill."

"A thousand thanks." Atsuko sighed happily. "Ed and Ted are doing their part, which is lovely. Now I'm going to do the same. Chat up the big money folks while making everyone feel special." She beamed. "How I do love an event."

She waved at someone and hurried away.

"Carol!"

Carol saw her friends approaching. Silver, Natalie and Wynn walked over, each holding a glass of champagne.

"I'll be right back," Mathias told her.

"Sure." She smiled at her friends. "You came. Thank you."

"Are you kidding?" Silver hugged her. "We wouldn't miss this. Very swanky."

Silver had pulled her platinum blond hair up on her head. She wore a silky dress that clung to every perfect inch of her body. Natalie had on a dress that came to midcalf. While the background was black, the swirling pattern was every shade of red. She looked like sexy fire. Wynn had a sparkly top over black pants.

"I never get out during the week," Wynn said with a laugh. "Or much on weekends. You'd think dating a single mom would be more appealing to men, but that doesn't seem to be happening. So I'm very happy to be with you."

Carol couldn't believe they'd all come. She expected to see Violet, and Pallas would be there with Nick, but these three had gone above and beyond.

"Thank you again for the wonderful origami giraffes," she told Natalie. "They're brilliant and adorable and so original."

"I'm pretty happy with how they turned out," Natalie admitted.

"And you!" Carol looked at Wynn. "I can't believe you printed all those pictures so quickly."

"I've got game," Wynn teased, then raised her eyebrows as she shook her head at Silver. "What did you do, young lady?"

"Very little. I'm here for the food."

They all laughed.

Mathias returned with two glasses of champagne. Carol took one but hesitated before taking a sip.

"I'm not sure alcohol is a good idea," she admitted. "I have to give a speech later."

"Then you'd better drink at least one glass," Silver told her. "It will take the edge off. You have notes?"

Carol patted her small bag.

"Then you're all set." Silver looked at Mathias. "Can we trust you to keep her from overindulging?"

"You can."

Anything else he was going to say was silenced by the sudden electricity that moved through the room. Everyone turned to look toward the entrance. Carol's stomach clenched as she braced herself for the inevitable onslaught.

Ceallach Mitchell had arrived.

CHAPTER NINETEEN

The combined sale price of Ronan's and Ceallach's two pieces was 1.27 million dollars. Bidding had been fierce, with three international buyers bidding by phone. Nick's carvings had gone for double what was expected and Natalie's animal origami collection had sold for nearly two thousand dollars—a record amount for her. Ulrich's statue and the photographs had also sold.

Mathias checked his watch for the eighteenth time in as many minutes, wishing the night would end. He told himself Millie and her herd were secure for the rest of their lives and then some. The goal had been achieved. Carol had given a charming, heartwarming speech that had probably been responsible for the increased windfall, although some of it had no doubt come from the underlying tension everyone had felt.

Nick wandered over. "How you holding up?" he asked.

"I'm just here as Carol's escort. I'm fine."

Nick's expression told Mathias he didn't buy that crap for a second, but thankfully he didn't say anything.

"Pallas has Del and Maya's wedding this weekend," Nick said instead. "She left early so she could be rested."

"You should have gone with her. It was a great excuse to get out early."

"I wanted to see what would happen."

Translation—Nick had been worried about him.

"I don't have any skin in the game," Mathias pointed out. "You should be with Ronan."

"Del and Aidan are running point."

Aidan and Shelby had arrived that afternoon. Poor timing on their end, Mathias thought.

"He's an asshole," Nick said conversationally. "We all know it. This was never supposed to be about him. It was for a good cause."

"Everything is about him. Our inability to learn that lesson is part of our problem."

Ceallach had claimed the spotlight from the second he'd walked into the gallery. He'd posed for pictures, had talked about his work until Atsuko had been forced to intervene. He'd ignored all his sons, the other work and everyone who wasn't with the press or there with a big checkbook.

"You should have brought your piece," Nick said. "That would have shut him up."

Mathias appreciated the support even though he knew it wasn't true. What he'd done was good, but there was no way it was in his brother's league...or his father's.

He was okay with that. He was proud of the work and one day he would give it to Atsuko to put in the gallery. But not tonight. Not when Ceallach was around. The old man had already destroyed too much.

He visually searched the crowd and found Carol talking to Natalie. He read exhaustion in her posture and turned to his brother.

"Go home to your girl. Carol's done and I'm going to get her home."

Nick slapped him on the back. "It's only forty-eight hours, give or take. We've been through worse."

"It gets harder as we get older."

"You got that right."

Nick headed for the exit. Mathias started for Carol. He passed his mom and Ronan on the way and caught a few words.

"You never call me," Elaine said, her voice thick with emotion. "Ronan, please."

Mathias's step slowed, then he shook his head and kept moving. Some problems he could solve, but certainly not that one.

As he approached Carol, he felt the strain of the evening fade away. They'd done it—Millie was going to get her herd. Carol had made it happen.

As if sensing his approach, she turned. Their gazes locked. Wanting slammed into him, nearly stopping him midstride.

Damn she was beautiful, he thought, forcing himself to start moving again. She was everything he'd ever wanted and nothing he could have. Sometimes life was a bitch.

"There's your ride," Natalie said with a yawn. "I'm going to head home. I'll talk to you after the wedding. Let me know how it goes. Oh, and I want a picture of Sophie in her dress."

"I promise," Carol said with a laugh. "I'm not sure Maya has considered the possibility of being upstaged by a very pretty beagle."

She slipped her hand into Mathias's and they walked out.

"Tired?" he asked.

"Exhausted, but also happy. Everyone had a great time. My dad and uncle were thrilled with the outcome. Violet looked so pretty. Ulrich was charming."

"Not really. It's the accent."

She grinned at him. "If you say so."

They drove back to her place. After parking in her driveway, he walked around and opened her door. Carol got out and turned to him.

"Thank you for coming with me tonight. I felt so much better knowing you were here with me."

You're welcome was the expected response. Mathias told himself to say it, get in the car and go home. But he couldn't seem to say the words. Or leave. Instead he leaned close and kissed her.

She responded immediately, kissing him back. As their tongues tangled, she made a noise in the back of her throat that had him hard and ready in two seconds. What was it about this woman that got to him? What combination of features and personality and just her-ness made him unable to stop dreaming about her?

He broke the kiss and leaned his forehead against hers. "I want you," he breathed. "Not because of what happened before or for any other reason than I desperately, hopelessly want to be with you." He straightened and looked into her eyes. "But it's completely your call."

Life was all about choices, Carol told herself. Little ones and big ones. Which way to turn, what college to go to, whether or not to go out with someone, study for a test or not. And sometimes there really wasn't a choice. Perhaps a week ago, she could have been rational, could have told herself all the reasons why making love with Mathias was a bad idea. Why she might get hurt or find herself dealing with more than she could handle. Now there was no choice. She loved him and making love with him wasn't anything she could refuse. Her body might respond to him but her heart needed him.

She took his hand in hers and led him to her bedroom. They didn't speak until after she'd turned on the lamp by her bed and slipped off her shoes.

"You're so beautiful," he whispered, reaching for her.

"I'm not."

"You are. I've always thought so. Sometimes in the morning I see you walking with Millie. What do you think inspired my giraffe piece? It wasn't just Millie. It was you."

She'd never considered herself an inspiration. Not for anything. Oh, she worked hard, was a good friend, a lovely sister and daughter, but an inspiration? That was left for people far more special than her.

"You doubt me," he murmured as he pressed his lips to her cheeks, her nose, her forehead. "Never doubt me."

Words designed to shatter the last of her defenses. She gave herself over to him, accepting that whatever was going to happen, she would be stronger in the end for having allowed herself to truly love him.

He returned his mouth to hers. They kissed slowly, deeply, tongues stroking, dancing. His hands roamed her body, moving up and down her back before settling on her butt and squeezing. She arched into him and her belly brushed against his erection. Desire flared, hotter, brighter, sending shivers rippling through every part of her.

She pushed at his suit jacket. He shrugged out of it and it fell to the floor. His tie followed, then his shirt. She put her hands on his bare chest and felt the warmth of his skin. She wanted to touch him everywhere, do all the things she hadn't been able to do before, when they'd been together last time. She'd been too caught off guard, too not ready. And he'd been too drunk.

She looked into his eyes and saw clarity there tonight. Awareness of what they were doing and how it would be. He watched her touch him, passion sharpening his features. She wondered how far she could go before he would react.

She moved her hands lower, sliding down to his belt. She unfastened it and then undid his zipper.

"While there's nothing I would like more than you to

touch me like that," he said with a slight smile, "we're both going to be disappointed by the outcome. And the speed of that outcome."

She laughed. "I would have thought you would be more legendary."

"Not when I'm with you."

Her belly clenched. How she wanted those words to be true. How she wanted him to love her back. But the odds were slim. Still, she would take tonight and deal with the consequences later when the realization of her love wasn't so new.

She stepped back and opened her nightstand drawer. Inside was a box of condoms. She pulled them out, then turned back to him. "I think it's time to get serious. Just to be clear, intercourse first."

He groaned. "You're never going to let me live that down, are you? It wasn't my fault."

"Regardless of fault, I'm saying what I want. Don't get me wrong—last time was great. I just missed not having the full show."

Emotions raced across his face. Before she could reassure him, he pulled her close and kissed her. At the same time, he reached behind her and unzipped her dress. The fabric pooled at her waist. Carol shoved it down, then stepped out of it. Mathias drew her against him as if he couldn't have her far away, then wrapped his arms around her. She buried her face in his shoulder.

They stood like that for the longest time—their bodies pressing together, her breasts flat against his chest, his arms holding her tight. She ached for him but also didn't want to let go. Being held like this—having their breathing synchronized, their heartbeats in unison, was the most intimate moment of her life. She pressed her hands flat against his back and let the warmth of him flow through her.

After a few minutes he began to kiss her again. Slowly.

Deeply. As his tongue slipped inside her mouth, his hands reached for her bra. He unfastened it, then tossed it away. He moved his hands against her breasts, causing her breath to catch as he rubbed her tight, sensitive nipples.

Need grew. Not just for her release, but also for him to be inside of her. She wanted to know what that felt like—his body over hers, his arousal filling her. She wanted the heat, the friction, the growing hunger. She wanted to be able to have that memory forever.

She stepped back and pushed her panties to the floor, then pulled back the covers to her bed. By the time she'd turned back to him, he had his shoes and socks off and was pushing his pants to the floor. His briefs went with them.

She gave herself a second to enjoy the show of a very naked, extremely aroused Mathias, then slid into bed. He pulled a condom out of the box and joined her.

He tossed the condom on the bed, then reached for her. Even as he kissed her, he moved his hands up and down her body. He lingered on her breasts before slipping his fingers between her legs and finding the very core of her.

"You're wet," he whispered.

"Funny how it works that way."

He smiled. "It's nice."

He slipped a finger inside of her. At the same time he rubbed his thumb against her clit. Tension flared and her breath caught. He quickly found a rhythm that nearly robbed her of conscious thought. Nearly.

"Stop," she gasped. "I want you inside of me. I mean it. We can do all this other stuff later."

"Other stuff?" He shook his head. "It's the best part."

"Not always." Not when it hadn't happened before. "Be inside of me."

There was no way she could explain why it was so impor-tant to her. Not without admitting her feelings. Because she loved him, she needed them to bond in that way. She needed to feel him taking her. Yes, it was old-fashioned or traditional or any other number of words, but it was also important.

He studied her for a second, then nodded. He rubbed her one last time before reaching for the condom and slipping it on. After shifting so that he knelt between her thighs, he braced his hands on the bed.

She reached between them and guided him inside. He was so hard and thick, she felt herself stretching to accommodate him. He moved slowly, giving her time. Nerve endings whimpered in anticipation as every part of her focused on the thrilling pressure.

He pushed all the way in, then withdrew just as slowly. Fire shot through her. Fire and need and pleasure and relief that it was finally happening. She gave herself over to what he was doing, trying desperately to remember everything. She wanted to be able to relive this moment again and again. The only flaw in her plan was the fact that each stroke aroused her just a little more. She couldn't seem to stay in her head—not when her body was reacting so strongly. She wrapped her legs around his hips and hung on.

There was something about the way he filled her. Or maybe it was the heat, or how his body felt as she ran her hands up and down his back. Maybe it was the intense gaze of him watching her watch him. Maybe it was just dumb luck. Regardless, she found herself getting closer and closer. Her body swelled and he went in deeper. He added a kind of grinding push at the very end, bringing him up against her swollen center, taking her that much closer to her release.

She gathered all her strength, all her focus and told herself to hold back. She could come later—she was sure of it. Only then he started moving faster and pushing harder and it was all too good, too perfect, too exactly what she needed to—

Her orgasm claimed her with an explosion that had her calling out his name. She moved her hips as he filled her again and again, drawing out her pleasure until there was nothing left. Only then did he let go, filling her one last time and exhaling her name.

They clung to each other, letting their breathing return to normal. She memorized the scent of him, the way his body covered hers, the sound of his voice as he whispered her name. Then she promised herself that whatever happened, this moment would surely be enough.

Friday morning came far too quickly for Violet. She and Ulrich had spent the previous night making love with a tender urgency that had nearly brought her to tears. Even as she found pleasure in his arms, she'd been aware of the ticking clock that brought his departure closer and closer.

She was going to visit him in England—that was for sure. She didn't know when, exactly, but she wanted to go and see him. And his grandmother, although she had to admit that her attention was more firmly on the duke than the dowager duchess.

She sat up slowly, not wanting to wake him. He had a long trip in front of him—first the drive to Los Angeles, followed by the flight back to London. He would be traveling nearly twenty-four hours. Hopefully by the time he called her from Battenberg Park she would be done crying, or at least able to fake a happy voice.

Sunlight spilled into the room. She studied his high cheekbones, the shape of his mouth. What had she been thinking, falling for him? He was going to leave and she was going to be destroyed. Okay, maybe not destroyed but certainly hurt and lonely and sad.

He opened his eyes and smiled at her.

"Good morning."

"Good morning, yourself." She did her best to sound cheerful. "You should try to sleep longer. You're going to be ex-hausted."

"I don't want to waste any of my time with you. I can sleep on the plane." He reached up and touched her face. "Darling Violet, how much you've come to mean to me."

"I feel the same way." She faked a smile. "And to think this started with you accusing me of stealing."

He winced. "That was a mistake."

"Oh, I don't know. It was memorable, if nothing else."

He rolled on his side to face her. "Have you forgiven me?"

"Of course, although I do plan to tease you about your mistake for a long time."

"As you should." He nodded at the dresser. "I have some-thing for you."

She held in a sigh. "A goodbye gift? You're just so thought-ful. Oh, thank you again for the carving you donated last night. Millie is going to have quite the trust fund."

"I'm sure she'll handle it well. Despite her propensity to cause car accidents, she seems like a sensible young woman." He raised an eyebrow. "Aren't you going to see what it is?"

No. If she got up and opened the drawer, she would have to deal with the gift. The goodbye gift. If she ignored it, maybe he wouldn't leave.

Recognizing the flaw in her logic, she gave in to the inevi-table and stood, then crossed to the dresser. She pulled open the top drawer and saw a long, slim black velvet box.

So not a ring, she thought, giving in to disappointment for a nanosecond before telling herself not to be a fool. She hadn't known Ulrich long enough for him to propose. While she knew he cared about her, she wasn't sure how far that caring went. He was a duke. He would be looking for some-one special.

She picked up the box. "Is this it?"

He nodded. "Yes. I used to carry all my possessions in velvet boxes, but it grew tiresome."

She grinned. "You think you're so funny."

"I am so funny."

She returned to the bed and sat next to him. Her wispy nightgown didn't offer much in the way of coverage, but that was all right. Ulrich had seen every inch of her. She no longer had anything to hide.

She opened the box and gasped when she saw six sparkling buttons. They were in the shape of flowers and looked amazingly like...

"Cut glass?" she asked, her voice shaking.

"No."

"I didn't think so." She looked at him. "Ulrich, you can't. These are diamond buttons. They're a part of your heritage. They belong at Battenberg Park. I really appreciate the gesture, but there's no way I can accept."

He rolled onto his back and stared at the ceiling. "I have a great-aunt who married one of Queen Victoria's sons." He glanced at her. "Maybe it was a great-great-aunt, or maybe she married a cousin. Regardless, those buttons are from the Victorian era. From all I've been told, they're very her."

She tried to hand him the box. "Thank you. They're lovely, but I couldn't possibly accept."

"Of course you can." He sat up and leaned toward her. "Violet, you'd never sell them. I want you to have them. I want you to have a piece of my world with you and this was the best way I could think of to make that happen."

Once again she was fighting tears. She kissed him, doing all she could to memorize the feel of his mouth against hers.

"You are a wonderful man."

"I'm glad you think so. Promise you'll keep the buttons."

"I promise."

She drew back and looked at them. The diamonds winked

back at her. They were lovely. One was a little larger than the others, perhaps to be worn at the neck. Before she could remove it from the box and study it more closely, Ulrich took the box from her and set it between them.

"You know I have responsibilities back home," he said quietly.

"The estate, your tenants, the village, the tourists and guests, not to mention your grandmother. Yes, you might have mentioned one or two responsibilities."

He smiled. "This is sass, isn't it?"

"It might be." She drew in a breath. This was the moment to do and say the right thing. She wasn't going to be selfish—she was going to say what he needed to hear. "Ulrich, I understand. You're more than a man."

One corner of his mouth turned up. "Especially in bed."

She smiled, kissed him, then straightened. "This time together has been wonderful. I wish it would never end. But the truth is you can't stay. You do have responsibilities. You have a heritage and people who depend on you. It's a big deal. Whatever happens, know that I've had a wonderful time. I've fallen for the amazing man who danced with me all those years ago. Whatever happens, I'll have that forever."

His eyes darkened. "About that dance, it pains me that I can't remember."

"I'll remember for both of us."

"You know I won't forget you now."

"Yes. And I'll come visit and maybe you can come back here."

His mouth straightened. "I don't think so."

She blinked. "I don't understand."

"I'm not going to visit you here, Violet, and I hope you won't be visiting me in England." He shook his head. "Damn, I'm saying this all wrong. What I mean is I have a legacy and I want you to be a part of that. I won't want to visit you because I want you to come with me to England. I love you, Violet. Please say you love me back and that you're willing to marry me."

She stared at him and her brain desperately struggled to understand what he'd just said. Had he... Was that...

"Did you just—"

"Ask you to marry me? Yes."

She flung herself at him and wrapped her arms around his neck. "Yes," she whispered as he hugged her back. "Yes. I love you and I want to marry you and just yes."

He kissed her, his mouth claiming hers.

"Thank God," he whispered. "I didn't know how I was going to convince you if you said no."

"Were you genuinely worried?"

"A little. My grandmother said you were very sensible and unlikely to fall for the likes of me."

"She did not."

He smiled. "She did not. She wished me luck and hoped you would say yes." He reached for the velvet box. "Now there's a bit of a surprise in here."

"With the buttons?"

He opened the box and took out the largest of the five buttons. As he pulled it free of the satin lining, she realized it wasn't a button at all, but a ring.

"The bit about Queen Victoria was the truth," he told her as he slid the ring on her finger. "And I do know which aunt it was and who she married. In fact it's rather an interesting tale, if you'd like to hear it."

She stared at the ring on her finger, then at the man who had placed it there. She slid down onto her back and pulled him with her. "Maybe later," she murmured.

"My thoughts exactly."

CHAPTER TWENTY

Carol watched Mathias hoist Millie's breakfast up the pole. The leaf-covered branches looked especially green and tasty this morning, but maybe that was the result of the previous night.

He hadn't left. She'd thought that he might, but Mathias had stayed the night. Sometime around dawn, he'd gone home for a shower and a change of clothes, but he'd returned in time to go with her to work. When she'd asked about him heading to the studio, he'd told her work could wait.

She didn't want to read too much into his words. They'd had a great time, they were both still recovering from the aftershocks. While she wanted to believe he was all in, her head warned her to be careful. Mathias didn't believe in long-term relationships—not the romantic kind. She knew all the reasons and while she could dispute them, what she thought didn't matter. He was the one who had to be willing to change his mind.

Her phone chirped. She pulled it out of her pocket and glanced at the text from her sister.

Got a second?

Sure. What's up?

Ulrich proposed. Just now. Okay, an hour ago. He loves me and wants to marry me and I said yes! I'm happy. So happy.

Carol stared at the message. Her heart neatly split in two with one half thrilled for her sister and the other half already missing her. She began typing before the disparate sides could reconcile.

OMG! Seriously? That's fantastic. I'm so happy for you. I hope he knows how lucky he is to have you.

He does. I'm a little worried about moving so far away. Tell me it's going to be okay.

Baby sister, it's going to be magical. We'll all come visit and you're going to be like the queen!

LOL. Not exactly the queen, but the woman Ulrich loves, which is even better. Talk soon?

Yes. Spend the day with your hunky, English fiancé. I'll see you tomorrow at the wedding.

You know it. Love you.

Love you, too.

Mathias checked the chain, then walked over to her. "Do you ring a bell or something? How does she know the buffet is open?"

"It's a timing thing. The animals all get fed about the same time every day."

She pointed and he turned. Millie walked around the trees, moving toward the pole with her leaves.

"She's something," he said, taking her hand.

"She is." She waved her phone. "I heard from Violet. Ulrich proposed and she said yes. She's moving to England."

Mathias looked at her. "You okay? I know you're close to your sister. You're going to miss her."

"I am, but she sounds really happy and with Skype and email, we'll still stay in touch."

It wouldn't be exactly the same, but it would be close.

Mathias put his arm around Carol. "I'm happy for her," he said. "Maybe you'll get to wear a tiara at the wedding."

"I hadn't thought of that, but you're right. I'd look good in a tiara."

He chuckled. "Yes, you would."

He kissed her and they walked back to her golf cart. She supposed he could have been freaked out by the news. Would she expect the same of him or something like that? But he'd taken it in stride. What she couldn't figure out was why that was. Because he was comfortable with her? Or because he knew taking things that far was never going to happen to him?

"But I don't want to," Mathias grumbled. He knew he sounded like a toddler being told to eat his vegetables, but he didn't care. There was no amount of broccoli in the world that compared with having dinner with his family.

Carol's expression was kind but firm. "It's the rehearsal dinner. You have to be there. What will Del think if you don't show up?"

"Logic is for men."

She raised her eyebrows. "I know you're dealing with a lot right now, so I'm not going to punish you for saying that."

"Thank you."

He sat next to her on the sofa, tugged her close and kissed her. "I know a better way to spend the evening."

She kissed him back before easing away. "No."

"But there wasn't a wedding rehearsal. We don't need a dinner." Del and Maya weren't having any attendants, unless he counted Sophie.

"Are you always like this when you don't get your way?" Carol asked.

"Mostly. Is it charming?" Because the last thing he wanted to do was have her questioning whether or not she wanted to be with him.

"Yes, but it's still not going to work. You need to go to the dinner."

"Come with me."

"No. It's a family dinner."

"Maya's going to be there."

Carol sighed. "Nick isn't bringing Pallas and they're engaged. You and I are only sleeping together. I'm not coming with you."

He wanted to argue the point, but had a feeling doing so would impact his charming status. Still, he felt compelled to add, "Pallas can't come because of work. She still has a few things to do for the wedding. You're done with work."

"I am and that doesn't change anything. I'm having a quiet dinner at home. You can join me when you're done, if you'd like."

He kissed her again. "You're stubborn and bossy." When her smile never wavered, he sighed. "Fine. I'll go, but I won't like it."

"This dinner isn't about you. It's about Del and Maya."

She was right, but that didn't make walking away from her any easier.

At three minutes to six, Mathias drove the short distance

to his house. For reasons not clear to him, the family had decided to eat in. Maya and Elaine were going to cook and then they would all gather around the large table in his dining room. He walked in to find Nick and Ceallach standing toe to toe in the living room.

"You could have been great," Ceallach yelled. "Instead you work with wood. It's ridiculous. Do you know I found out you help out at that wedding place? What's wrong with you?"

Mathias stood in the doorway. It would be so easy to back out, to pretend he'd forgotten about the meal. Then he remembered what Carol had told him—this was about Del and Maya. He had to do his best to keep the peace.

"Hey, Dad," he called.

His father glanced at him, then turned back to Nick. "Even your brother still works with glass."

Nick's expression hardened. "Even, Dad? You always have to put down Mathias. You think we're fooled, but we're not. We all know who's better and it's not you."

Ceallach's face reddened. "He makes dishes."

"Because of what you did. You couldn't stand he's more talented so you destroyed his work. You're a hell of a father."

Mathias moved to Nick's side. "It's okay," he said quietly. "I'm done fighting that battle."

Ceallach turned on him. "You never tried. You never took me on. You're nowhere near as good as me, but you could have been something. Instead you gave up."

Mathias glared at him. "You're saying that it was a test? You did what you did as some perverse test of my character?"

Ronan walked into the living room. "Elaine said to stop yelling."

"Yeah, that's gonna work," Nick muttered. He looked at Mathias. "He's just saying that. You know he's still messing with you."

Mathias did know. He might not fully understand his father or the damage he'd done, but he could grasp the broad strokes of what had happened. He would have sworn that after all this time, he would be better at handling it, but his father still had the ability to get to him.

"You three have disappointed me," Ceallach said. "I expected more of my sons."

"Not nearly as much as we expected of you," Nick shot back.

"You have two other sons," Mathias added. "They're good men with great characters. You know what, Dad, I think the reason you don't want to deal with them is that you know you had nothing to do with who they are. At the end of the day, you're still an asshole and they're still good guys and you can't stand that."

His father started for him. "You dare to speak to me that way?"

Mathias had never been one to fight, but right now he was more than willing to take on his father. "I dare a whole lot more than that."

Ceallach raised his fist. Nick got between them. Mathias had no idea where this was going but before he could find out, Ronan grabbed his arm and dragged him back.

"There's no win in this," his brother told him. "Not for you."

Because Mathias had never been the fighter in the family. That job was Nick's. Maybe it was time for things to change.

"We all need this to end," he growled.

"Maybe, but not this way. The only person you're going to hurt is yourself."

Elaine walked into the living room, her eyes filled with tears. "Stop it!" she demanded. "Stop fighting. This is supposed to be a happy dinner. Del and Maya are getting married tomorrow. You have to stop fighting all the time. We're a family. We should be nice to each other."

"Kids learn from their fathers," Nick said as he glared at his father. "Tell him to quit ignoring his two oldest sons and quit browbeating the rest of us."

"Stop being a girl," Ceallach said disdainfully.

Nick lunged for him. Both Ronan and Mathias pulled him back. Aidan and Del appeared and got in front of their father.

"I won't have this," Elaine shouted. "Stop it. Do you hear me? Stop it!"

"She's right," Mathias told Nick. "There's no point. You'll never win. You won't break even. Worse, she'll side with him and you'll be the bad guy. Don't bother. That's the advantage of growing up, bro. We don't have to care about him anymore."

Their mother hurried forward. "Don't say that," she told Mathias. "He's your father. He can't help who he is."

"You believe that, Mom?" he asked. "Do you actually believe the mighty Ceallach Mitchell can't change his behavior?"

She looked from her husband to her son. "I just want us all to get along."

Mathias felt the flood of emotions. He took a couple of deep breaths, then let the feelings wash over him. Regret, he supposed. That was the biggest one. Not so much for what had been lost but for what could have been. Imagine if they'd been a family, if he and his brothers had grown up supported by their artist father. They could have been great together. Instead each of them had been forced to make his way alone.

No, he corrected. Not each of them. Until a few years ago, he and Ronan had had each other. They'd been a team. The twins.

He looked at his mother. She was getting older. She'd battled breast cancer a couple of years ago and had beaten the disease. That took courage. But she'd never been able to stand up to her husband. Not for herself and not for her sons.

"What?" his mother demanded, glaring at him. "What are you thinking?"

"Nothing."

"Tell me." Her lower lip trembled. "You think this is my fault, don't you? You think I should have stood between each of you and your father. You think I betrayed you." She raised her head. "I didn't. I made sure you were all right. I was a good mother, but at the end of the day, Ceallach is my husband."

And that matters more.

She didn't say the words, but then she didn't have to. They all knew what she was thinking. Worse, the sentiment wasn't a surprise. Each of them had known it all their lives. Dad came first, even when that meant the back of a hand across the face...or shattered glass on the floor.

"Leave her alone," Ceallach growled before Mathias could respond. "She's done more than enough."

"It only took thirty-five years for you to defend her, Dad. Impressive." Nick's voice was thick with sarcasm.

Ceallach lunged for him. Mathias pulled his brother back. He was exhausted—from not sleeping, from dealing with his family, from the fight that never seemed to end.

"Let it go," he told Nick. "He's not worth it. That's what we never saw. He's not worth it and he never was."

"Mathias." His mother's expression turned pleading. "Don't say that."

Mathias ignored her. He waited until Nick nodded slightly, then glanced at Aidan and Del. They both nodded their agreement. Finally he looked at Ronan.

"I don't have a dog in this fight," Ronan said lightly.

Fury built up inside of Mathias. Fury born of too many questions and too much uncertainty.

"Damn you," he growled. "Do you have to be a jerk?"

"I learned from the best." He looked at their father. "At least I have that."

Meaning what? That he wasn't like the rest of them because Elaine wasn't his mother? That there was no repairing what had been broken? That they were never going to be close again?

"I'm out," Mathias said as he walked toward the door. He reached for the handle, then turned back and met Del's gaze. "I'll be at the wedding tomorrow. I promise."

"I never doubted that," his brother told him. "It's okay. We'll be fine."

Mathias made his escape. As he walked to his car, he wondered if Del and Maya had already counted the hours until they got to escape to their honeymoon. He doubted they would be encouraging a family reunion anytime soon.

When he started his car, he thought about where he should go. Back to Carol's made the most sense and yet...

He hesitated before heading into town. Work was safe, he told himself. If the glass cut him or burned him, he was at fault, not it. People were different. They couldn't be trusted. People who were supposed to love you betrayed you. He'd always known that and nothing he'd experienced in the past few weeks had changed his mind.

Carol told herself everything was going to be fine. The trick was believing it. Something had happened to Mathias at the family dinner the previous evening. Somewhere around ten he'd texted her and told her he was going to be working through the night and that he would see her at the wedding. All of which should have been fine, but wasn't. Why hadn't he come over? She wouldn't have cared if it was four in the morning. She loved him and she wanted him in her bed.

It wasn't just sex, she thought as she walked into the wedding venue and made her way to the bride's room. It was about being close to him and knowing he was okay. Right now she wasn't sure what was going on, but she knew in her gut something had happened. Something bad. The question was what it was and how it had affected Mathias.

She turned the corner and saw her sister walking toward her. Violet caught sight of her and started to run. Carol did the same and they met in a big hug.

"How are you?" Carol asked, her concern about Mathias pushed aside for a few minutes. "Are you happy? Excited? I hope so because I'm really excited for you. Have you decided when you're flying to England? Have you told Dad? Have you told Mom? Did Ulrich ask Dad's permission to marry you? Do I have to call you *my lady*? Is there a ring?"

Violet laughed, then hugged her again. "That's a lot of questions." She drew back and held out her left hand.

Carol gazed at the flower-shaped diamond setting. The style had an elegant, old-fashioned air and totally suited her sister.

"It's beautiful," Carol breathed. "Are you happy?"

"Over the moon," her sister confessed. "I'm so excited. Ulrich is flying home tomorrow and I'll join him in a couple of weeks. I talked to Mom this morning and she's flying over to England next month. We've been to see Dad and yes, Ulrich asked if he could marry me. It was very sweet and Dad nearly cried. Uncle Ted so lost it."

Carol grinned. "Did you take pictures?"

"Of our uncle sobbing? No. It seemed tacky." She hugged Carol a third time. "Leaving you is the worst part. I love us living so close together and hanging out. You have to promise I'll still be your favorite sister and that we'll talk all the time and text and Skype and visit." There was humor in her voice, but also worry.

"I promise. You will always be my favorite sister." They walked toward the bride's room. "I'll help you pack and I have room for you to store your stuff until you can send for it all. What about your place?"

"I'm not ready to sell it. I think I'm going to lease out the shop and the loft above. Thursday night Silver mentioned she was looking for a small office and a new place to live, so we're going to see if we can work something out. I'd love to rent to a friend."

"Silver would be a great tenant." For all her wild ways, she was a responsible business owner.

They knocked on the door to the bride's room. A voice called out for them to enter. They found Elaine helping Maya with her dress, two older women Carol didn't recognize and a whining Sophie with her leash tied to a chair. Her brown eyes begged for help as much as her howls of outrage.

"She was getting underfoot," Elaine explained. "There's just so much dress. I didn't want her getting tangled or tearing lace."

"She's not taking it well," Carol said, walking over to the dog. "Don't worry. I'm happy to be the beagle wrangler. Violet, where's her dress?"

"Right here." Violet pulled the beagle outfit from her tote bag and passed it over.

Carol took it, then turned to the older ladies. "Hi. I'm Carol and this is my sister, Violet. We're friends of the family." Which wasn't exactly true. They were more friends of three of the brothers and Carol was sleeping with Mathias, but none of that seemed like a good introduction.

"I'm Eddie and this is Gladys," the shorter of the two white-haired women said. "We're with the bride."

"They're my flower girls." Maya smiled. "My best friend is ready to go into labor any second and couldn't make the wedding, but I've known Eddie and Gladys for a long time, too. They're my family."

Eddie and Gladys exchanged a look. "I never thought we'd be family again," Eddie said, her voice thick with emotion.

"That's very sweet, Maya. Now which of your future broth-
ers-in-law are still single?"

"Mathias and Ronan," Maya said with a laugh. She turned
to Carol and Violet. "Watch those two. They are on the wild
side and have a thing for younger men."

Carol wanted to say that Mathias was taken, but the unex-
plained growing sense of foreboding had her playing along.

"Good luck, then," she murmured.

Violet shot her a questioning glance. Carol ignored it and set
her bag on the vanity, then dropped to her knees by Sophie.

"All right, pretty girl. Let's get you wedding-ready."

Violet joined her and together they got the wiggly dog into
her bridesmaid dress. Carol had to admit Violet had done her
usual stellar job, fitting the garment to the beagle's muscu-
lar shape. The dress hung low enough under her belly to be
dress-like but didn't get in the way of her walking. Sparkly
buttons decorated her back.

"You're beautiful," Carol told Sophie who thanked her
with a quick lick.

Pallas walked into the bride's room and took in the activ-
ity. "Maya, you are the most beautiful bride. Your photographer friend has finished with Del and his brothers, so it's time
for him to immortalize you." She saw Carol and Violet with
Sophie. "I see your canine attendant is ready to go, as well.
Excellent. Sophie's already met the dog sitter, so when the
ceremony is over, she'll go have her own private dog party."
She smiled at Eddie and Gladys. "You two are going to steal
all the attention, but Maya swears she's totally fine with that."

"Del will only have eyes for his bride," Gladys said with a
sniff. "Maya, you're lovely."

"Thank you."

Maya stepped back from the mirror. Her dress was done
up the back and fit her perfectly. Her hair had been styled in
an updo and her veil was waiting to be slipped on.

Elaine stood behind her, gazing at her in the mirror. "I have a surprise for you, Maya. It's your something borrowed." She drew a flat velvet box out of her tote and opened it. A diamond necklace winked back at all of them.

"Ceallach gave it to me after Mathias was born," Elaine said with a sigh. "He's always been so sentimental."

Violet and Carol exchanged a look. Sentimental, Carol wondered. Or maybe just feeling guilty because his long-term mistress was also pregnant and about to give birth. But if it made Elaine happy to think there was another reason for the gift, then she should go with that.

Elaine fastened the necklace around Maya's neck. The diamonds sparkled against her skin. Violet walked over and adjusted the bride's dress. "You're perfect," she murmured. "Enjoy every second of your day."

"I intend to," Maya said with a laugh.

Carol and Violet took Sophie's leash and led her out of the bride's room. Their job was to walk the beagle down the aisle in front of Eddie and Gladys, then hand her over to the dog sitter. Once the pet portion of the event was finished, so were their duties. Mathias had already promised to save her a seat next to him. Carol knew that Ulrich would be doing the same for her sister. There was no reason to worry, only she couldn't seem to quiet her head. Thoughts kept swirling as she wondered about the real reason she hadn't seen Mathias the night before.

She reminded herself that right now, there was no way to ask. She would get through the wedding, then deal with whatever was going on later. With luck, Mathias would laugh and tell her she was being silly. That everything was fine and as soon as they could get away, he would take her back to her place and prove it over and over again.

She crossed the first two fingers of her free hand and hoped she wasn't wishing for the moon.

CHAPTER TWENTY-ONE

Despite living in a destination wedding town, Carol rarely got to attend any weddings and she almost never participated in them. So it was fun to walk Sophie to her place by the bride, then hand over her leash to the dog sitter waiting just by the urn of flowers. The woman would stay there until after the ceremony, then lead Sophie out the back way and take care of her until Elaine and Ceallach returned to Mathias's house.

Mayor Marsha Tilson of Fool's Gold was standing with Del, smiling happily as they waited for Maya to start down the aisle. The petite older woman wore a pale pink suit and pearls.

Carol had already found where Mathias was sitting. She tried to catch his eye as she walked Sophie down the aisle, but he wasn't looking at her. When she sat next to him, he gave her an absent smile—one that dropped the temperature in the room about fifteen degrees. Where was the handsome, happy lover she'd known just yesterday?

But this was his brother's wedding and there was no way to ask. Carol faced forward and tried to focus on what was happening. She watched Del and Maya exchange vows, then a kiss. As they started down the aisle, Eddie and Gladys threw rose petals at them.

"Are you staying for the reception?" Carol asked as she and Mathias joined the stream of people walking toward the open double doors.

"Sure. Del wants us all there." He put his hand on the small of her back and guided her toward the tables and chairs set up under an open canopy. "How about there?"

He pointed to a round table far from the center of the room.

"Is there going to be a head table? Do you have to sit with family?"

"Nope. I'm all yours."

Words to ease her growing tension. Maybe she was imagining things, she told herself. Maybe everything was fine.

She took the seat he held out. When he sat next to her, she reached for his hand. But instead of lacing his fingers with hers, he gently withdrew from her touch and put his arm on the back of her chair.

"I'm going to stay at my house tonight," he told her. "Everyone's heading out early in the morning, so I should be there to say goodbye."

"Of course." She spoke as calmly as she could and did her best to keep her face from betraying her turmoil. "I'm sure you're looking forward to getting your life back to normal. Family is always a challenge."

"Not yours."

"That's true. We're drama free in the Lund household."

"The Mitchells have drama enough for all." He glanced around. "It's great to see Eddie and Gladys. They're cool old ladies with very quick hands." He chuckled. "Back in Fool's Gold they're known for taking advantage of any man not smart enough to stay out of their way."

"What does that mean?"

"They hug, they pinch, they give butt pats. On their best

days, they're more than willing to ask a guy to take off his shirt. More, if the man in question is willing. They have a cable access show that rates the butts of men around town." He leaned close and lowered his voice. "Naked butts. You text in who you think it is."

By comparison, Happily Inc seemed really tame, she thought. "And all we have is a wild animal preserve. Did you ever, um, model?"

"They asked, but Ronan and I never got around to sending in pictures." He frowned. "Or taking them, because how do you get a picture of your own butt? You'd need someone to do it for you."

Carol glanced at the two old ladies sitting with Ceallach and Elaine. "And they look so sweet."

"Don't let that fool you." He pointed. "The bar's open. Want to get something to drink?"

"Sure."

She was curious about the signature cocktail and would've liked a second to talk to her friend Silver. But as they walked over, Carol realized that Mathias was very careful to keep his distance. They didn't touch, didn't even brush arms. It was as if the past few days had never happened. Something had changed. She had no idea what, nor did she know how to ask. Worry returned and with it the fear that she was going to lose Mathias before she'd truly had a chance to be with him.

Saturday morning Mathias was up at dawn, not that he'd ever really been asleep. Del and Maya had spent the night at a hotel before heading out on their honeymoon. His parents were gone by nine that morning, with his mother hugging him tight even as she watched to see if Ronan would show up to say goodbye. He didn't.

Ceallach, Elaine and Sophie drove away in their rental car. They would catch a flight from Palm Springs up to Sacramento, then drive home to Fool's Gold. Mathias walked back into his now quiet house and told himself everything would finally get back to normal. His cleaning service would be by first thing Monday to erase all traces of company. In a few days, he would be able to put the last few weeks out of his mind. Except...

He missed that damned dog. He kept expecting to run into her, literally—Sophie didn't have any need to get out of the way. But she wasn't underfoot, or getting into cabinets, or jumping on chairs to eat off the table or snoring in his ear at night. She wasn't anywhere, and the house seemed colder and less hospitable because of her absence.

Worse, he missed Carol. He ached for her. While he could have easily gone home with her after the wedding, something had stopped him. A gnawing sense of concern in the back of his mind. Being with her again would be dangerous—he knew that. She was a temptation, but one he'd managed to resist. He just didn't think he could hold out for long. He needed her—needed to see her, talk to her, touch her, make her smile. He wanted to know she was okay and that all was right in her world. She was his air, the reason his heart beat. And yet...

He couldn't stay with her. He knew that. It made him a coward, but it was still true. Being with her would mean risking everything. He would have to believe in her, trust her. Worse, he would have to trust himself and he couldn't do either. He'd been taught to be wary his whole life. First by his mother, then his father and finally by Ronan. His brother's betrayal had been the worst of all. Funny how he'd learned that from family, rather than from a romantic relationship, but regardless of the delivery system, the lesson had been learned.

At least the Millie problem had been solved. Thanks to the sale of both his father's and brothers' artwork, there was money for the purchase and transport of the herd, along with funds for a veterinarian and upkeep for the next twenty-five years. He and his brothers didn't need to drive the giraffes cross-country after all. All the animals would be safe. Mayor Marsha had come through with the permits and last he'd heard, the first of the giraffes would arrive in a week or so. Everything was in place.

Which meant he didn't have an excuse. Not to wait any longer. Not to hope or wish or dream. There were no possibilities, just the truth he could no longer ignore.

He grabbed his car keys and walked out of his house. Five minutes later he pulled into Carol's driveway. He didn't give himself a second to reconsider—he wasn't going to back out. He had to protect himself and he owed it to her to get this done sooner rather than later.

She answered only a few seconds after he knocked. She wore jeans and a T-shirt. Her feet were bare, as was her face. Gone was the glamorous beauty from the auction and the wedding. The woman he knew and, well, liked, was back.

She smiled when she saw him. "Is everyone gone? Life back to normal?"

"They left. I think I'm going to miss Sophie. What's up with that?"

She stepped back to let him in, but he didn't want to go into her house. There were too many memories, too many temptations. He needed to say it and then get the hell away from her before he changed his mind.

When he didn't move, her smile slowly faded.

"What is it, Mathias? Why are you here?"

He almost told her he loved her. That he couldn't stand to not be with her because they were so right together. But he couldn't. It would be a disaster for both of them—he'd had that proven to him over and over again.

"I can't do this anymore," he said instead. "I'm not that

guy. I'm into bridesmaids, not relationships. We both know that. It was great while it lasted, but it's over."

Color drained from her face as her eyes filled with tears. But she didn't cry. He waited—no, hoped—she would call him on his crap. He wanted her to grab him and shake him, telling him he was stupid and a coward, but that she was brave enough for both of them. That she would get him through this because they belonged together and in time he would learn to trust her enough to offer his heart. But until then, she would love him and stay with him.

Because if she said that, or something like that, he would be okay.

Mathias acknowledged that made him a total douche, but he would be a douche for Carol, if she would have him. Only she didn't say any of those things. Instead she cleared her throat before speaking.

"I figured it was something like that," she said in a small, sad voice. "Thanks for being honest with me and telling me to my face. I was afraid you were just going to disappear." A single tear ran down her cheek. "Goodbye, Mathias."

Her door closed in his face and he was left with absolutely nothing.

"I'm not going," Violet said as she sat on her sofa. "At least not right away. I can head over to join Ulrich in a few weeks, when things have settled down."

Carol did her best to stop crying. She knew that her tears were a big part of her sister's decision. Or the actual reason.

"You won't," she said firmly, wiping her cheeks with her fingers and attempting to smile. "You're going to finish packing and then you're going to get on that plane and go join the man you love."

Violet grabbed her hands. "No way. You're my sister and I love you. You need me."

"No. What I need is to pull myself together. I'm sorry I've upset you."

"You didn't. And don't pretend to be fine. I hate Mathias. I wish I could beat him up."

"You couldn't and you shouldn't. This isn't his fault. He feels what he feels."

Violet grimaced. "He's a total jerk. He hurt you and I'll never forgive that. You're wonderful and amazing. What's wrong with him?"

Not being wanted by Mathias had hurt far more than Carol had ever imagined. She was still having trouble drawing full breaths.

She stayed in her house the whole weekend, only emerging on Monday morning because she had to get to work and take care of her animals. She'd done her best to be brave and cheerful. Her dad and uncle had been fooled, but when she'd shown up Tuesday to help Violet pack, her sister had taken one look at her and demanded to know what had happened.

"It's not about me." Carol admitted the truth it had taken her three days to figure out. "It's about him and his past. He won't get involved because he doesn't trust not being abandoned and betrayed. He and I talked about it before. I know what he thinks and what he's afraid of. Telling him I won't hurt him is meaningless."

"But you never *would* hurt him," her sister insisted.

Carol managed a tiny smile, then sniffed. "I would. Of course I would. People who care about each other still get wounded. It's the nature of relationships. The difference is if I were to upset you, you'd call me on it. Or I'd see it myself. Either way, I'd apologize and try to do better. But it's never been like that for him. He doesn't know that there's a process or if he does, he doesn't trust it. I should have remembered."

"You're taking this all on yourself. It's not about you. It's about him."

Carol thought about the other uncomfortable truth she'd realized. One that was harder to admit. "I'm just as bad as he is," she admitted. "I believe I'm not special."

Violet hugged her. "Don't say that. You're the most special person I know."

"Thanks, but you know what I mean. I learned that lesson too well and when I get scared or hurt, it's where I retreat to. When Mathias was telling me he wasn't going to see me anymore, all I could think about was not being good enough to keep him. That and trying to keep from bleeding to death. I was shocked and in pain and I couldn't move, couldn't react. Now I keep thinking that maybe I should have fought him. Called him on his ridiculous beliefs and fought for my position."

"Do you think it would have made a difference?"

"I don't know." That was the worst of it, she thought. Not knowing. Had being a coward cost her everything?

"Tell him now. I'll go with you."

Carol squeezed her sister's hand. "You are very good to me," she said. "Thank you for that. I will talk to him, but I need to get stronger and more sure of myself. I need to get through this."

It wasn't that she felt she needed to process more pain. Rather, she had to earn her way back. Not for him, but for herself.

"I'll be okay," she promised. "No matter what. So you're going to keep packing."

"I don't want to leave you."

"I don't want to be left, but I do want you to go."

They hugged for a second time. Carol let the love wash over her. Healing seemed so very far away, but at least there was the promise that she would get better. She knew she had some decisions to make. She could either live her life in fear, or she could fight for what she wanted. The decision was hers.

With or without Mathias, she had to make the right one or she would also fall short of who she wanted to be.

The FedEx wild animal shipping division did an excellent job of giraffe delivery. Carol watched as Mrs. Santora walked delicately down the ramp leading to her new home. Like Millie, Mrs. Santora was a Somali giraffe, native to northeastern Kenya, southern Ethiopia and Somalia. There were estimated to be less than five thousand in the wild.

Mrs. Santora hesitated, as if not sure what to do.

"It's okay," Carol said softly. "You're safe now."

Like Millie, Mrs. Santora had lived a solitary life for several years. While she was a bit older than Millie, they were both relatively young. Carol hoped they would form a strong and lasting friendship.

For the first few days, Mrs. Santora and Millie would be kept completely separate. Once Mrs. Santora was more comfortable in her surroundings, they would be allowed to see each other from a safe distance. Carol hoped that within a month or so, they would be the start of the new Happily Inc herd.

"I have the best leaf-eater treats," Carole told her. "The zebras are a little wild, but you know how they get. We have gazelles and a water buffalo. I want you to be happy here. Do you think that's possible?"

Mrs. Santora looked at her. She blinked, her long lashes sweeping up and down.

Carol smiled. "I'm going to take that as a yes."

Mrs. Santora walked into her enclosure. There were several branches hanging from a sturdy pole. The giraffe moved toward them, sniffed once, then took a single leaf and chewed.

"That's my girl," Carol whispered. "Welcome home."

Mathias took his morning coffee out onto his patio. The mornings had gotten colder as October stretched into early

November, but the afternoons were still warm. He watched wisps of fog snake along the ground and thought about going in for his sketch pad, only he knew there wasn't any point. He was done creating anything beyond his dishes and bowls. Whatever muse Carol and Millie had inspired had long since moved away. He'd tried making a few things, only to fail miserably. His skills were still there, but not the heart of the piece.

Today was the day—the big giraffe reveal. Everyone in town knew and later there would be a celebration in the office of the preserve. By virtue of his location and dumb luck, he had a front seat to the pre-game show.

A little after seven, Carol's electric golf cart came into view. Thick branches covered with leaves were stacked on the open back. As he watched, she and her father hoisted the branches up onto three tall poles grouped together. They secured the chains, then returned to the golf cart and backed away. When they were about fifty yards from the poles, they stopped and waited. Mathias watched along with them.

It only took a few minutes for Millie to appear. She walked toward the poles, two giraffes just behind her. They all reached the poles and began to eat.

Millie's herd, Mathias thought. Carol had made it happen. Two of the giraffes were already here and settled in. Two more would be arriving within the week. Once they were ready to make friends, there would be five giraffes in total.

He'd heard from Nick that the two newcomers had adapted more quickly than anyone had dared to hope. The local news had run several stories on Millie's growing family and the story had been picked up nationally. More donations were flowing in to fund expanding the preserve. Apparently there was talk of starting a breeding program for a few endangered grazing animals. He'd also heard that a couple of botanists were going to see what they could grow outside of Happily Inc as a way to help save endangered plants.

Carol must be proud, he thought. She'd accomplished so much with only a little help. He was glad for his part in what was happening. He wondered if she thought of him much at all or if she'd put him behind her. As for himself, he was living on the ragged edge.

He'd known being without her would be tough, but he'd figured he would start to bounce back in a few weeks. No such luck. He couldn't sleep, couldn't eat. It was as if Carol was his entire world and without her, there was no reason to get up in the morning. He was going through the motions because he didn't want to hear any crap from his brothers, but he was starting to think they weren't fooled.

He told himself he needed to get back on the horse, so to speak. That he should find some pretty bridesmaid and make sure they both had a good time. Only he didn't want to. His bed might be cold and empty, but the only way to fill it was with Carol.

He missed her. He missed her laugh, her smile, her touch, her warmth. He missed talking to her and laughing with her. He missed knowing he could look forward to going to The Boardroom with her. Sometime when he hadn't been paying attention, she'd become everything, and without her, there was nothing.

Which left him at a crossroads. What did he do? Assuming he was going to get over her was one possibility, but based on what had happened so far, he had his doubts. That left sucking it up and taking a chance. Something he'd never been willing to do before. But maybe he no longer had a choice—not when Carol was on the line.

He watched her and her father drive back to the main barn, then turned his attention to Millie and her herd. They were so beautiful in the morning light. Both awkward and elegant, completely out of place on the edge of the California desert, yet completely at home.

His cell phone chirped. He pulled it out of his pocket and stared at the single word text.

Well?

Atsuko had been pushing him for weeks. She wanted to have a one-man show for him. Worse than that, a one-man show with a single piece. The statue he'd done of Carol and Millie.

While he appreciated her support, he didn't understand the point. He was never going to make anything like that again. As for selling it, he had his doubts. Did he want it to go to someone else? Although keeping it was pointless and based on what had happened, or not happened between them, there was no way Carol would want it.

Sure, he texted back, then turned his back on the giraffes and walked into the house.

Carol's stomach was not happy. The churning, cramping pressure made it hard to relax. Not that she'd thought she would be able to be anything but nervous, but her tummy's emotional meltdown wasn't helping.

Mathias's show was that night. She'd been invited, along with everyone else she knew. When she'd sent her regrets— because there was no way she could face him in such close quarters in front of all her friends, plus what if he brought a date—Atsuko had asked her to stop by the gallery before the event. Because there was something Carol had to see.

Which all sounded mysterious, and not in a happy *I have your favorite flavor of ice cream* kind of way. But Atsuko had been amazing with the fund-raiser and had made Carol's dreams of a herd possible, so saying no wasn't exactly an option. Telling Atsuko she'd already seen enough of Mathias's work, thank you very much, wasn't polite, or true. Honestly, she would love to spend the rest of her life looking at his creations. Which was why three hours before the event, she parked in front of the gallery and told herself she was strong and powerful and going inside would be no big deal.

She'd already circled the block, checking for Mathias's Mercedes. It wasn't there. As the star of the show, he would wait to show up until the evening started. It was just going to be her and Atsuko. There was no reason to worry. Not that her stomach was listening.

She got out of her Jeep and went into the gallery. The main room was empty and relatively dark. She looked around, trying to get her bearings.

Once again the display cases had been rearranged. Most of them were gone. The few that remained were filled with examples of his everyday work. Dishes and vases and bowls. There was a collection of his more whimsical pieces and samples of his new Millie-inspired dishes.

Atsuko appeared from the shadows and smiled. "Carol. You made it. I'm so glad. Just give me a second to put the lights on."

She walked to the wall and played with the switches. For a second the gallery went completely dark, then three overhead lights came on in the center of the room, illuminating a low pedestal and the piece sitting on it.

Carol stared, unable to move or breathe. Tears filled her eyes and her throat tightened. What had he done?

The glass statue was in two parts. There was a beautiful Millie about three times the size of the one Mathias had given her. The features were all there, the markings, the essence of movement. Millie bent her long neck, as if to touch the woman standing in front of her. A woman who looked so familiar.

Somehow Carol found herself standing right next to the piece, even though she couldn't remember walking toward it. She stared at the face, at the clothing and recognized herself. She was reaching up to Millie as Millie leaned down. They were connected—two different species bound by trust and affection.

How had he done this? And when? The logical side of her was in awe of his brilliance. The technique, the talent. The man was incredible and the world a better place for what he created. But the rest of her saw something else. Something more.

At first she didn't want to believe. No, she told herself. That wasn't true. At first she was *afraid* to believe. Afraid to trust what both her heart and her eyes beheld. Because the true genius of what he'd done wasn't in the beauty, or the movement or the connection, it was in the love. His love for both his subjects radiated from the very core. It grew until the viewer had no choice but to feel it, too.

She let the warmth wash over her, chasing away fears and doubts. She'd always worried about not being special enough. She'd lived an emotional half-life because of that fear. She'd nearly lost Mathias because she hadn't been brave enough to tell him the truth and expect the very best of him.

Emotions grew and clashed and swelled before settling into a certainty that eased her stomach and soothed her heart.

"Thank you," she told Atsuko. "I have to go."

She drove to Mathias's house and ran to the front door. She tried to think of what she was going to say, but she couldn't focus enough. Not with the truth right there. Did he know what he said with his art? Had it been a message or happenstance?

He opened the door and stared at her in surprise. "Carol?"

He had on suit pants and a white shirt. Because he was getting ready to go to his showing. Because he was a famous artist and she was just—

No. No! She wouldn't assume, wouldn't be less than. He loved her and she loved him and that was what mattered.

She pushed past him and walked into the living room, then turned to face him. The room was silent. Fear was there, but she ignored it as she stared into his familiar face.

He looked tired, as if he hadn't been sleeping. She hoped he'd missed her as much as she missed him. They belonged together and if he wasn't ready to admit that, she was going to have to convince him.

"I get it," she told him. "Now that I've spent time with your parents, I have a small understanding of what you went through as a kid. It was crazy and frightening and you were never sure what was going to happen next. All you could depend on were your brothers. You had talent, and while you wanted to be successful, you weren't sure that was okay. Then your dad made it clear it wasn't. You were torn between who you were and who it was safe to be. But no matter what, you had Ronan. You were a team. Then one day he was gone, too."

Mathias stood on the edge of the living room, not moving, but not looking all that comfortable, either. He didn't speak, didn't respond in any way. She had no idea what he was thinking. Obviously he wasn't going to declare himself and save her the embarrassment of possibly being wrong. Only that was a good thing. He had his demons, but she had hers, as well. She had to believe she was special enough to have what she wanted and this was her moment of reckoning.

"I get why you've been reluctant to trust anyone else. You don't want to be hurt or emotionally abandoned or deceived. What is it you always say? Betrayed. You've been holding yourself apart, thinking that would keep you safe. Only you know what? It doesn't work. Cutting yourself off only shrinks your world until there's nothing left. Some people can hide who they are, but you're not one of them."

She took a step toward him, sucked in a breath and said out loud, "You love me."

A muscle in his jaw twitched, but otherwise, he didn't move.

"You love me," she repeated. "I'm sorry I didn't see it before. It's everywhere. You were the one to get Ronan to donate a piece, you always look out for me. You're caring and kind. You took in Sophie and yes, I know that doesn't have anything to do with loving me, but it speaks to who you are. And it's not just that you took care of her, it's that you missed her when she was gone."

She took another step toward him. "I saw the sculpture, Mathias. What you created. It's there. Your love. I can see it and feel it. I should have known before. That's on me. I was too caught up in not being special, so I couldn't see what was right in front of me. I've been a fool. Worse, I let you go. You were testing me before. Not on purpose, I don't think, but because you had to be sure and I let you down."

She smiled at him. "I always thought love was about being worthy, but it's not. It's about being willing to be loved and to love in return. I love you, Mathias. I have for a long time. We belong together and if you need me to keep proving that, I will."

She stopped talking and waited for him to say something. Fear flickered, but she pushed it away. She had total faith in both herself and him. That was how this was going to work. There was no room for doubt—not anymore.

The seconds ticked on. Finally the tension left his body and one eyebrow rose.

"You sound pretty sure of yourself."

"I am."

"What if you're wrong?"

"I'm not. I love you, Mathias. If you need some time to—"

She never got to finish her sentence because he pulled her

close and claimed her with a kiss that told her everything she wanted to know. He wrapped his arms around her and held on as if he would never let go.

"I've missed you," he breathed. "I'm sorry I didn't get it before. You're right. I do love you."

She smiled. "That's a relief."

He chuckled. "When did you go see the piece?"

"Atsuko had me stop by just now. The second I saw it I realized what you were saying."

He rested his forehead against hers. "I've been an idiot. I couldn't see what was right in front of me."

"I'm the one who was too scared to admit anything."

He kissed her again. "Carol, it's not you, it's me. I've been in love with you from the first second I saw you."

She blinked. "You have?"

"Yup. It was the third day I was in this house. You and Millie walked out into the morning light and I was a goner."

She felt a little shiver of delight. "You never said anything."

"I was terrified."

"You slept with other women."

"Not since the night when we…"

"When we had sex and you passed out and didn't remember?" she asked sweetly.

He groaned. "We need a better name for that night, but yes. Since then."

"Good. Because tragically, that was the best sex of my life. Until, you know, the times when you were awake."

"Yeah?"

"Don't go fishing for compliments. You know you're a god in bed."

"You like that about me."

"I like many things about you."

His humor faded. "I love you, Carol."

"I love you, too." She kissed him. "So this probably means we're dating."

"It does."

She sighed. "I have a boyfriend."

He laughed and hugged her before gently easing her toward the stairs.

"What are you doing?" she asked, even as she ran up the steps beside him.

"I think you already know."

"You have your event."

"There's time." At the landing, he touched her cheek. "You'll come with me, won't you?"

"Of course." She would go anywhere with him, do anything.

"That's my girl," he said before pulling her into the bedroom and slowly closing the door.

Across town Atsuko hummed happily to herself as she attached the red "Not for sale" tag to the base of the pedestal. At the other end of the valley, Millie and her herd stood together in the late-afternoon light. All was well in her world. Her lonely giraffe heart had been healed by the gift of new family and the promise of more to come.

EPILOGUE

The dining room at Battenberg Park could easily seat fifty...
or maybe a hundred. Mathias had never thought much about
British history or peerage, but it seemed being a duke wasn't
a bad thing. Sure, there were a lot of rules and he would bet
taking care of the old house was an ongoing challenge, but
he had to admit the sense of continuity would be kind of interesting. The downside was living in England in the winter.

While the temperatures in late February were technically
above freezing, there was a dampness that seemed to creep
into every corner of every room. Roaring fires did little to
chase it away. On the bright side, it meant Carol cuddling
closer at night and there was no way he was going to complain about that.

They'd flown over to England to be with Violet and Ulrich
in the week leading up to their wedding. Friends and family
would arrive on Thursday before the ceremony and reception
on Saturday. The former would take place in a beautiful old
church on the grounds of the estate while the latter would
be in the large ballroom. Because hey, every duke needed a
ballroom. But tonight it was just the four of them sitting at

one end of the huge table. They were having a tasting dinner, finalizing the menu for the reception. Small portions of different courses were being passed around and commented on. He and Ulrich were mostly in it for the meal, while Carol and Violet made the actual decisions.

He watched the two sisters compare notes on a savory meat pie.

"It's a ridiculous thing to serve at a wedding," Violet admitted. "But I know it's one of Ulrich's favorites."

"I can have it any day of the week," her fiancé said mildly. "Darling, whatever makes you happy."

"You make me happy," Violet told him.

Their eyes met in one of those intimate gazes happy couples often shared. Mathias liked to think that he and Carol looked at each other the same way.

They'd been together nearly four months. Each day was better than the one before. He was working on new projects—spending as much of his time creating "art" as making his dishes. Carol was busy with the new herd of giraffes. Come spring, the botanists would arrive. Nearly five acres had been put aside for an attempt to grow endangered plant species. She was working with the newly hired veterinarian and there were ongoing discussions about bringing in a male giraffe.

This getaway was the only one they could manage for the next few months. After the wedding, they were going to spend a week in the Caribbean before heading back to Happily Inc.

"I'm going to check on the next course," Violet said as she rose.

"I'll help." Mathias rose and went with her into the kitchen. But before she could speak to the cook, he drew her into the corner.

"Quick question. Is it tradition here for the bride to toss the bouquet?"

Violet's green eyes widened and her mouth dropped open. Then she shrieked and wrapped her arms around him.

"Really? Are you going to—"

He pressed his index finger to his mouth. "I'd like to keep it a secret for now."

Violet nodded vigorously. "I swear, I won't even tell Ulrich until after you've proposed. About the bouquet, I have no idea, but everyone already knows I'm American, so they're used to my odd quirks. I'll say I have to do it and then toss it to my sister. It will be great fun." She glanced around, then lowered her voice even more. "When and where?"

"I've arranged for a private seaside dinner on the beach next Monday." He had the ring upstairs. He'd designed it himself.

Violet hugged him again. "I'm so happy for both of you." She grinned. "Ulrich and I want to start our family right away. It would be so great if you and Carol did the same."

Kids. They'd talked about a family. They both wanted children and he was hoping for a little girl, just like her mom.

"I'll see what I can do," he murmured.

Violet laughed. "That's the spirit. I'm really happy for both of you."

She went to speak to the cook while he returned to the dining room. Carol smiled when she saw him. As always, the sight of her set his world to rights. He'd been lucky to find her. Funny how sometimes she joked about being his second chance girl, but he knew he was the one who'd been given a second chance to find happiness. And now that he'd found her, he was never, ever letting her go.

★ ★ ★ ★ ★